WHITE LINE RAZOR

CONCHO BOOK SEVEN

A.W. HART

WOLFPACK PUBLISHING
—— EST 2013 ——

Text copyright © 2023 A.W. Hart
Special thanks to Charles Gramlich for his contribution to this novel.

Published by Wolfpack Publishing
9850 S. Maryland Parkway, Suite A-5 #323
Las Vegas, Nevada 89183

Paperback ISBN 978-1-63977-144-8
eBook ISBN 978-1-63977-998-7
LCCN 2023941224

WHITE LINE RAZOR

CHAPTER ONE

Two roads to choose from. Both dirt. Texas Ranger Concho Ten-Wolves took the one that branched to his right and led toward the bank of the Rio Grande River. Dust spun up behind the wheels of his white Ford F-150, fogging the air of an early summer afternoon. He was off the reservation and on the prod.

He'd spent his morning testifying in the case of Tallulah Whiteheart. It hadn't been pleasant. Tallulah was a prominent citizen of the Kickapoo Traditional Tribe of Texas. She lived on the same reservation outside Eagle Pass, Texas where Concho lived. He'd tied her into a smuggling operation and a murder, and it looked like she was going to spend a long time in jail. Her daughter, Isi, was likely going to jail, too, although not for as long.

Some people on the reservation appreciated Concho's work. The Whitehearts—Tallulah and Isi, along with Tallulah's husband Sam and her son Pete—liked to throw their weight around and they'd made enemies. But they also had friends who blamed Tallulah's fall on the lawman rather than the woman's own behavior. Some of those friends had been heckling in the courtroom today, and a call warned that more Whiteheart allies awaited his return to the Rez so they could scream and rant and waive signs.

On top of it all, local and state media had fastened their suckers on the unusual story, which involved a child mummy, and news crews were everywhere. He'd barely escaped the courthouse after the trial and had no urge to confront more reporters waiting for him on the reservation.

So, he wasn't going home. Not yet. He'd drive around a while, maybe even find a place to park where he could sleep in his truck. After court, he'd headed out of Eagle Pass in the opposite direction from the Rez and taken a few roads only dimly familiar. He still wore the linen dress pants, starched white shirt, and silver tie—loosened—he'd had on in court, but he'd brought a blue workman's shirt and jeans along to change into.

A rise in the road beckoned, as such rises always did. He topped it, his windows down on this warm, sunny day. On the other side of the rise lay Little Owl Creek, already dry even this early in the year. An old stone bridge crossed the creek and in the streambed below sat two vehicles, a dirty, emerald-green Jeep and an old jacked up Monte Carlo that hardly seemed built for the terrain.

Both vehicles had their driver side windows down to allow for communication. Two fuzzily indistinct heads leaned out of those windows; both jerked back suddenly when they heard the Ford approaching. Two engines banged to life.

Drug deal, Concho imagined.

The frustrations from the morning trial boiled away as the prospect of action kickstarted his body with adrenaline. He slapped the button on his dash to turn on his lights and siren and punched the gas. The Ford leaped ahead, barreling toward the rough dirt trail the other vehicles must have used to get down into the creek.

The driver of the Jeep flung his vehicle into gear and peeled out, his tires whickering on the dirt as they kicked it behind him into the breeze. He headed down creek where his four-wheel drive *might* find an exit.

The Chevy Monte Carlo had no such way out. The driver's side door flung open. A man hove into view, a shadowy figure in the glare holding something in his hands that glinted. The passenger side window was already down and another glint of light stabbed through it.

Guns!

Concho pushed the gas pedal to the floor. The Ford bounced and jounced. He hung on, manhandling the steering wheel. The gunman in the passenger seat of the Monte Carlo opened fire. Ten-Wolves saw the muzzle flash but heard no sound of a hit. Maybe he was moving too fast, or the outlaw was rattled. Or both.

Now, the driver swung *his* weapon to bear. It looked like some kind of SMG. Before he could fire, the reinforced grill of the Ford F-150 plowed into the Monte Carlo's front end. The blow knocked the smaller car backward and sideways. The driver went flying as his own door struck him. Concho had his safety belt on but the passenger in the car flung forward in his seat, slamming into the dash and losing his pistol outside the window.

Concho slapped his truck into park and bailed out, hands dropping to his waist to draw both of the Colt Double Eagle semi-automatic .45s hanging at his hips. The passenger recovered enough to throw open his door and reach down to grab for the lost revolver. Concho smashed his size thirteen boot into the door from outside. It pinned the man's arm. He shrieked.

The Monte Carlo's driver rose from the dirt where he'd been thrown. He still held his gun, a short-barreled SMG. Concho had no time to yell, "freeze!" He double actioned the trigger on his right-hand pistol. The .45 slug caught the driver in the chest, sending him into a backward stagger. He dropped his weapon and grabbed for the wound, then swayed forward and fell into the creek bed with a loud thwack.

The lawman turned his weapon on the passenger. A little smoke drifted out of the semi-automatic's barrel, stinging his nostrils. He could see the other man's pain-wracked face through the open window, though his arm still hung vised in the door against which the Ranger's big boot pressed.

"You have the right to remain alive," Concho said softly as he eased back the hammer on the Colt. "I suggest you not waive that right."

CHAPTER TWO

CONCHO KILLED THE STILL RUNNING ENGINE ON THE MONTE Carlo and tucked the keys in his shirt pocket. He pulled the car's passenger out and handcuffed him by his good arm to the toolbox in the back of his truck, then checked the driver he'd shot. No need for handcuffs here. The man was dead. Both perps were Hispanic, probably in their mid to late twenties. The driver had been heavily tattooed, the passenger not so much.

The emerald-green Jeep was long gone. Even the dust it kicked up was settling. It must have found some way out of the creek farther down. He'd check in a bit but right now he needed to make some calls on his cell phone, to the Maverick County Sheriff's Office and for an ambulance.

Once the wheels of justice ground into motion, the Ranger returned to the maroon and white Monte Carlo and inspected it. Other than an open and three-quarters empty can of Tecate cerveza, nothing in the car's interior suggested contraband. He pulled out the keys and unlocked the trunk, then popped it open.

"Hello!" he muttered. Contraband here. Plenty of it. And a big surprise.

Stacked neatly on the left side of the trunk were wrapped

bricks of what looked like cocaine. On the right side was a woman, alive but bound and gagged. Her short-sleeved white blouse and khaki shorts clung to her light brown skin with sweat. She'd been in the trunk for a while. He could smell her.

The woman, or girl maybe, had her head cricked at an awkward angle to look up at him. Above the gag, her dark, avocado eyes gleamed wide and terrified. She mumbled something through the scarf tied across her mouth. He couldn't make it out.

Concho always carried a Strider SMF folding knife in his pocket. He pulled it out and flicked the tiger striped blade open. The woman's pupils dilated even more, if that were possible.

"It's OK," the lawman said, tapping the silver badge pinned to the left side of his shirt. "I'm the good guy."

Leaning into the trunk, he slit the scarf at one side and gently tugged it free of the woman's mouth. Pent up saliva dripped from the corner of her lips to pool on the rough carpeting beneath her; she coughed.

"Thank...thank you," she murmured. Her accent suggested Arizona or New Mexico with an exotic undercurrent he couldn't place. He wondered if she were from one of the Indian reservations out there.

"Let me see those hands," he replied.

The woman turned her body a little. Her hands and feet had been bound with plastic zip ties. The one around her wrists was strapped too tight, leaving her fingers almost purple from lack of blood flow. He carefully sliced through the plastic tie and she moaned when her hands came free, immediately pulling them around in front of her to cradle against her chest.

Next, he cut the big zip tie constraining her ankles. She tried immediately to get out of the trunk but he put a hand on her shoulder to stop her. "Hang on. Let some circulation get back into your hands and feet before you move too much. It's safe. The men who kidnapped you are incapacitated."

"Thank you," the woman said again.

"You're welcome. What's your name?"

The woman's face took on a stricken look. She opened her mouth but no words came out.

Concho frowned. "You all right?"

She stared at him, then shook her head. "I...I'm not sure. I don't know who I am."

———

TERRILL HOIGHT, a deputy in the Maverick County Sheriff's Office, was the first policeman on the scene. He arrived in a flurry of dust in his Dodge Charger Interceptor. Stepping out of the car, he looked like a TV version of the heroic police officer, dressed immaculately in black jeans and a brown uniform shirt with badge gleaming. The tight shirt accentuated the gym-built muscles Hoight bore, but despite the celebrity look and the dash of manly sage cologne, the fellow made a solid officer who'd helped Concho out plenty of times.

The two men greeted each other with a handshake. Concho explained the situation and showed him the cell phone pictures he'd taken of the Monte Carlo's trunk. Hoight studied those, then studied the woman seated in the passenger seat of the F-150 with her bare legs hanging out the door. No recognition passed in either direction.

"Don't know her," Hoight said, shaking his head. "She Indi— I mean, Native American?"

"Looks it," Concho replied. "But she says she doesn't remember that either."

"Well, we can run a fingerprint kit on her. Maybe get a hit."

Approaching sirens made both men look up. The ambulance arrived and eased down into the creek. Two paramedics got out. Concho knew them both and let them in on the story.

"One man dead," he said. "The other probably has a broken wrist."

The two men moved off to double check as more sirens came

over the hill and two more police vehicles arrived, another Maverick County deputy and an officer from the Texas Highway Patrol, Texas's equivalent to State Troopers. The second Maverick County officer was Roland Turner, also a good man who Concho had worked with. Both newcomers gathered around the Ranger and he retold the story, including the woman's claim that she couldn't remember anything about who she was or why she'd been tied up in the trunk of a drug dealer's car.

"You think she's lying?" the trooper asked.

"I'm the suspicious sort," Ten-Wolves said. "But I'm going to leave that to you fellows to figure out. This is not really my bailiwick and I'm on another case already. I did check the Monte Carlo for anything to identify the woman. Didn't find anything but you'll probably want to check again. And I couldn't see the license plate on the green Jeep that got away but I called in a BOLO on it with a rough description." He slapped Hoight on the shoulder. "First I'm gonna drive down the creek, though. See if I can find where the Jeep got out. Then I'll head on. As soon as I file my report, I'll copy the sheriff's office and the Texas Department of Public Safety."

"Just spell my name right," Hoight said, grinning.

"What makes you think I can spell any better than you can?"

"Probably all the book readin' I've seen you do."

Ten-Wolves laughed. "Just for cover." He excused himself and went back to his truck. The woman looked less terrified than earlier but still not comfortable.

"Maverick County has the jurisdiction here," he told her. "See that man?" He pointed out Terrill Hoight. "He's going to take care of you."

"What's going to happen to me?"

"First they'll have a doctor check you over." He didn't mention they'd do a rape kit to determine if she'd been assaulted. "Afterward, they'll try to find out who you are. They'll run your fingerprints and check whatever other sources they can think of to help identify you and get you back to your people."

"What if they don't believe me?"

"They'll still do the same job. And treat you fairly. You'll be in good hands."

"Can't...can't you help me?"

He smiled as gently as he could. "I'll file my report so they'll know everything I know. And I'll check on you in a couple of days." He shrugged. "But I've got another case I'm finishing up."

"I wish it was going to be you. You believe me, don't you? About not being able to remember?"

"I'd like to," Concho said. "But I'm afraid I get lied to quite a bit in my line of work."

"I'm not lying."

"All right. Just tell them what you've told me. And if you remember anything at all, share it with them. Right away."

The woman looked deflated, but nodded. She slid out of the Ford and Terrill Hoight came over to take her arm. The perp with the broken wrist had already had the bone set by the paramedics and been shut into the backseat of Hoight's car. Concho would let the Maverick County Sheriff's Office take care of that interrogation, too.

Ten-Wolves climbed into his own truck and started the engine. The grill was bent from where he'd rammed the Monte Carlo but the damage was only cosmetic. He had a mechanic friend on the reservation who could fix it up like new.

Pulling around the Monte Carlo, he started down the creek, following the tracks of the Jeep that had fled. One glance out the window showed him the woman standing by Hoight's squad car. Hoight was talking but she didn't seem to be listening. Her gaze followed Concho. He tried to give her another reassuring smile, then turned away.

Not his business now. Or so he told himself.

CHAPTER THREE

THREE QUARTERS OF A MILE DOWN THE MOSTLY DRY CREEK BED, Concho found where the Jeep had climbed the bank to escape. The scars it tore in the slope were clear to see, along with a beaten path that cattle must have left here as they came to drink.

He turned the Ford onto the same trail and gunned the engine. The big truck stormed the hill, its tires digging in and spinning dirt out behind them. He jounced and jolted, but went up...and out.

He pulled to a stop on top of a grassy rise. A meadow lay in front of him where a small herd of twenty or so Longhorn cattle grazed indifferently, paying him no mind. He frowned. The cows didn't look to have been disturbed any time recently so where had the Jeep gone?

The air flowed fresh through his open window, but he could feel the summer heat beginning to flex its muscles. Shifting the truck into park, he climbed out to search for tracks. The soil was dry and the grass short, but he knew how to read sign. The Jeep must have stopped here for at least a few minutes. The marks from booted feet had scuffed the dirt, although they'd left no clear prints he could photograph.

Two men, it looked like. One had smoked a cigarette and

discarded the butt. He smelled the tobacco. Grabbing an evidence bag out of the glove box, he used a twig to scrape the butt into it, not that he expected to get much from it.

Another frown curved his mouth as he tried to make out the path the Jeep followed away from this place. He would have expected the escaping outlaws to go straight across this field, likely the shortest route to any local road. The tracks indicated they hadn't. Instead, he realized, they'd turned back to the west along the creek bank, back in the direction they'd come from.

Alarm bells began to jangle in Ten-Wolves' head. A little ridge rang along the bank here, and if the Jeep stayed down behind it no one could spot it from the creek's bed. That meant...

The Ranger leapt for his truck, threw himself into the front seat. His cell phone rested in a charging holster on the dash. He grabbed it, flipped frantically through his contacts to find Terrill Hoight's number. Stabbing the call button, he listened to it ring.

"Pick up. Pick up!"

Hoight's voice answered, "Ten-Wolves?"

"The Jeep's headed back your way," Concho shouted. "Get the girl down."

Before Hoight could respond, the whip-fire of a rifle shot sounded through the speaker. The phone whined and went dead.

Concho thrust his silent phone back into its holder and slammed the Ford into gear. Punching the gas, he powered along the grassy trail left by the Jeep. The way was rough. The Jeep had probably taken it slowly but the lawman hurried and the truck bounced all over the place.

He glanced at the phone, willing it to ring. It didn't. He spotted the Little Owl Creek bridge ahead and stomped his brakes, sliding to a stop in a flurry of dust. Leaping out of the vehicle, he ran to the edge of the creek bank, waving his hands above his head to indicate he wasn't a shooter.

Below, he could see the Monte Carlo and the police cars.

Activity boiled around the back of the ambulance. The state trooper was crouched behind his patrol car, looking Concho's way with his gun drawn. But he recognized the Ranger and lifted a hand in acknowledgement. Ten-Wolves stepped over the edge of the bank and slid on his boots down into the creek bed. An avalanche of dirt and pebbles followed him. He ran toward the trooper.

"What happened?"

The man straightened from behind his car. "Two shots. From up on the bank where you were just standing. Did you see 'em?"

Concho shook his head. "It was the Jeep, but they're gone." He glanced toward the ambulance where a roil of activity continued. "Who got hit? The girl?"

"No. Hoight! I was looking right at him. He was on the phone, then suddenly turned and shoved the girl down on the ground. Something hit him and I heard the shot, but he threw himself on top of the woman. Another quick shot and I opened up at the muzzle flash, though I didn't see a person."

"They must have been lying prone. Did you hear a vehicle?"

"Yeah, they took off. I saw the top of it, I think. A flash of green."

Concho was already running toward the ambulance. Roland Turner, a black deputy and a friend of Hoight's, stood at the back of the vehicle. His face showed anguish. A smear of dirt and blood crossed his cheek.

"How bad?" Concho asked.

"Don't know," Turner said. "I saw a lot of blood. Good thing the paramedics were here."

Concho rubbed his face with a big hand. "I should have considered this possibility. Were they shooting at the woman? Could you tell?"

"Pretty sure."

"Where is she now?"

"I locked her in the back of my squad car. Told her to lie on the floor."

"Good. You call it in?"

"Yeah. Should be hearing the sirens any minute."

Concho puffed out a huge breath, turned to his left, then to his right, not knowing what to do. Both paramedics appeared at the back door of the ambulance. One climbed down and started around toward the front of the vehicle. The second looked frazzled. The left leg of his black uniform pants hung sodden with blood.

"What's happening?" Concho asked.

"We've got him stabilized. Headed for the hospital now." He started to pull the back doors closed.

The state trooper rushed for his patrol car. "I'll open the way!" he shouted.

"Is he going to make it?" Concho called to the paramedic before the doors could shut.

The man paused. "The bullet caromed off his shoulder blade and nicked his right carotid artery. We've got the bleeding stopped but he needs a lot more blood than we have to give him."

"*Is* he going to make it?"

"I don't know," the man said. He shut the doors.

The ambulance and the trooper's car roared to life and pulled out with the ambulance following the police. Ten-Wolves and Turner were left watching. Helpless.

CHAPTER FOUR

TEN-WOLVES HUFFED A LONG, FRUSTRATED SIGH AS HE TURNED toward Turner. "I should have anticipated it," he said.

"You couldn't have known the other perps would come back to try an ambush," Turner replied. "No one could have."

"I should have suspected." He punched his right hand into his left. "I let myself be distracted. And now a good man lies shot."

Turner opened his mouth as if to say something, then closed it and shook his head. "What next," he finally said. "We've got to follow this up."

It was what Concho needed to hear. There were still things to do to make sure whoever shot Terrill Hoight did not get away with it. His mind turned to the task at hand.

"I need to talk to the woman," he said. He started toward Turner's squad car.

"What do you want me to do?" Turner asked.

The big lawman paused. "Up the creek bank," he said, pointing to the place he'd come sliding down moments before. "My truck's up there. Probably close to where the shot came from. Would you go up and see if you can find any sign? Maybe a shell casing?"

Turner nodded. "Will do." He moved away while Ten-Wolves continued toward the deputy's vehicle.

Concho pulled open the back door of the car. The young woman lay across the floorboards. She glanced up at the creak of the door, terrified, then calmed a little when she saw who it was. He slid into the back seat and pulled the door not quite shut. The woman shifted to the other side but remained on the floor.

"Are they there?" the woman asked.

"Who?" he asked, his voice cold.

She gestured with the back of her hand. "Them. The shooters."

"They're gone. And the ambulance took Deputy Hoight to the hospital."

The woman-girl blinked. She couldn't be much over nineteen. If that. "Is he...going to be all right?"

"They don't know." Concho was aware of the harshness in his voice but he didn't care. "He took a bullet for you. He could have died. He still might."

The woman's lower lip quivered. If she were acting, she was good at it. "I...I...I didn't want him to do that. I didn't know."

"There was a Jeep here this morning. At least two men in it. They drove off when I showed up. Got out of the creek up the bank a ways. Then, instead of running like just about any criminal would, they snuck all the way back up here and took a shot at you. I want to know why."

"I don't know. I told you, I can't remember anything. I never even saw this Jeep anyway."

"You saw the men who kidnapped you. Two men in a Monte Carlo. Drug dealers. What do you remember about them?"

"Nothing. All I remember is waking up in the trunk. I didn't even know it was a trunk at first. I thought I was buried alive. I was trying to scream but there was a gag in my mouth. I couldn't tell you how it got there. I—"

"What *do* you know?" Concho roared.

The girl froze, startled. She burst into tears.

Ten-Wolves' rage boiled, then abruptly evaporated. He sagged. "I'm sorry," he said. "The deputy who was shot. He's a friend of mine. I'm worried about him."

The girl looked up, sniffling. She wiped her eyes with the backs of her hands. "I'm sorry, too. I wish...I could help."

"You still may be able to. We'll just have to find another way."

Sirens began to wail in the distance. The cavalry coming.

"Is this still outside your juris...jurisdiction? You're going to let the others handle it?"

The lawman shook his head. "Not anymore. It just got personal."

———

Leaving the nameless young woman to sit in silence, Concho climbed out of the back of Roland Turner's cop car. A new ambulance and two more police vehicles arrived. He went to explain the situation to them. Turner came down the bank of the creek and found him, showing him an evidence bag. Inside lay a brass shell casing.

"You found it!" the Ranger said, slapping Turner on the shoulder. "A piece of good luck finally."

"Definitely one of the two fired at us," Turner said. "The brass was still warm and I could smell gunpowder residue. Didn't see the other one."

"Looks like a .308. Probably bolt-action so the second empty might still be in the gun."

"Yep. A hunting rifle, you think?"

"Likely." Concho frowned as he studied the casing. "What are those lines drawn across the brass?"

"Glad you asked," Turner said. He took out his cell phone and punched up his pictures, swiping to one particular image, which he enlarged to show. "The casing was marked with this."

Concho stared. "A half folded straight razor. What kind of criminal takes the time to etch something like that on a bullet casing?"

"Got me," Turner replied with a shrug.

"I wonder."

"What?"

"Did you and Hoight pick up the shell casings fired here in the creek? By me and the other two perps?"

Turner understood the direction of the Ranger's thoughts. "We did. No etchings. I would have noticed."

"Send me that photo. You've got my phone number?"

"In my contacts," Turner said. He swiped a couple of buttons on his cell.

Concho heard the ping of his phone indicating he'd gotten the picture. "Thanks." He looked around. The paramedics from the newly arrived ambulance were loading the dead body of the one perpetrator into the back of their vehicle. The injured criminal still sat locked in the back of Terrill Hoight's Charger.

"Time to talk to an outlaw," Concho said.

"You want me along?"

"No. Can you take charge of the crime scene? And see if there's any way to get a helicopter to do some scouting runs around. Maybe spot that Jeep."

"Will do."

Concho headed for Hoight's black and white Charger. He could see the man whose wrist he'd broken lying down across the back seat. The fellow hissed as Ten-Wolves jerked open the door and leaned in.

"Whatcha doing, man?" the outlaw asked in a hoarse whisper. He pronounced 'man' like 'main.' "They gone? They gone?"

"Who?"

Because of his broken right wrist, which was encased in a thick wrap, the perp hadn't been cuffed. He threw up his left arm as if indicating all of the outside world. "The shooters, man! They gone?"

Concho let a grin show, the shark-like grin he used at times to discombobulate his enemies, and sometimes his friends. "I don't know," he said. "Let's find out." He grabbed the man's good arm and jerked him upright, then began to drag him out of the back seat.

"No, no, no," the man squealed, his Hispanic accent deepening as he struggled against being pulled out of the car.

The fellow certainly didn't seem much like a hardened criminal, and he was no match for the lawman's strength as Ten-Wolves yanked him out and shoved him up against the rear of the vehicle. He tried to duck down behind Concho's six-foot-four-inch frame but the Ranger grabbed his collar and held him still. The man's face showed stark terror.

"One, two, three," Concho counted. He shrugged. "You're not dead yet so I guess the shooters must be gone."

"Pendejo negro!" the outlaw snapped, his face flushed with anger.

"I'll take that as a compliment coming from you," Concho snapped back. "Now, tell me who they are? These shooters you're so concerned with? Good friends, I guess?"

"Al Diablo contigo!"

The big Ranger gave the man a shake and leaned closer, his smile growing bigger and sharper. "I already don't like you very much. You need to be more worried about me than your buddies."

"I don't have to talk to you."

"Maybe you'll want to after your trigger-happy friends learn just how much heroin you lost for them in the trunk of your car."

"I don't know anything about any coca—" the man started, then stopped as he realized he'd been tricked.

"Oh yeah," Concho said. "My bad. I meant cocaine." He grinned again. "Thanks for correcting me. I'll make note of it."

The outlaw merely shook his head.

"Now, let's talk about something else," the Ranger said. "Who's the woman you had locked in your trunk? And why did your 'buddies' in the Jeep try to kill her?"

CHAPTER FIVE

AN ISOLATED TEXAS FARMHOUSE WITH A BARREN FRONT YARD. Two barns. One big, one small and rickety. A broken and rusted windmill to one side and a few withered old oaks rising behind the single-story dwelling. A dusty, ten-year-old Peterbilt tractor trailer rig stood to one side of the yard, its rear doors open with a ramp running up into the cargo area of the trailer. A big man in his mid to late fifties—maybe six two and two forty—paced impatiently back and forth beside the truck.

A glint of light caught the man's attention as it sped down the dirt road leading to the house. A 2022 green Jeep Wrangler 2-Door Sport 4X4 turned into the yard and pulled up behind the semi. One man got out and the driver skillfully used his rear-view cameras to back the Jeep up the ramp into the truck.

The first man and the newcomer immediately began pulling down the ramp to stuff in beside the Jeep. The driver came hopping down to lend them a hand. In a moment, the trailer's back door was shut and the Jeep hidden from view.

The big man glanced at the sky, then snapped an order, "Inside!"

The two men from the Jeep, both looking to be in their twenties, followed the older man into the farmhouse. All three were of European descent and resembled each other enough in build and hairiness to be kin.

"You're late!" the older man snapped once inside the house, which consisted of one long wide room up front with a kitchen, bathroom and three bedrooms behind.

"Some asshole cop interrupt—" the biggest of the two young men started to say.

The older man slapped the younger across the face. "Don't curse in my house, Boy. Your mama would not approve."

The slapped young man rubbed his reddened cheek and looked sheepish. "Sorry, Pa. It's just, a policeman in a pickup came ramming into our meeting with the Mexes. They still had all the stuff in their car so we took off, figuring where there's one pig there's more."

The man called Pa huffed an angry breath. He stalked over to a heavily scarred oaken table and pulled out a chair to sit. The younger men joined him.

"I don't care none about the coke," Pa said, "but what about the girl?"

The two young men exchanged glances. The biggest one, who was taller and heavier than his pa and who'd been driving the Jeep, finally said, "We circled back around to take care of it but Justin missed his shots."

The smaller of the two young men shook his head. "Taylor's wrong. I didn't miss. The first bullet went right where I wanted it to go but a cop threw himself in the way just as I pulled the trigger. No chance at the girl after that. The other shot was just to keep their heads down while we got outta there."

"Same cop?" Pa asked.

"No," Justin said. "Maverick County Deputy." He grinned slyly. "But I reckon he won't be bothering us no more."

"How'd this deputy know to throw himself in the way? He see you?"

"Not a chance," Taylor said. "We were down behind the creek bank. But he had his phone to his ear. I think someone warned him right before Justin fired."

"Who would have warned him?"

Both young men shrugged, but Taylor added, "The first cop. I think he was a da...a Jig. His truck wasn't there when we got back to the site. I'm thinking now he followed us and maybe figured we'd doubled back."

"What about the Mexes?"

"We heard shootin' as we drove away. When we got back we saw one of the greasers dead on the ground. Pretty sure it was the one we knew as Diego. Figured the other was in the back of a squad car but we didn't see him. Didn't have a lot of time to look."

Pa scratched at his clean-shaven chin. "Relief to hear Diego is dead instead of in custody. The other Mex was supposed to just be a hired hand. But I don't trust that. He needs to be gone and I have his name from Diego, who agreed to that before we did business. Biggest worry is the girl. If you tried to kill her and failed, she might talk despite what the Mex was holding over her. Specially since he's dead hisself."

"Hel...heck, Pa, she won't remember nothing with all those drugs in her," Taylor said.

"Maybe she won't," Pa replied. "Maybe she will. But we can't take the chance she recalls anything about your brother Derrick sampling the merchandise."

"You want us to kill her, Pa?" Justin asked. "And the second Mex?"

Pa considered but then shook his head. "You boys screwed up enough already." He slapped his knees and rose to his feet. "You'uns lay low. There's chili and Shiner in the icebox. I've got some calls to make. One in particular. Get a professional in on this. Get it done quick."

————

THE PERP with the broken wrist tried to stare Concho down and failed. "Look, man," he said, glancing away from the Ranger's brown-eyed glare as he answered the question put to him. "I don't know nothin' about that girl. Diego, he brought me in on a deal he had going. I knew it had to do with the cocaine but he never said nothin' about no kidnapping." He shook his head back and forth. "I wouldn't a had anythin' to do with that. Mi Madre, mi hermana, they kill me for that."

"So tell me about Diego."

"Man, I don' know." He snickered. "Maybe you better ask him, no?"

Concho leaned a little closer to the man and breathed lightly into his face. The fellow recoiled. "I'm asking *you*," Ten-Wolves said. "Diego isn't taking any calls."

The perp's bravado failed him. He shivered. "Diego Guzman Cabello, man. He don' work nowhere I know of. Goes back and forth to Mexico. I know he deals but I never hung out with him. But I needed some dinero now. Got bills to pay."

"Where'd you meet Diego?"

"Church, man."

Concho wished he had the ability to arch an eyebrow but settled for a hard frown instead. The outlaw got the message.

"No, no, it's true, man. He wanted to date my sister. Came to church for that. We got to talkin'."

"Looks like a bad mistake."

The fellow gave no response.

"What about the men in the Jeep?" Concho asked.

"Two white guys. I didn't know 'em. Diego did."

"Any description you can give me?"

"Only could see the driver really. Big dude. About your size. Really hairy."

"Hairy? How so? Long hair? A beard?"

"No, no. No beard. Short hair on his head. His arm, though. He had his sleeve rolled up and it was like he's wearin' a bear suit under it."

Concho nodded. "That's useful. So, what's *your* name?"

The man hesitated, then sighed. "Martino. Salas. What you gonna do to me, man?"

"Not up to me. The coke's bad enough but kidnapping...." Ten-Wolves shook his head back and forth. "That's heavy time."

"But I didn't know about the woman," Martino protested. "You believe me, don' you?"

"Doesn't really matter what *I* believe."

"But I helped you. I told you everything."

"And I'll testify you cooperated. That'll help. If you keep cooperating."

"Sure, man, sure."

"Speaking of which, I need you to identify an image for me."

"What image?" Martino asked suspiciously.

Concho pulled out his cell phone and swiped to the etched image of the straight razor from the shell casing officer Turner had found. He showed it to Martino. "This mean anything to you?"

Martino twitched; his eyes shifted back and forth. "Uh...no, man. I never seen anything like that before."

Concho closed the screen and slipped the phone into his pocket. "OK," he said. He gestured toward the police car. "Back inside for now. I'm sure some other officers will have questions for you. Just be as cooperative with them as you've been with me."

Martino nodded. "Sure, man." He slid into the back seat of the car and the lawman closed the door before walking over to Roland Turner.

"Anything?" Turner asked.

"Some names on the two Hispanics," Concho explained. "Two guys in the Jeep. Both white. The driver had a very hairy arm."

Turner arched an eyebrow. "Anything else?"

"Yeah, the fellow was pretty talkative until I showed him the picture of the straight razor on the shell casing. Then he clammed up. He recognized it, though. I'm sure of that."

"It's a start," Turner said.

"Only the finish matters," Ten-Wolves replied.

CHAPTER SIX

A WRECKER ARRIVED TO HAUL THE MONTE CARLO TO POLICE headquarters for the investigation. And there were four police vehicles to escort Martino Salas and the nameless young woman to the hospital and then to the Maverick County police headquarters where Salas would be arrested and the woman held in protective custody until her identity could be established. Concho imagined that was enough folks for the job, so when everyone pulled away from the crime scene, he stayed behind. He'd promised the woman a visit tomorrow.

After everyone left, he climbed up the side of the creek bank to his truck, then stood looking over the scene where the shot that wounded Terrill Hoight came from. He found nothing Roland Turner hadn't found, but he did see where the Jeep had parked, and the divots in the soil and grass where they'd peeled out after the shooting.

The tracks of the fleeing Jeep held to no road but cut across the field. Ten-Wolves slid into his truck and followed. Half a mile later he came to a barbed wire fence penetrated by a cattle grate. He jounced across the grate onto a narrow dirt farm road leading off to the east.

A look back the way he'd come showed no sign of Little Owl

Creek Bridge. The field across from him had been left untended long enough so it was overgrown with persimmon bushes. The fleeing Jeep must have taken the road. Concho followed slowly, checking repeatedly to each side for any sign of a turnoff or for anything unusual that might strike his eye. He didn't expect to see anything but had gotten lucky before just by keeping his eyes open when others had theirs shut.

He reached a dead end, at least as far as a trail was concerned. The dirt road joined with a paved county road. To his left, the new road ran almost straight north, though it probably eventually turned back west toward Eagle Pass. To his right, the road curved to the southeast, toward the Rio Grande.

Which way would the Jeep have gone?

The Ranger sighed. His stomach growled. He'd eaten a big breakfast of eggs, bacon, and hashbrowns before the trial but nothing since. Fortunately, he'd planned ahead. He turned right and cruised along that road until he saw an old gas well. Pulling off onto the access road for the well, he parked under the shade of a big oak.

Getting out, he stretched and took a quick bathroom break. The well wasn't working; the afternoon lay quiet. A little breeze stirred his long black hair, which he'd tied off behind his head with a turquoise band gifted to him from a friend. It was peaceful here but his spirit was not at peace. Too much had happened. He took out his cell phone and placed a call.

"Fort Duncan Regional hospital," a woman's professional sounding voice answered. "How can I help you?"

"Hi, this is Concho Ten-Wolves. I'm a Texas Ranger and I was call—"

"Oh yes, Officer Ten-Wolves," the woman said, her voice becoming animated, "we all know of you here. I just read an article on you in *Texas Monthly Magazine*. A great write up." The woman paused, then added, "You're something of a hero around here after what you did for those people at the mall."

Concho felt his cheeks heating up. The woman was talking

about the terrorist attack on the Mall de las Aguilas, which he'd broken up nearly a year ago. He'd tried to forget it but no one else in the local area seemed to want to.

"Uhm, yes, uhm, thank you," Concho said, discombobulated and with his train of thought in shambles.

"But forgive me," the woman said, "you must have had a reason to call and here I am babbling. What can I do for you, Sir?"

"Uhm..." Concho puffed out a quick breath and got control of himself. He didn't enjoy being a local celebrity but if he had to use it to get what he needed, then so be it. "I was calling to check on a Maverick County deputy brought in with a bullet wound. His name is Terrill Hoight."

"Hoight," the woman said. "OK, let me just check what I have."

Clicking sounds came through the phone from fingers hitting computer keys. The woman's voice came back.

"Yes, Officer Ten-Wolves. Deputy Hoight was brought in about an hour ago and taken immediately to surgery. I have it listed here that he's out of surgery and in our intensive care unit. His condition is marked as 'guarded.'"

"Can you tell me what that means?"

"Hmmm, if you...can you hold just a moment? I know one of the nurses in ICU and she might be able to give me more information. We don't normally do that except for relatives, but in this case..."

"Sure," Concho said. "Thank you very much.... Can I ask your name?"

He could almost hear the woman blushing over the phone. "Well, I'm...I'm Helen Riley."

"Helen you're being a tremendous help. I'll be happy to hold."

"Yes, Sir. Just a moment. I'll check with my friend and get right back to you."

"OK."

The line clicked. Concho kept the phone to his ear. A few black flies started to swirl around him and he swatted at them, then climbed back into his truck and rolled up the window.

The woman's voice came back. "Officer Ten-Wolves, you still there?"

"I'm here, Helen."

"I talked to my friend. She said Deputy Hoight is actually conscious and doing well. They're still giving him blood to replace what he lost but she thinks he's going to be fine. She said not to 'quote her on that,' but she's very experienced so I think she probably knows."

Concho let out a heavy breath. "Wonderful news, Helen. I really appreciate your help here."

"Well, I'm very happy to give it."

"OK, Helen. I have to go but I might call back later to see if there have been any changes. Would that be OK?"

"Of course, I'll be on the desk until ten tonight."

"I'll remember. Thank you again!"

"You're very welcome."

Concho swiped off the call without saying anything else. Otherwise, the "thank you's" and "welcome's" would go on long enough to get awkward. He took a deep breath and relaxed. He'd been more worried about Terrill than he'd realized.

His stomach, which didn't seem to care about any worries he might have, growled again. "All right," he said. "Hold your horses." Opening his glove box, he took out a plastic container holding a brisket sandwich and a bag of Takis tortilla chips.

With a towel on his lap to catch any drip or chip fragment, he set about easing his typically prodigious appetite. Half a dozen big bites later, he was finished, and wishing he'd brought a second sandwich and another bag of chips. He washed it all down with a bottle of water and was about to get back on the road when his phone rang. The caller ID gave the name Maria Morales. He quickly swiped to answer.

"Hey, beautiful," he said.

Maria Marta Morales managed the Mall de las Aguilas, the mall of the eagles, in Eagle Pass. She was more than his girlfriend but something less than a fiancé. They'd dated once before and broken up, but this time they were taking it slower and had been together for nearly a year. As part of her job—and not an unusual occurrence—Maria was currently in San Antonio for a conference of mall workers and owners.

"Ranger!" Maria replied softly. As always, her voice did wicked things to his spine. "How did the trial go?"

"Not completely over yet but my part is mostly done. I think Tallulah is going away for a long time."

"Good. But what about you? I know this kind of thing bothers you."

Concho sighed. "I'm OK but there's a lot of upset on the Rez. Some protesting. Plenty of it directed at me unfortunately. *And there's the media.*"

"Ah, I was worried. Wish I was there for moral support."

"Me, too." He decided not to tell her quite yet about his other adventure of the day, being shot at. He didn't want to worry her. "How is your conference?" he asked.

"I think I'll live through it. But I won't enjoy it," she answered.

"I'll have something for you to enjoy when you get home. You'll *probably* live through it."

"Mhmmm," Maria replied, her voice doing the throaty thing that drove him crazy, "dare I take a guess?"

Concho felt his face flushing and chuckled at himself. "Don't know why I try to play the innuendo game with you. You win every time. I can't take the tension."

Maria laughed. "Well at least you can beat me in arm wrestling."

"One point for me and a hundred for you."

"I'll give you some points back when I see you," she whispered.

Concho flushed again. He reached up and loosened his tie a

little more than it already was. "When you coming home?" he asked to change the topic, although he knew the answer.

"Not till Monday. Just about four days away."

"That's five days too long."

"We'll make up for it."

"Yes."

"Listen, I have to go, but why don't you stay at my apartment a few days. At least the protestors won't be able to find you. Maybe not the reporters either."

"I appreciate that. Maybe I will."

Maria chuckled. "Just make sure you leave the toilet seat down when you're finished."

"I've been eating brisket so you'll be lucky if I leave you a *toilet*."

"Oh God! Now you win. I'm going, goodbye."

She hung up, laughing.

Concho chuckled too as he stuck his cell phone back in its holder on his dash. After completely removing his silver tie, he tossed it into the extended cab area of the Ford. He started the truck, but then killed the engine again as a stray memory struck him like a blow.

He'd learned of late to pay attention to such memories. They often seemed to provide insight into his cases, as if his subconscious mind picked up hidden clues and tried to call them to his attention. Leaning back against his seat, he closed his eyes and let reverie take him. This time, it drew him a long way into the past.

CHAPTER SEVEN

Georgia, 2009, US Army Ranger School

"*I can whip any man in here!*" *Tommy Dougall shouted as he pushed up from his table in the Staghorn Saloon and Grill. "And I've got a hundred bucks to prove it."*

Concho Ten-Wolves sat at the same table as Tommy. He sighed, knowing what was coming. The country music band on stage kept playing but a quiet began to spread out from their table to others nearby, like a ripple on a pool of water.

"*He's drunk!*" *Concho yelled. "Pay him no mind."*

"*I am indeed inebriated," Tommy yelled as a counter, "but that jus' means I can whip any* two *men in here at the same time."*

Saturday night. The Staghorn was full, mostly with soldiers stationed at Fort Benning just down the road. Several soldiers rose as if to accept Dougall's challenge. Most of them decided to sit back down or head to the bar for another round instead when Ten-Wolves stood up beside Tommy.

Concho reached six four and weighed two-thirty. Tommy

was an inch taller and twenty pounds heavier. They looked pretty formidable standing side by side, especially since Concho was sober enough to give everyone around him a glare that warned, "back off!"

Three months before, at age twenty, Ten-Wolves had graduated from Haskell Indian Nations University with a major in languages. He'd joined the Army Rangers immediately and been sent to Fort Benning, Georgia for training. He'd made a few enemies there, and a few friends. One of the few friends was Tommy Dougall, though except for their large sizes they seemed to have little in common.

Tommy was a white Georgia farm boy. Concho was a half black and half Kickapoo Indian from Texas. Tommy was loud and boisterous, a big drinker and big eater. Concho had the eating part but was quiet and thoughtful and hardly ever drank more than two or three beers at a sitting. He'd drunk four tonight and could feel the effects, though no one else probably recognized it.

Two men who'd stood up at Tommy's challenge, though, didn't sit back down or go to the bar. Ten-Wolves studied them and didn't like what he saw. Soldiers. Probably in their late twenties, though he didn't think they were stationed at Fort Benning. Both were six feet or a little above and built as lean as panthers. They wore fatigues and green berets on their heads.

"Let's sit down," Concho said in an aside to Tommy. "You've made your point."

But Tommy was beyond any analysis of the situation. He glared at the two Green Berets. "Don't care if you're special forces bullcrap or not," he snapped. "I'm a ranger and I can still whip both of you."

"Where's your money?" one of the two asked as he and his friend approached.

"Look, he's drunk," Concho said. "Give him a few minutes to calm down and we'll buy you fellows a brew."

The two soldiers might have been twins in size and build but one had short black hair under his beret and the other short wheat-colored hair. The dark-haired one curled his lips in a smirk. "Sure, if he gives us the hundred dollars he promised."

Irritation tightened Concho's muscles but he forced himself to remain calm. "That's not happening," he said softly.

Tommy then did what drunk Tommy often did. He roared, "Come take it Little Man!"

The black-haired one's left arm blurred as he snapped an open-handed blow toward Tommy's throat. Concho blocked it. Tommy blinked. The soldier stepped back in surprise.

"You making this your business?" the dark-haired one snapped. "Not a good idea."

The soldier with the light-colored hair squared off against Concho. Ten-Wolves gave him a glance, then looked back at the first soldier, who seemed to be the leader of the two.

"There isn't any business. You gentlemen sit down and I'll take Tommy outside. We'll all end our evening without anyone getting bruised or broken."

The light-haired soldier lashed out with a foot, smashing his boot against the table behind which Tommy and Concho stood. Beer bottles went flying. The table crashed into Concho's legs, staggering him backward. Dark-hair chopped again at Tommy; the blow connected, an open hand to the right side of Tommy's neck. The big man's muscles on that side spasmed. He grunted.

Concho grabbed the edge of the table, hurled it back at the two Green Beret's. Both men dodged aside. Tommy swung a roundhouse blow that would have felled a horse if it had struck. Dark-hair slipped the blow and struck twice. Lightning fists exploded in Tommy's face. The big man staggered back, crashed down onto another table whose legs folded under the weight.

Light-hair launched a kick at Concho. He blocked it. Another kick followed; Concho blocked again. He snapped a fist toward the man's face but the Green Beret was fast. He slipped the punch and smacked a left up into Ten-Wolves' ribs. The Ranger grunted, and his simmering anger ignited. His right hand plucked up a chair by the back and sent it swinging.

Light-hair threw his right arm up and ducked behind it. The chair hit him and shattered. Concho charged. Tommy tried to get up and the dark-haired special forces soldier kicked him in the face before turning toward Concho.

Ten-Wolves grabbed light-hair at arm and shoulder. The man chopped with his free hand into Concho's shoulder but had no leverage to make the blow count. Concho picked him up bodily and hurled him ten feet across the room into a ring of other watching soldiers.

Dark-hair turned on Concho, launching a blur of flashing hands. A fist caromed off the Ranger's chin; another blow hacked into his cheek, cutting the skin against the cheekbone and spattering blood. He shook his head as he staggered backward, throwing his arms up for defense.

Dark-hair's eyes were intense, burning, as he leaped in. He sent a kick stabbing into Ten-Wolves' thigh. The muscle there spasmed. The Green Beret had the momentum but he made a mistake. He threw a punch that slammed into Concho's blocking hands.

Concho viced the man's wrist. He twisted, flinging the fellow away from him. But now light-hair regained his feet. He snapped a kick into the Ranger's gut. Concho turned at the last second so the kick didn't completely steal his air. It still bent him over and left his face wide open for a roundhouse kick.

Tommy rose with a fresh roar and lunged to wrap both his big arms around light-hair, pinning his arms to his sides. The Green Beret bludgeoned his head back into Tommy's face. Tommy's nose shattered; blood sprayed. But he held on, which gave Concho a moment to punch the other soldier in the face with one big dark fist. The man wilted. His legs folded. Tommy let him drop.

The dark-haired Green Beret was on his feet. His right

hand gripped a long brown beer bottle and he snapped it against a nearby table, shattering the bottom of the bottle to leave jagged edges of glass stabbing out like scalpels.

"Enough!" someone shouted.

The band had long since fallen silent, and now the raucous yells of the crowd died away. Concho spun around to see who'd shouted. Another Green Beret stood facing the scene. He was an officer, a captain according to his insignia. A calm anger boiled off him as he walked toward the center of the fight.

The light-haired soldier who'd been knocked out stirred. Tommy, suddenly chastened, reached down and grasped the guy under the shoulders and hauled him to his feet. The man snapped to consciousness. He jerked away from Tommy and threw up his fists. The Green Beret captain grabbed his wrist and shoved him away.

"Coleman!" the captain snapped. "You and Hendricks get out of here. Move!"

The dark-haired soldier dropped his broken beer bottle, then grabbed his friend by the arm. He gave a yank and the light-haired man followed him, stumbling a little on still shaky feet.

The captain stopped in front of the two rangers. His gaze studied them.

"Captain!" Concho said, straightening his shoulders.

"Jack Travers," the officer said. "Who are you two yahoos?"

"Tommy Dougall," Tommy said.

"Concho Ten-Wolves."

Travers ignored Tommy. "Ten-Wolves," he said. "What tribe?"

"Kickapoo."

Travers nodded. From his high cheekbones, the complexion of his skin, and his anthracite eyes, the captain probably had some Native American in him, too. Not Kickapoo, though. Maybe Apache.

"You don't appear to be drunk," Travers said to Concho.

"No, Sir."

Again, Travers nodded. He wore his dress uniform, complete with tie. Unsnapping the pocket of his jacket, he fished out some folded greenbacks, which he tossed to Tommy. The big man caught the money with surprise.

"Well, gentlemen," Travers said, "carry on!" He turned and stalked out.

Tommy unfolded the currency. His swollen lips moved as he counted it. He glanced at his friend and spat out a fragment of tooth. Then he grinned. "And I made my hundred! That's a lot of beer."

Concho shook his head. "He must have watched the whole thing. And only interrupted when his man produced a weapon."

"Who cares," Tommy said. "A hundred bucks. A hundred bucks!"

Ten-Wolves pulled the table they'd originally been sitting at back upright, though it leaned precariously to one side on a bent leg. He grabbed an unbroken chair and sat down heavily.

"You're buying," he said to his friend. "And I'm drinking."

CONCHO OPENED HIS EYES AND SAT UP STRAIGHT IN HIS TRUCK AS the reverie ended. He frowned as he tried to consider any possible meaning to connect the images from so many years ago with the case that had just fallen into his lap. He couldn't see any, though his thoughts kept circling around the image of the straight razor on the shell.

The slugfest in the Staghorn had certainly marked a big change in his life. Three days later, he and Tommy and their entire unit shipped overseas to the fighting in Afghanistan. Tommy didn't even last a month before an improvised explosive device—IED—took him out. It hadn't been the last time he'd seen Jack Travers, though. Maybe there was something there, too, though he couldn't imagine what at the moment.

Starting the truck, he threw it into gear and peeled out. Giving up any hope of stumbling upon the perpetrator's Jeep, he turned back toward Eagle Pass and Maria Morales's house. It was getting late and he felt hungry again. And he had a report to prepare. Maybe writing down his thoughts would jolt loose some clues to help him with what promised to be another strange case.

CHAPTER EIGHT

MESKWAA WOKE FROM A NAP AND SAT UP ABRUPTLY. IT WAS LATE afternoon. He'd fallen asleep in the warm sun on one of the benches on the ramada porch of his wickiup, the traditional Kickapoo hut he'd built for himself a few years previously. He owned a more modern trailer, too, but seldom spent much time there, especially when the weather was nice.

Meskwaa was a Kickapoo term for "red," and that was the name everyone knew him by. It wasn't his full name. He was old now and didn't remember who might still be living who knew the rest of it. It did not matter to him.

Most everyone considered Meskwaa to be a Naataineniiha, a medicine man. He made no such claim for himself. It was only that, at times, he knew things, and he used that information to help good people when he could. Of late, he'd been able to use his knowledge and visions to help Concho Ten-Wolves, who he sometimes thought of like a son.

Now, he'd experienced a vision in his sleep that revolved around Ten-Wolves in some way, though he didn't yet understand how. He pushed himself to his feet, his muscles and bones protesting. He remembered when he'd once been young and could move with the fluid grace of a panther. Those days were no more, particularly after his encounter some months before with the big Indian named Whirlwind, who'd held him prisoner for several days before Ten-Wolves came to free him.

Stepping through the doorway into the main part of the wickiup, he paused to let his eyes adjust to the gloom. Even with the blanket covering the door tacked up out of the way, the interior remained full of shadows. The hut had no windows and no smoke hole. The loose construction of sotol stalks that made up the walls, along with the cattail and river cane roof, allowed for plenty of ventilation when he did build a fire. He had none now, of course, though he could smell the residue of old ones.

He went to a bench upon which many items lay piled, from feathers to tortoise shells to broken tools. He scooped up a sketch pad and a big thick pencil he'd bought at a little store in Kickapoo Village, not very far away on the reservation.

Sitting down on another bench, he quickly sketched the image from his sleep. It had not been a dream, only a silver and pearl image floating against a midnight background. He put the finished sketch down and fished a rather bulky cell phone out of a hide pouch tied to the belt of his deerskin trousers.

Staring at the phone, he felt his lips curling in distaste. He did not like such things but Ten-Wolves and Robert Echabarri— the young sheriff of the Kickapoo Tribal police—had insisted he keep it and he'd done so. It was a simple gray plastic phone with very large numbers on the front.

Pressing the button on the side to turn the phone on, he waited until it completed its strange wake-up rituals. He could see a small numeral at the top of the phone that read three percent and frowned. He'd forgotten to charge the thing, but perhaps it would work well enough for one call. He pressed another button, something Robert Echabarri called a "speed dial."

The phone rang. Once, twice, three times. Robert Echabarri answered. "Meskwaa!" Echabarri said. "Are you all right?"

The old man could hear a lot of noise in the background of

the call. Angry people shouting and chanting. "I am better than you it would seem," he said.

Echabarri sighed. "We've got a bunch of protestors in front of the office and they're starting to get rowdy."

"What are they hating the Ten-Wolves for now?"

"How did you know.... Never mind. He testified in court today in the Tallulah Whiteheart case. Apparently it was pretty damning."

"I am sure he told only the truth."

"That doesn't matter to some people. These folks are waiting for Concho to come back on the Rez so they can scream at him. But what about you? Why did you call? Everything all right?"

"I am fine but there is something I wanted to talk to Ten-Wolves about."

"His number is in the phone I gave you."

"Yes, but it is hiding from me. I only remembered how to call you. Besides, I have not fed this phone thing and I think it is about to die of starvation."

"Well is it an emergency? I talked to him earlier to warn him about the protestors but I'm not sure he's coming back to the Rez tonight. If he's smart, he'll just stay away."

Meskwaa considered, waiting long enough for Echabarri to ask," Did I lose you?"

"I am here," Meskwaa said. "I do not think it is an emergency. Tell him to come see me when he can."

"All ri—" Echabarri was saying when the phone buzzed and went dead.

Meskwaa took the phone from his ear and stared at it. He shook his head, then went back to the junk-piled bench to look for the thing called a 'phone charger.' "Let us hope," he muttered, "it is truly not an emergency."

———

ROBERTO ECHABARRI LOWERED his cell phone as the call with Meskwaa went dead. He stood just inside the front entrance to tribal police headquarters, a long, one-story building at the corner of Chick Kazan Street and Nakai Breen Avenue on the Kickapoo reservation.

Through the glass door, he could see a crowd of twenty or so people yelling outside. Most held signs, with such slogans on them as JUSTICE FOR TALLULAH, POLICE CORRUPTION, and ARREST TEN-WOLVES. He'd already told them twice to disperse and been ignored. He didn't have room in his jail to arrest them all, and that would be an unwise move anyway. He'd hoped they'd eventually give up and go home, but that didn't seem to be happening.

In a fresh effort to facilitate the crowd's dispersal, he opened the door and yelled out, "Ten-Wolves is not coming back to the reservation this evening. You have no reason to be here. Please move along so we can go about the business of the police."

The yelling and sign waving only intensified. Someone shouted, "Free Tallulah Whiteheart!"

"Tallulah is in jail in Eagle Pass," Roberto shouted back. "I couldn't release her if I wanted to."

"Arrest Ten-Wolves," another voice shouted. "Justice. Justice!"

A few individuals at the front of the crowd surged forward. Roberto shut the door in their faces and locked it. Fists banged on the glass. He turned away. His glance crossed that of Nila Willow, who sat behind the dispatch desk. Nila was the first female officer to work for the Kickapoo Tribal police. Echabarri had appointed her. She was a woman of few words and all she did now was shrug.

Timbo Corbett, another of Echabarri's deputies, who was only one quarter Kickapoo and could have passed for white with his sandy brown hair, had more to say.

"Want me to get the tear gas?"

Roberto shook his head. "It's getting late. They'll get hungry soon enough and move along."

"At least let me pepper spray a few," Corbett responded.

"Timbo," Roberto said. "We're not doing that. Make yourself useful and give Arturo a call. Make sure he's doing OK keeping an eye on Ten-Wolves' trailer. Tell him we'll send someone to relieve him in a few hours."

"You're the boss," Corbett said, as if he didn't really believe it to be true. But he pulled out his cell phone and moved off.

Roberto gave Nila a nod and went into his office. He dropped heavily into his chair, then realized he still held his own phone. He swiped up a number and placed a call.

CHAPTER NINE

THE BROTHERS TAYLOR AND JUSTIN MODINE DID WHAT THEIR father ordered them to do. They went into the farmhouse kitchen and grabbed a couple of Shiner bock beers from the fridge. Taylor took the lid off the big pot of chili simmering on the stove, all meat with no beans. But plenty of peppers. He dished up two thick bowls.

Justin stepped over to the kitchen doorway to look back into the living area. He watched their father open the front door and stalk outside, his cell phone in one hand. When he turned back around, Taylor held one of the bowls of chili out to him, with a spoon already in it. He took it but didn't immediately eat.

"Pa and his professionals," he snorted. "Hell, the second Mex is gonna be right in the middle of pig central. The girl, too. No one's gonna be able to get to them. We better just hope they keep their mouths shut."

"People get killed in jail all the time," Taylor replied after a belch.

"The girl ain't gonna be in jail," Justin said. He air quoted. "She's a 'victim.' They'll be lookin' after her like she's a glazed donut."

Taylor laughed at his brother's gibe. "Maybe that drug the

Mex gave her will do its job and she won't remember what happened to her."

Justin took a thick bite of chili and chewed. He spoke around the mouthful. "From the pictures the Mex sent us, she was a looker. For an Indian. Sorry to lose out on that."

"At least Derrick got some," Taylor said.

"Don't he always?"

Taylor only nodded. He finished inhaling his chili and set the empty bowl down on the counter, letting his spoon clatter into it. Bottles of Shiners didn't have twist off caps but he twisted his off anyway and slugged a few huge swallows. His hazel-brown eyes grew shiny and his jaw worked back and forth as if powering his thoughts.

"You got some kind o' idea?" Justin demanded. "Spit it out!"

"One thing Pa mentioned but didn't follow up on," Taylor said. "The collateral Diego was holdin' over the girl's head."

Justin snapped his fingers. "Right!"

"We get that and we'll be sittin' pretty."

"You know where to find it?"

"I do. Pa let it slip on a phone call he didn't think I could hear. We best not tell him, though. Till it's done."

"What the old man don't know won't hurt him," Justin replied. He began shoveling his own chili down but had to use a bottle opener to get at his beer.

———

IT WAS after 6:00 PM but still light out as Concho pulled into the parking lot of Casa Del Sol, the house of the sun. This was the building where Maria Morales lived in Eagle Pass. It was a nice complex, with three wings of large, somewhat expensive apartments. Maria lived in 214, on the second floor of Wing B.

Taking his laptop and the change of clothes he'd still had no time to don, he locked his Ford and climbed the stairs to 214. Someone down the way played loud hip hop music but it wasn't overly distracting. He and Maria had long since exchanged keys to their places so Concho let himself in and shut the door behind him, deadening most of the sound.

A pleasant scent in the apartment struck him first. Maria often wore a perfume that made him think of blackberries and cream. Even though she hadn't been here in a few days, the scent lingered. He liked it very much.

The apartment had a large, tastefully decorated living area with a smaller kitchen and dining room behind it. There was a lot of clutter; Maria was not the neatest of housekeepers. Stairs led up to the bathroom and two bedrooms, one of which Maria used for a home office.

Setting his belongings down on the couch, he walked into the kitchen and opened the fridge. Two bottles of Modelo Especial sat against the right side of the fridge and he pulled one out. He didn't drink much, and he preferred Modelo's darker brew when he did, but he figured he'd had a tough day and deserved a beer. His phone rang as he used a bottle opener to pop the lid off the Modelo. He saw Roberto Echabarri's name and swiped to answer.

"Yes?"

"You're not coming back here tonight are you?"

"No. Staying at Maria's place."

"Good idea. The protestors want your head."

"Well, I don't use it a lot but I'd prefer to keep it anyway."

Echabarri chuckled. "Meskwaa called here a bit ago."

"Oh?"

"Yeah, he asked you to come see him when you can."

"Nothing about why?"

"No, but he said it wasn't an emergency."

"All right, I'll stop by and see him tomorrow. By the way, you know Terrill Hoight don't you?"

"Yeah, good officer."

"He was shot today." Concho explained what happened after he'd finished testifying at Tallulah Whiteheart's trial, and about the young Indian woman who claimed to have no memory of who she was or why she was locked in the back of a car.

"How can one man attract such mayhem?" Echabarri asked.

"If I believed in astrology, I'd tell you I was born under a bad sign."

"I'm just glad I'm not you. Hoight going to make it?"

"I hope so. I called the hospital a while ago and they said he was doing all right."

"Glad to hear it," Echabarri replied. "By the way, I've got Arturo Ramon watching your place. Wouldn't want you to get burned out again."

Concho sighed. He remembered when his old trailer had been burned. He'd lost a lot of irreplaceable personal possessions, as well as a book collection he was very fond of. He'd been slowly replacing most of the latter and didn't want to lose it again.

"Anyway," Echabarri continued. "I'll call you tomorrow. Hopefully, you'll be able to get back on the Rez without too many protestors in your way."

"Thanks. For everything."

An awkward silence followed. "No problem," Roberto finally said.

They hung up, and though Concho felt the pangs of hunger again he first set his laptop up on Maria's dining room table and typed up his report of the day's adventures. He emailed a copy to Dalton Shaw, his boss and the newish commander of Texas Rangers group D. He copied the email to Isaac Parkland, the sheriff of Maverick County, who Terrill Hoight and Roland Turner worked for as deputies. He also copied the Texas Department of Public Safety, and then sent it off to one more destination—Special Agent Della Rice of the FBI.

Della Rice, who'd been named after the actress and singer Della Reese, had at one time been assigned to investigate Concho for possible corruption. She'd cleared him of those insinuations and the two had become friends. Of a sort. At least they'd come to tolerate each other and work well together when needed. Since this case involved a kidnapping and possibly the transportation of a kidnap victim across international borders, the FBI needed to be informed.

Concho closed his laptop and was heading for Maria's fridge to look for something to eat when the doorbell rang.

CHAPTER TEN

TEN-WOLVES FROZE AS THE BING-BONG OF THE DOORBELL ECHOED through Maria's apartment. No one knew he was here except Maria and Roberto Echabarri. Neither of them would have told anyone.

He'd taken his guns off. They lay on the table. He stepped back to them and pulled one Double Eagle free of its holster. Most likely, whoever was at the door was an innocent, perhaps one of Maria's neighbors, or a friend who didn't realize she was gone. It could also be a reporter, or a protestor from the trial, neither of which would likely pose him any real danger. But it could be something more sinister. He'd learned to be cautious this past year. Several attempts had been made on his life.

He eased his way across the apartment, avoiding the spots on the floor he knew from experience squeaked. He tried to peer through the curtains on the front window but couldn't directly see the outside of the door. The bell rang again.

"Who is it?" he called, making sure not to stand directly in front of the door where someone might shoot through the wood.

A gasp came in answer, and then a voice. "I...I was looking for Maria. Is...is she home?"

Concho stepped silently to the door and pressed one eye to

the peephole. A young Hispanic woman in her early twenties stood outside. She wore a thin dress and had her arms crossed over her chest. She shivered, though surely not from cold on this summer night.

"Just a minute," he said through the door. "I'm Maria's boyfriend. Let me open up."

He lay the pistol on the small knickknack table to one side where Maria kept her keys, then twisted the lock to open and pull back the door. The woman outside gasped again as she saw his size. She shrank back and he lifted his hands, open palmed to show her he meant no harm.

"It's all right," he soothed. "I'm afraid Maria's not here right now. Can I help you?"

As she'd stepped back, the woman moved more directly beneath the outside light. The big man's mouth tightened as he saw the swelling on the right side of her face, just under the eye. She'd been struck there, and recently.

"Oh, uh, no, I just.... Well, I didn't realize Maria was gone. I'll come back another time."

"Ma'am," Concho said as the woman started to turn away. She looked back at him, her eyes hollow and pregnant with emotion. He continued: "You can see by the badge on my shirt that I'm a lawman. If you need help, I'm happy to offer it."

She glanced at his shirt. "I...I, uh, yes, I know. Maria...told me about you. And I've...read about you."

He smiled as gently as he could for her. "Maria's a pretty good judge of character isn't she? And she trusts me. You can, too."

The woman shook her head emphatically. "Oh, no, it's OK. Nothing's...wrong."

"Hey, bitch!" a man's voice shouted from down the row of apartments. "Where'd you go? Get in here and make us somethin' to eat."

The woman nearly jumped off her feet. Her face flashed fear and she looked quickly away. She grabbed the skirt of her dress, bunching it in her hands. "I've got to go," she said. "Thank you. I'll talk to Maria later." She hurried off, not quite running but not far from it.

Concho felt like spitting. He quickly reached up and unpinned his badge, tucking it into his pants pocket. His handcuffs still hung at his belt and he slid the case that held them around toward the back where it wouldn't easily be seen. Then he strode after the woman, moving silently for all his size.

The woman hurried toward a man-shaped shadow standing outside another apartment half a dozen places down. The loud music from earlier came from the partially opened door behind the shadow. The fellow grabbed the woman's arm, hard. She winced.

"Excuse me," Concho said.

The man—in his mid to late twenties—turned, surprise and shock showing on his face that he hadn't seen or heard the big fellow coming who now suddenly stood beside him. "Who you?" he demanded. When Concho didn't immediately answer, the fellow glanced accusingly at the woman. "You know this dude?"

Concho wanted to slap the faux mean look off the man's face but had to handle this delicately or everything would backfire on the woman. "I don't know *her*," he said quickly. "I came to talk to you."

Again, the fellow showed surprised. "Whatcha lookin' for me for?"

"The music," Ten-Wolves said, offering a deliberately weak smile as he gestured toward the apartment door, which carried the number 219. "Wonder if you could turn it down a little?"

The man snorted through his nose. He relaxed, thinking he understood now what the scene was about. "What's the matter, brother? You don't like good music?"

Concho was playing this whole situation by ear. He needed to escalate it in some fashion that didn't implicate the woman. And the man had just given him a way—a misunderstanding. "Brother?" he asked sharply.

The man frowned. "Brother, man." He gestured back and forth between them. "You know, the skin tone, man."

Concho let his tacked-on smile fade, let his own mean look start to surface. "You insulting my mother?" he demanded.

The other man blinked. His mind was off balance, kept that way from the first moment of this interaction. He spluttered. "No, man. You know it's just what people say."

"*My* mother would never have given birth to a scumbag like you so I think you just insulted her. And that means you insulted me!"

The man grunted as the Ranger's words registered. His lips curled in a snarl and his hand darted toward his pocket. He came out with a butterfly knife, started to flip it open. Concho grabbed his wrist, squeezed hard. The man cried out as the wrist bones ground together. His fingers spasmed; he dropped the knife, which clattered on the concrete walkway.

Concho wrapped a fist in the man's oversized t-shirt and spun him around to press him against the black iron railing along the outside of the walkway. The fellow's legs came off the ground. He yipped in surprise, but before he could do anything to resist, the Ranger grabbed his ankle. In the next second, the man found himself hanging upside down over the railing with a long drop beneath him. He screamed.

The woman shouted, "Please don't drop him!"

"We'll see," Concho snarled. He held the man by both ankles and gave a vigorous shake so coins and keys fell out of his pockets and plummeted to the sidewalk below.

The door to apartment 219 swung fully open. Ten-Wolves turned his head but immediately the six-inch barrel of a large revolver was shoved close to his face. The African American holding the nickel-plated gun was big but young, probably no more than seventeen. From the looks, he might have been the real brother of the fellow Concho had hold of.

"You let him go?" the gunman's voice snapped, his words a little higher pitched than the youth probably wanted.

The Ranger released one hand on the dangling man's ankles. The fellow dropped half a foot and shrieked, "No, no, no!"

"Please?" the woman shouted.

"Bring him back, bring him back up," the youthful gunman yelled.

Concho shrugged. "You need to choose your words carefully here," he said. "Say what you mean."

"Pull him back up here," the gunman ordered, trying to get control of his voice.

Concho shrugged again. He hauled the first man up by the legs. When he had him lifted high enough, he grabbed an arm and pulled him back over the railing, then dropped him with a thump on the concrete where he lay gasping for breath.

Glancing back at the gunman, Ten-Wolves said, "There. Happy?"

The young man's arm shook. Things weren't going the way his mind had envisioned them. He tried for bluster to raise his courage. "Give me one good reason why I shouldn't blow your head off."

Concho smiled his shark smile. "I'll give you two," he said.

The youth recoiled a short step. "What? What?"

"One, you and your brother here just pulled deadly weapons on a Texas Ranger. And that's not going to end well for you."

"What? You ain't no Ranger."

"Off duty. Badge in my pocket. But I'm very much an officer of the law."

The young man shook more now. His eyes darted left and right as if seeking escape.

"You want to hear the second reason?" Concho asked.

The gunman licked his lips. He didn't seem to know how to respond but threw out a, "What?"

"That Ruger Blackhawk you're holding is a single action revolver."

The man blinked, confused. "So?"

"So...you haven't cocked the hammer."

The youth frowned. His pupils dilated. He glanced down at the gun and started to lift his thumb. Concho was faster. His hands blurred as he grabbed the long barrel of the Ruger and twisted it savagely to the side. In the next instant, the Ranger had the revolver in *his* hand. Now *he* cocked the hammer, the sound almost as loud as a gunshot in the gathering darkness.

"Like this," Concho said. "So it can be fired." He pushed the big hollow bore of the weapon to within an inch of the youth's face.

The young man cowered back. "No, please!"

Ten-Wolves took a slow, deep breath. He eased the hammer down on the pistol. "Up against the railing," he ordered both men. They immediately obeyed. He took out his handcuffs and cuffed their wrists together.

"What...what are you going to do with them, Officer?" the woman asked.

"They're going to jail for assaulting a lawman."

He grabbed the older brother by the arm and started dragging the two of them along the walkway toward the stairs. After stuffing the Blackhawk into his belt, he fished his cell out of his pocket and called the Maverick County Sherriff's office.

"Officer needs assistance," he said when the call was answered. "Casa Del Sol parking lot. Not an emergency but no need to dawdle."

CHAPTER ELEVEN

AN SUV CONTAINING TWO MAVERICK COUNTY POLICE OFFICERS arrived to take custody of the men Concho had arrested. He handed over the Ruger and the butterfly knife as well and told the officers he'd be in shortly to file charges.

After the SUV drove off, Concho went back up the stairs of the apartment complex and walked down to 219. The woman leaned against the railing. She hadn't left that spot except to go inside for a few seconds to turn down the music. She didn't look directly at him as he stepped to the railing near her. He'd pinned his badge back on.

"I...I didn't want them arrested," she said.

"My call. He'd hit you, and I imagine it's not the first time. But they don't ever need to know you had anything to do with it. I arrested them for assaulting me."

"They'll just get out."

"Not right away. You've got some time."

"Time for what?"

"Look, no one owns your life but you. I can't tell you what to do. But if he's hit you before, he will again. If you want out of the situation, I'm here to help. I know a women's shelter. It's safe. You can pack a bag and I'll drive you there right now. Or, even better, if you have family, go home. Don't leave anything behind to tell him how to find you."

The woman sighed as she considered. "My family is in San Antonio. Mi Madre and Padre. But they're old. I don't want to burden them."

"Do they love you?"

The woman seemed shocked at his bluntness. Then tears filled her eyes. "Si," she said. "Not sure why."

"So it's not a burden to go to them. I'll drive you to the bus station."

"I...I don't know."

"Think about it," Concho said. "I've got to go down to the police station to file my charges. It'll take a while and I'll make sure they won't be able to make bail until tomorrow afternoon. I'll be back here well before then and you can tell me what you want to do. I'll take you wherever you want to go."

The woman nodded. She looked at him. "Jaiden is not a bad guy," she said. "He's just...unhappy. And he lashes out."

"Unhappiness is no excuse for taking pain out on someone else. And you don't deserve to have it taken out on you."

She sighed. "I'll think about it."

"OK." He gazed at her. "What's your name?"

"Valentina. Valentina Caamaño."

"Well, Valentina, I'll be back in a few hours. I'll check on you then."

The woman nodded again but didn't say anything else. Concho turned and walked back to Maria's apartment. He buckled on his guns and went down to his truck to drive to the Sheriff's office. The woman still stood at the upstairs railing as he pulled out of the parking lot. He didn't wave. Nor did she.

———

AFTER FILING charges on the two men he'd arrested at Casa Del Sol, Concho decided to check on the woman he'd found bound in the back of a drug dealer's car earlier in the day. The Maverick County Sheriff's office had only a few cells in the front part of the building, for special cases. The woman certainly qualified, since she wasn't officially under arrest but in protective custody.

Isaac Parkland—the Sheriff—who was a good friend, had gone home for the day but the Ranger knew his way around. He walked the building's back corridors until he came to a metal door guarded by a newly hired deputy he'd yet to be introduced to.

The young man sat behind a desk but immediately straightened and rose as he saw the Texas Ranger Cinco peso badge and recognized the wearer. "Sir!" he saluted.

"Take it easy," Ten-Wolves replied. "I was hoping to speak to the young woman in protective custody here."

The man hesitated, then nodded. "Of course, Sir." He pulled a key out of his shirt pocket and turned to unlock the door.

"I guess they're referring to her as Jane Doe," the Ranger said.

The young man flashed him a white grin as he said, "Some are calling her Jane Running Doe."

Concho frowned. The officer saw it and his smile fled. "You know...uhm, because she's...uhm, Native American," he tried to explain.

"I get it," Concho said, his brown-eyed gaze never wavering from the hazel eyes of the officer. "But I'd prefer not to hear it again."

The man blushed heavily. "I'm sorry, Sir. I know you're—I wasn't thinking."

"No. I don't reckon you were" He slapped the officer lightly on the shoulder. "But you will next time. What's your name?"

Again, the young man straightened. And almost saluted. "Keegan, Sir! Kerry Keegan."

Concho smiled to take a little sting out of his criticism. "It's OK, Kerry. We all have moments when our thinking Stetsons aren't on. Make sure you list my visit on your records. I'll talk to Sheriff Parkland about it tomorrow."

"Yes, Sir!"

Keegan opened the door and held it for Concho to pass through, then closed it behind him. Beyond the door stood a short corridor with two sealed rooms on either side. This area lay in the heart of the building and none of the rooms bore windows, though plenty of ventilation holes were cut in the Plexiglass walling them.

Jane Doe sat on the cot in the first room on the right, the only occupied one of the four. She still wore the same clothes as earlier, though it looked like she'd been able to take a sponge bath at least.

"Hello," Concho said.

The woman put her hand to her mouth, then lowered it. "I thought you weren't coming until tomorrow."

"I had to come tonight for a different reason. Thought I'd stop by and see how you're doing. What did the doctor say?"

"He...well, I guess you know they took me to the hospital first. They said I didn't have any...concussion to explain my memory loss. They took a blood sample for drugs. And they uh...." She looked away and he knew she was thinking of the rape kit examination. It couldn't have been pleasant.

He let her move on from that thought. No need to discuss it until they got the results. "Do you remember ingesting any drugs?" he asked.

She shook her head. Rising from her cot, she walked over to the stand in front of Concho, with only the Plexiglass between them. "I'm...glad you came. It's lonely here."

The Ranger nodded. "I'm sure it is, but it's for your protection right now. The sooner we're able to identify you, the sooner we'll be able to get you into some more comfortable surroundings."

A faint smile twisted Jane's lips. "Unless it turns out I'm some kind of criminal, of course."

Concho vented a low chuckle. "Yeah, unless that. So, besides 'out of here,' what can I get you?"

She glanced around, then gestured to some magazines piled on the chair by her cot. "They gave me some things to read but..." she shrugged.

"You like to read?"

The woman's gaze darted across his and away, like a quick bird flitting through thick brush. "I don't know. I don't remember what I like to do. Or not to do. I'm pretty sure I don't like being cooped up."

"Me either. You know, I live on the Kickapoo Reservation just outside Eagle Pass. I've got a huge mesquite tree in my front yard. I like to sit underneath it when the weather's good."

"Sounds nice. But why are you telling me this?"

"I've got a feeling you've been on a reservation yourself. Something about your accent. Maybe the Navaho Nation in Arizona. That mean anything to you?"

Again, Jane's eyes did the darting thing. She shook her head. "Not that I recall."

"All right. I'm gonna go, but if you think of anything you want to tell me, let the officer outside know and he'll give you access to a phone. Call anytime."

"OK. Thank you. When do you think I can get out of here?"

"Wouldn't be a good idea right now. You've already had one attempt made on your life."

She crossed her arms over her chest and sighed. "It's just..." She threw her hands up in the air. "I can't stand it here. I want out."

"I understand. But be patient. I know it's hard. Work on your memory. Help us catch them."

"I worry."

"About what?"

"I don't know." She shrugged and turned away.

The Ranger headed for the door, considering what he'd learned in the last few minutes. Almost certainly the woman had *some* memories, which meant she was telling at least a few lies. It felt, though, as if she were telling them less to protect herself and more to protect someone else.

It was also very likely she'd been drugged during her ordeal, which meant she might have only fragmentary memories of what happened to her in the last few days. Not the time to confront her about either issue. Let her calm down some more. Let any memory fragments solidify. Let her start thinking about trusting someone.

Back in the corridor outside, Concho spoke to Kerry Keegan behind his desk. "If she says anything about calling me, let her. Anytime, day or night. And make a note about that in your log for whoever spells you here."

"Yes, Sir. Will do. And..."

"And what?"

"I'm...sorry about earlier. About what I said."

Concho nodded. "I understand," he said. "We're all trying to do better." He was pretty sure that wasn't true for everyone, but it probably was for this young officer. And that needed to be acknowledged. He'd seen too many bad men. The decent ones had to be encouraged.

CHAPTER TWELVE

IT WAS ALMOST 10:00 PM AND FULL DARK BY THE TIME TEN-Wolves left the police station. The parking lot lights cast an orange, sodium vapor glow over everything, harshening the night. A few bats didn't seem to mind as they swept curlicues through the strange light after insects.

The lawman could smell tarmac and exhaust and was eager to get back to Maria's apartment and the scent of her blackberries and cream perfume. As he approached his Ford in the lot, a familiar voice called to him. He turned to see Roland Turner approaching, his shoes clicking on the concrete.

"Glad I caught you," Turner said.

"Figured you'd already gone home," the Ranger replied.

Turner sighed. "Too much going on. And too worried about Terrill."

"I called about him. He's out of surgery and doing better."

Turner nodded. "Glad to hear it. Sounds like good news but I don't trust hospitals. Too much can go wrong in one of those places."

"You're right."

"I stopped you because I imagine you want to know what we've found so far."

"I would. Figured I'd have to get it from Isaac tomorrow."

"I put a report on Sheriff Parkland's desk but I can give you the gist."

"Please."

"Our Jane Doe has no head injury that might explain her memory loss. She's physically healthy. A few bruises on her arms and legs but nothing to indicate a beating. They took a blood sample for a drug test but said we won't hear until tomorrow."

Ten-Wolves nodded, though he'd learned much of this from the woman herself. "What about the rape kit?"

"They did one. DNA results will take a while but they told me the woman had sex more than once. No tearing of the vagina so it could have been consensual."

"Or she was drugged for it."

"Possibly. Circumstantial evidence points to our two perps. One or both. But we'll have to be sure."

"What else?"

"The Monte Carlo was clean except for the cocaine in the trunk. We found nothing connected to the woman other than a few of her hairs. We've got cell phones from both perps. They're locked but our tech expert is on it."

"Good."

"The dead perp. You already know his name is Diego. He's got a long sheet of crimes, but nothing as serious as kidnapping. We haven't been able to find any address on him, though. Don't know where he was staying. We got nothing on Martino Salas. He's local and seems to have been clean before this."

"Gotcha."

"I also did a database search on that image of the straight razor."

Concho perked up. "And?"

"Nothing. I even tried running tattoos but no sign of it associated with any criminal activity I can find."

Ten-Wolves huffed a heavy breath. "Too bad, but I still think that might be our *in* for this case. The symbol meant something to the man who etched it on the shell casing. And that was a mistake, the only one they've made so far. Was the Diego body taken to the coroner?"

"Yep."

"Good again. Earl Blake knows what he's doing. Maybe he'll be able to tell us something from his examination."

"All right," Turner said. His face turned grim. "I want these guys. Bad enough to taste it."

"We'll get 'em. I guarantee it. They've already made one mistake. They'll make more."

————

AFTER ARRIVING BACK at Casa Del Sol apartments, Concho knocked on the door to 219. Valentina Caamaño answered. She'd taken a shower and used some makeup to hide her bruised cheek as best as possible. A suitcase rested on the floor next to her.

"You've decided," Concho said.

The woman nodded. "I'm going to San Antonio. Home."

"For the best." She picked up her suitcase and he took it from her. "You need anything else?"

She shook her head, then closed the door behind her. It locked with the sound of finality. She sighed but straightened her shoulders. "I'm ready."

Half an hour later, Concho stood on the bus station platform and watched a blue and silver Greyhound coach pull out for San Antonio, about a hundred-and fifty-mile ride. He waved, though he couldn't see if the woman waved back or not. As he turned away, a large white man whose bulky layers of clothing had seen better days approached. The Ranger studied the fellow cautiously, though the man's first words put him a little more at ease.

"Sorry to ask you, my man," the fellow said. "But I ain't eaten in three days. Could you spare a little somethin' somethin'?"

The beggar's eyes matched the tale he told. They looked listless and dull. And the face and short dark hair were dirty enough, although the odor clinging to the man wasn't very strong. Concho seldom believed such stories entirely but it didn't really matter to him. Helping was cheap enough, and maybe sometimes it fed the truly hungry. Pulling out his wallet, he fished out a twenty and handed it over.

As the man reached for it, the long sleeve of his ratty black jacket pulled back over his wrist. The arm above the wrist grew thick with reddish-brown hair. A tattoo decorated the meaty portion of the hand behind the thumb. Startlement froze the lawman.

CHAPTER THIRTEEN

AFTER TELLING THEIR PA THEY WERE GOING TO SPOTLIGHT SOME deer, Taylor and Justin Modine headed into Eagle Pass to grab themselves some "collateral." Justin kept asking where they were going and Taylor just kept grinning and refusing to say. Finally, though, they cruised down a street called Mesa and Taylor pulled off into an abandoned lot and killed the Jeep's engine and lights.

"Here?" Justin asked.

"You got it, little brother. There's a couple of ski masks in the glove box. Hand me one. We'll use 'em, but first we're going to sit here a while to make sure the coast is clear."

Justin did as ordered, then turned and leaned into the back seat. A Remington 700 bolt action hunting rifle chambered for the .308 cartridge lay under a blanket in the floorboard but he ignored that and picked up a vinyl briefcase. Placing the case in his lap, he opened it to reveal two Glock 17s nestled inside. The pistols were only 9mms but each held seventeen shots. A lot of firepower if needed. Two silencers rested in their own slots in the case. He began threading them onto the weapons.

"Silence is golden," Taylor said as he watched.

"And deadly," Justin added.

―――――

CONCHO GLANCED QUICKLY AGAIN INTO the beggar's eyes as the man took the twenty he'd been offered. That gaze was no longer listless. An intensity burned in the brown irises now; a glitter danced in the pupils. The man had seen his response to the tattoo.

"Interesting ink," Concho said softly. "Mind if I ask where you got it?"

The man turned and fled, leaving the twenty-dollar bill to flutter to earth behind him. Caught off guard, Ten-Wolves was already six steps behind when he took off after the runner. The beggar leapt off the elevated concrete loading dock for the buses and landed three feet down in a narrow alley full of overflowing garbage bins.

Concho followed. The runner hooked his hand into the back of a broken chair in passing and hurled it toward the Ranger. Refuse clattered. Ten-Wolves dodged. The man darted through a gap in the wooden fence bordering the alley. Concho followed, found himself in an empty lot overgrown with brush and full of trash. It was dark and smelled of urine, but the pounding footsteps of flight led him onward.

Fifty feet across the lot, another wooden fence loomed. Boards were missing in places, leaving gaps in the perimeter. A shadow appeared at one of those gaps, darted through. Concho kept trailing the runner but the man knew this area and he didn't. He stumbled over debris, losing ground. A feral cat squalled at him as he passed.

By the time Ten-Wolves flung himself through the same hole in the fence as the runner, the man was gone. The Ranger found himself standing on a grassy border along a small subdivision of Eagle Pass. Three paved roads stretched out in front of him, purple lit by street lights. Rows of small houses, all nearly identical except for trims and external landscaping, faced him.

Dogs had gone wild across the entire subdivision. Their barks and howls made it hard to hear any retreating footsteps. If there were any. The man might have gone to ground. He could be in one of the houses, or possibly hiding behind a car or in a back yard. Who knew where to look?

Drawing his right-hand Colt, the Ranger stepped forward onto the closest street. His eyes darted left and right, scanning for any sign of the man he pursued. But now, lights began to come on in many of the houses. People appeared in doorways, some of them muttering angrily.

Shaking his head, Concho holstered his pistol. From the first house on his right, a man came out of his yard onto the sidewalk. He carried a baseball bat. Concho pointed at him. It's all right," he called. "I'm a Texas Ranger. Go on back in your house."

"How do I know you're tellin' the truth?" the man with the bat shouted back. "We've had plenty robberies in this neighborhood. Maybe you're the one doing them."

"Maybe I'm looking for the one doing them. Go back in your house."

The man kept coming, and several other men stepped out onto the sidewalk in front of their houses, too. Several carried weapons. No guns, but one fellow swung a pipe wrench back and forth in his hands. Another had, of all things, a samurai sword. The neighborhood looked to be a mix of white and Hispanic. The color of Concho's skin might not endear him to these folks.

The Ranger sighed. His search for the man with the tattoo had ended for now. The fellow was long gone or hidden where he couldn't be easily sniffed out. And all the people gathering outside their houses would interfere with any search anyway. Threatening to arrest those who didn't go back inside was not a good idea. That would only create an uproar and he didn't want to have to shoot someone to protect himself.

Turning, he started back toward the vacant lot. The man with the bat kept following. Concho turned around as he reached the gap in the fence. The bat man paused. Ten-Wolves gestured for him to come closer.

"You better get outta here," the man snapped, but he didn't accept the invitation to approach.

"I've got a question," Concho said. "You know this neighborhood don't you? And the people here?"

"I know 'em," the belligerent man retorted. "But I don't know you!"

Ten-Wolves flicked the badge on his shirt. The man could surely see its shine under the street lights, although he probably couldn't make out any details. "I told you, I'm with the Texas Rangers. I chased a man into this neighborhood who may be associated with a crime. You see anyone in the area with a tattoo of a partially opened straight razor on the back of his right hand? Behind the thumb? It's silver and black."

The man seemed confused at first with the question, but then shook his head. "Nope. No one here has anything like that."

Concho nodded. "OK, thanks for your cooperation." He stepped back through the hole in the fence into the vacant lot. The man with the bat didn't follow. The lawman had enough to chew on anyway.

How strange was it for that tattoo to appear on a man here at the bus station when earlier in the day a similar image had been found etched on a spent shell casing at a drug and kidnapping scene? Why had the man run when Concho asked about his tat? Unless he was somehow connected to that earlier crime? If so, why was he at the bus station now, and why approach someone wearing a badge to beg for money? Concho doubted the fellow was truly homeless. He'd had another reason than begging for being at the station, but what could it be?

Ten-Wolves didn't believe in coincidences. There was

meaning here. If he could find it. Shaking his head in confusion, he headed for his truck. The twenty-dollar bill the man had dropped was nowhere to be seen. Someone else must have picked it up. Or else it blew away in the wind, the ubiquitous Texas wind that eventually buried everything in this land.

CHAPTER FOURTEEN

DANIEL KING MODINE, BETTER KNOWN TO MANY AS "PA," whether they were related to him or not, sat at his dining room table shoveling chili into his mouth from a big wooden bowl when his cell phone rang. It was just after 10:00 PM.

He was expecting a call back from a phone message he'd left earlier in the day for someone regarding the affair of the woman currently called Jane Doe. Not that he'd mentioned her in the message, of course. However, the caller ID told him this was someone else—his third son, his eldest, Derrick.

"You get a hit?" Pa asked.

"Afraid not. Got trouble instead."

Pa frowned. "What kind of trouble?"

"I was at the bus stop. Looking for a potential target. This big black dude showed up with a Mex woman. Put her on a bus. Figured him for a pimp or somethin' and I wanted to check it out in case he was gonna be trouble. I was doing my homeless act so I rolled up to ask him for some dough. Saw right away he weren't no pimp. A real live Texas Ranger. Badge and guns and all. On top of that, I recognized him."

"Recognized him? Whatta you mean?"

"You know that big jig who busted up Darrel Fallon's play at the Eagle Pass Mall about a year ago? When he was gonna take it over and blow it to kingdom come?"

"You're not saying it was the same Ranger?"

"Very same. His picture's been all over the place since. I even remember his name. He's half Kickapoo injun. Lives on the Rez down here. Name of Concho Ten-Wolves."

"How'd you play it?"

"Was gonna play out the beggar angle but it went bad. He saw my tattoo. The one on my right hand. I could tell right away he recognized something about it and was suspicious. So I took off. I lost him but it has me shook up. I'm gonna lay low until tomorrow before I come home."

"How could he have *recognized* anything about your tattoo? That don't make any sense."

"Don't know, Pa. But he did. He even asked me about where I'd gotten it. Before I took off."

"You must be mistaken."

"I'm not. And from everything I've read, this guy's trouble. I've even heard he's got like...uhm, Indian sense. I don't know what you call it. Like he sees stuff that's gonna happen before it does."

Pa snorted. "Boy, get that nonsense out of your head. Ain't no magic in this world except the Lord's and the Devil's."

"Maybe his is from the devil?"

"I told you to shut that nonsense off. *If* he recognized your tattoo, there's some normal reason behind it. I can't figure out what. I don't know anyone wearing that tat has been taken by the cops. I'll check around. You do what you said. Lay low. But get back here as soon as you can. We've got some planning to do."

"Yeah, Pa. Gotcha."

Pa swiped off the call without saying anything else. He sat at the table, the last bites of his chili forgotten. *Concho Ten-Wolves.* He'd heard the name, of course. Everyone around this part of the state had.

And he didn't like it that the man appeared curious about the straight razor tat. It probably meant nothing, but maybe when he talked to his contact about the Jane Doe and Mexican gangbanger problem he'd mention the Texas Ranger problem along with it.

Three birds with one stone so to speak. Or three bullets for three problems. Two of them Indians. All three undesirables. Culling the herd.

————

1:15 AM. Mesa Street. Eagle Pass. A quiet night in one of the poorer suburban neighborhoods. Movement showed in the small backyard of 1224. Two shadows wearing ski masks darted across to the back of the house. They eased open the screen on the porch and advanced cautiously across the board floor.

A gloved hand pressed a yellow suction cup against one of the small squares of glass in the rear door. A single sharp tap with a gun butt broke the glass loose from its frame, but the cup held it as the hand reached through to unlock the door from inside.

The Modine brothers slipped into the house, into the back hallway. A nightlight to the right indicated the bathroom, with a small laundry area full of unfolded clothes next to it. On the left was likely a bedroom. Closed.

Taylor Modine grasped the doorknob to the closed room and turned it gently. He eased the door back, pausing to listen when it gave a creak. Uninterrupted breathing came from inside, the quick snick of a sleeper. He smelled faint perfume and baby powder.

Easing the door back farther, Taylor stepped through as silently as the deer hunter he often was. His brother, Justin, followed. Another nightlight glowed here, from a pink unicorn riding a rainbow.

A single bed rested against the wall by the door. An adult

sized shape huddled there under wadded sheets. Against the other wall stood a cheap crib with white bedding that looked pink under this light.

Bingo! Taylor murmured silently to himself. He started toward the crib while motioning Justin toward the bed.

The floor creaked; the person in the bed still didn't wake up. But from the crib came a soft cry. Taylor took two quick strides and reached down. He could see the child in the crib. It was less than a year old. Maybe a lot less. He didn't really know how to judge. It had kicked off its blanket but wore a little pink nightdress that hung past its toes.

Taylor scooped the little thing up with his left hand while cupping its mouth and nose with his right to muffle any noise. The surprised child tried to squall. The sound came out past Taylor's hand as a high-pitched hiccup.

The adult in the bed sat up abruptly. "Qué?"

A young woman. Latina. She had long hair dyed red. Justin slammed the butt of the pistol he held down on her head. She folded like a fitted sheet, all flopping knees and elbows.

"Let's go!" Taylor snapped.

Holding the squirming child, he darted past his brother and out the door. Justin trailed him. Taylor had almost reached the back porch when an old woman cursed at them in Spanish. He twisted his head to look over his shoulder.

The light in the hallway flickered on. The brightness stabbed his eyes, bringing stinging tears. A Latina grandma of seventy or eighty stood at the end of the hall in a long white nightdress. She held a shotgun in both hands but the light blinded her old eyes worse than it blinded the two brothers.

Justin shot her twice with his silenced Glock. Pfftt, pfftt. She gave a little stuttering moan and fell forward, dropping the shotgun with a clatter.

Justin turned toward his older brother. "No choice."

Taylor nodded. "There's still a witness, though."

Justin grunted an acknowledgement. He stepped quickly

back into the bedroom. Taylor heard another shot, this one a little louder than the first two as the silencer degraded. It still wasn't loud enough to alert the neighbors.

Taylor stepped out onto the back porch with the kid still in his arms. Its attempted wails had turned to phlegmy sobs so he removed his hand from over its mouth and awkwardly patted its head. Justin should have been right behind him but a moment passed, and another.

Frowning, Taylor leaned his head in the still open back door and hissed, "Justin. Where are you?"

"Hold on," Justin hissed back.

"Speed it up!"

Justin came out of the bedroom. He'd tucked his pistol in his belt and hurried toward Taylor. His grin stretched wide and feral. "Another win over the heathens," the younger Modine said.

"What did you do?" Taylor demanded.

"Nothing good," Justin replied, as he slammed through the screen door and ran for their Jeep. Taylor had to follow.

CHAPTER FIFTEEN

CONCHO AWOKE IN MARIA'S BED. ALONE. HE LAY THERE WISHING she was next to him, that he could throw his arm over her and cuddle close. He was more of a cuddler than she. He missed it when she was gone.

Shaking his head, he sat up. He normally woke at 6:00 AM but it was only 4:00. He hadn't slept well, and it was more than the fact that he couldn't completely stretch out in Maria's bed without his feet hanging over the bottom. Too much occupied his mind—Jane Doe, the straight razor tattoo, the connection between the beggar at the bus stop and his earlier gunfight at Little Owl Creek Bridge. There were other things, amorphous and indistinct. Thoughts and feelings he couldn't name.

He rose, showered, and dressed, finally putting on the jeans and blue cotton shirt he'd been hauling around with him since yesterday morning. The only food readily available in Maria's fridge were some small containers of yogurt. He made a face but ate two of them, one with blackberries, one with blueberries, and drank a grape Powerade.

By 4:45, Ten-Wolves was in his truck and headed for the reservation. The protestors should be home asleep, and it was indeed quiet as he drove through a nearly deserted Kickapoo village. Even the Lucky Eagle casino, up a short hill to his right, had a mostly empty parking lot.

He turned down a dirt road leading out of town and it wasn't long until he came to a lone wickiup standing on a small plot of land. A battered trailer sat behind the traditional Kickapoo dwelling but all its windows showed dark in the pre-dawn. In contrast, a faint glow came from inside the wickiup. Meskwaa was home, and likely awake.

Concho didn't know Meskwaa's age. He was in his seventies at least, although the old man sometimes claimed to be over a hundred, or older. The Naataineniiha of the Kickapoo tribe was the closest thing to family Concho possessed on the Rez. He'd been friends with Concho's grandmother, who'd raised Ten-Wolves, and had seemed old then.

The Ranger parked his truck and climbed out. A shadow rose from the earth just outside the wickiup. A low growl reverberated through the rapidly graying morning. This was Dog, which was the only name Meskwaa used for the half-wild beast. Dog wasn't even fully dog; he was rangy and black-furred, and looked like some kind of wolf hybrid.

Months back, there'd been a half-wild man on the Rez, an Indian named Whirlwind. Dog had been Whirlwind's companion, but when Whirlwind disappeared, Dog stayed behind with Meskwaa. The two had become friends of a sort, though Dog didn't extend the cone of friendship to Concho.

"It's OK, Dog," Concho said. "I haven't shot you yet and didn't have any plans to do it this morning. Don't make me reconsider."

The animal growled louder as the Ranger started toward him. But then the blanket covering the door to the wickiup twitched and a thin old man stepped out onto the hut's dirt porch. "Dog!" the man said. "Your mistrust of the Ten-Wolves is misplaced. He is not as mean-spirited as he appears."

"Thanks," Concho said dryly.

Meskwaa grinned, his teeth shining white in the dawn.

"Consideration where consideration is due," he said. "But perhaps if you were to bring him a cheeseburger when you came to visit, he might be more accepting of you."

"Bring *him* a cheeseburger? Or bring *you* one?"

"Two cheeseburgers would not seem unreasonable."

"I'll try to remember next time."

Meskwaa shrugged. "I'll not hold my breath as they say." He gestured. "Come."

Concho trailed Meskwaa as the medicine man stepped back into his wickiup. Dog glared at him as he stalked past but didn't try to take a bite. The Ranger ducked to enter the small house built of sotol stalks. A large candle burned on the floor in the center of the room. Meskwaa moved behind it and folded himself into a seated position. Concho joined him on the other side of the candle, though he took a bit longer getting down.

A tin bucket of water sat to one side of the candle, with a dipper stuck in it. At Meskwaa's gesture, Concho scooped up a mouthful of the water and drank. He sat the dipper carefully back into the bucket. For a moment, he studied the old man. Meskwaa wore newish blue jeans and a black cotton shirt. A red bandana encircled his wrinkled neck. The medicine man was thin, thin, and seemed to have aged quite a few years in just the last few months.

Concho winced inwardly but didn't let it show on his face. "Roberto told me you wanted to see me," he finally said.

"Yes. I have had an experience."

"A vision?"

Meskwaa shrugged. He reached into the pocket of his shirt and pulled out the small doeskin bag in which he kept his filterless cigarettes. He merely held it, though, without opening it.

"I do not know exactly what it was, my experience," the old man responded. "I saw an image and knew it had something to do with you. I do not know what."

A sketch pad lay beside Meskwaa's knee. He flipped it open and took out the sheet of paper lying on top. This, he passed over to the lawman, who studied it in the candlelight. No mistaking this image. A straight razor, opened at about a ninety-degree angle—the same as the etching on an empty shell casing and the ink on a beggar at the bus station.

Concho started to hand the sketch back and Meskwaa gestured for him to keep it. He placed it on his lap. "I've seen it," he said. "Twice." He explained where.

Meskwaa grunted an acknowledgement. "This symbol is bad," he said. "It indicates great hate."

"What kind of hate?"

"The kind that wishes certain people dead."

"What people?"

"Anyone who is not with them."

"Doesn't narrow it down much."

"Every tribe knows its symbols. This is not ours but Waapeskyai."

"White," Concho translated. "You mean white people?"

Meskwaa shook his head. "Not all of them. The whites have tribes, too. This is only one such. Small, but dangerous. Hidden, but hungry for power."

"A terrorist group, perhaps?"

The medicine man shrugged. "I have given you all I know. Though perhaps more will come to me another time."

Concho nodded. A year ago he would have been polite when hearing such pronouncements from Meskwaa, but he would not have taken them seriously. Now he did. Too many times, the old man had been right about things he should not have known. The straight-razor image was just one more.

Sometimes now, Ten-Wolves even felt such things himself. Most days, it did not seem he'd changed much in the past year. On other days he scarcely recognized his own thoughts. He was becoming...becoming something other than he'd once been.

Much of it had to do with his heritage as a Kickapoo. He'd never denied that heritage. It had been his mother's and his grandmother's and he'd respected it. But he'd never truly *embraced* it. He didn't know if he could.

And there was another part to his heritage he'd scarcely considered. The African part. His father had been an African American named Donnell Blackthorne. He'd once seen Blackthorne's murdered body but had never met him in life, at least not that he remembered. He'd been raised on the Kickapoo reservation by his grandmother and grandfather on his mother's side.

His biological father had lived and died a criminal, though some said there'd been more to his personality than that. Concho also had a paternal grandfather who was still alive— Hamilton Blackthorne. Hamilton was also involved in criminal activities and the lawman refused to have anything to do with him.

But what did all that mean? How had it impacted him? Or had it? How could he reconcile all his disparate parts? Or did he need to? To a greater or lesser extent, perhaps everyone was torn between many histories.

Concho rose to go, his knees cracking as he stood. He held the paper image of the straight razor drawn by Meskwaa in one hand. The old man looked up at him and lifted an arm in a goodbye wave.

"Ketapaanene," Ten-Wolves said.

Meskwaa jerked. His eyes misted. "Ketapaanene," he replied. I love you.

CHAPTER SIXTEEN

AFTER LEAVING MESKWAA'S PLACE, CONCHO DROVE TO HIS OWN trailer on the reservation. It was after 6:00 in the morning now, with the sun blossoming orange-red over the horizon. As he pulled into his driveway, he found a blue SUV parked in his yard with words written across it in white: *Kickapoo Tribal Police*.

He stepped out of his Ford and the driver's side door of the SUV opened at the same time. Roberto Echabarri climbed out. Echabarri had been chief of the tribal police for less than a year. The responsibilities had aged him. He was only twenty-six but looked older. The gray, flat-crowned Stetson he wore atop his short, dark hair matured him even more.

"Ho," Echabarri said. He didn't look happy with the morning light.

Concho grinned. "You couldn't assign one of your deputies to watch my trailer?"

"They have been. I needed to take my turn."

"Ah, well, come inside. I'll make you breakfast. Maria only had yogurt at her house. I need bacon and eggs."

Echabarri chuckled, his mood improving. "I can just see you with those big hands eating out of one of those little yogurt containers. Kind of terrifying now I think about it."

"Terrifying and a little disgusting," Concho agreed.

He led the way to the trailer and entered. The place smelled like it had been locked up for a day. Musty. He opened some windows as he headed for the kitchen. Less than fifteen minutes later, the two lawmen sat across from each other at the dinner table shoveling down eggs, bacon and toast. Two eggs and four slices of bacon for Roberto, four eggs and eight bacon slices for Ten-Wolves. With toast.

"How's Terrill Hoight?" Roberto asked as he chewed.

"Haven't checked yet today. I'll call over after eight."

"And what about the Jane Doe woman?"

"Nothing new."

"Did you say she was Indian?"

"Yeah. Possibly Navajo."

"They doing a blood test?"

"Yep."

Echabarri finished his last strip of bacon and pushed back in his chair. "Well, I need to get back to the office. See if your fan club has arrived yet. They do seem dedicated."

"Sorry to add to your burden."

"Not your fault. I reckon it'll blow over."

"Hope so."

Slugging the last swallow of milk Concho had poured for him, Echabarri slapped the Ranger on the shoulder and left. Ten-Wolves finished his own breakfast and fetched his laptop from the truck. He had it set up and was typing an addendum to his last night's report on the Jane Doe affair when the sound of horns honking and engines roaring shattered his train of thought.

With his hands on his pistols, he stepped quickly across to his kitchen window and looked out. Two pickup trucks full of people with signs in their hands booked it up his driveway. He sighed as he recognized several of them. His "fan club," as Roberto Echabarri named them. These were the people who'd been protesting the arrest of Tallulah Whiteheart and calling for him to be fired.

Concho unbuckled his gun belt and lay it on the kitchen counter. If he needed those weapons for this scene, he wasn't handling it right. Striding to the door, he stepped outside to face the crowd.

"Bread and circuses," he muttered to himself. "Ancient Rome all over again."

———

IN A SERVICE ROAD motel off the I-35 in San Antonio, the man known as Snow snapped awake. Listening intently, he heard only the groaning whisper of the cheap window AC unit and a faint snick of breathing from his most recent bed companion. But there'd been another sound here a moment ago. The air tingled with it.

Sliding from the worn and rumpled sheets, he padded naked to the small motel table where his cell phone lay. The screen was dark but when he pressed the button on the side it lit up faintly to show he'd gotten a text message. He pressed to see it.

"Eagle Pass. Two heartbeats," he read. A cell phone number followed, which he memorized instantly. There was nothing else.

An almost imperceptible excitement dilated Snow's pupils. *Business. Finally.* He'd been inactive too long.

Padding to the bathroom, he did his business and dressed in jeans and a navy-blue T-shirt with faded white letters across the front that read *Hellspawn Walking.* He slipped his cell into his pocket and moved over to study the woman in the bed. She slept on, the sleep of the exhausted, with her short bottle-blond hair ratted around her head from where his hands had tangled during sex.

He leaned a little closer and sniffed her, and the combination of scents and sights brought a slice of poem driving hard into his awareness.

For the tequila breathed.

For the tasered soul.

Sweat-dank in a semblance of love.

He smiled. The woman hadn't been a very good lay but at least she'd been enthusiastic. That was worth something, he decided. He'd leave her a gift.

He turned away, slipping on his leather motorcycle jacket and plucking up his saddle bags before quietly leaving the room. He'd slept through the night and it was dawn outside, with the sun boiling over the horizon and the remnant sliver of the moon melting away.

His bike waited, purple in the lingering shadows, and he strapped the bags on it, then unlocked his full-face helmet and slid it over his head after tying up the long silver-blond hair that had given him his name. The morning was still cool and he pulled on a pair of leather gloves to keep his hands from stiffening up on the ride.

Straddling the bike, he punched the starter and listened to the low growl of the modified Honda Magna 750 engine, the sound so different from the raw-throated chuckle of a Harley. The woman was probably waking to the sound now, and he pulled from the motel's parking lot and onto the street before she could come looking. He didn't want to see her as he left; that might change his mind about giving her his gift.

He chuckled to himself as he thrust his boots up on the highway pegs and leaned back into the customized seat. Of course, the woman probably wouldn't even realize he'd left her anything. But he'd left her alive.

The road unfolded in gray as he headed south with the wind toward Eagle Pass, Texas.

CHAPTER SEVENTEEN

THE TWO PICKUPS FULL OF PROTESTORS PULLED UP TO BRACKET Concho's Ford, blocking his vehicle in. About a dozen men and women piled out of the trucks. None were armed with anything other than anger and some signs on wooden stakes.

"There he is!" someone shouted.

"Yes!" Concho replied. "Here I am. What do you want?"

"Justice!" rang from several throats.

Not everyone shouted, Concho noted. Nate Wronghorse, who he'd shared friendly words with in the past, stood at the back of the crowd. The sign in his hand drooped toward the ground and he looked ashamed.

Paid! Concho thought. Some of these people had been given money to be here, probably by Tallulah's husband, Sam. No doubt, they were meant to inflate the apparent numbers of the protestors. That meant.... The Ranger nodded to himself as he saw one woman also standing back from the others and recording the confrontation on her cell phone.

At the front of the group stood Letty Garcia. He might have known. Letty hated him for multiple reasons, but all originally stemming from her brother, Daniel Alvarado, who'd been chief of the tribal police for a short while before Roberto Echabarri took over.

Concho had exposed Alvarado as a criminal and the man had been killed by fellow criminals before he could spill their names. Letty blamed the Ranger, which made her a natural ally of the Whitehearts, who were now accusing him of selective persecution of Tallulah Whiteheart for her role in smuggling and murder.

Flanking Letty stood two young men of around twenty or so. Both were strongly built, with long black hair flowing. Concho vaguely knew them, though the last time he'd seen them they'd been kids. He didn't remember their names but they were cousins of Letty who'd been living south of the border for many years in the small town of Múzquiz, Mexico, where many Kickapoo dwelt.

People from the Texas reservation frequently traveled south to visit relatives in Múzquiz, and others came from Mexico to the US. These two young men hadn't been to Texas in a while, at least not that he knew of. He strongly suspected both men were members of the NATV Bloods, an Indian gang that operated across a number of reservations in Mexico and the States.

The gang had operated almost openly on the Texas Rez for a while until Concho and Roberto broke it up. Letty's son and daughter had been involved. It was likely these two cousins were as well. However, their purpose *here* was to serve as Letty's muscle. Concho made sure to make eye contact with each of them and offer a low-wattage version of his shark-tooth smile.

Manuel Night-Run also hung with the crowd. Concho sympathized a little with the young man. After all, he'd arrested the boy's mother and she was serving her jail time now. Others that he recognized by sight and reputation, if not through much personal contact, were Temple Escarra, Oscar Bigotes, and Atanasio Bluefeather. As far as he recalled, he'd never had a run in with any of those three.

Temple's presence disappointed him. She and her husband,

Tobias, ran a small knife-making company on the Rez and their blades were exquisite. He'd admired their artistry and bought an antler-handled hunting knife for himself. But the couple had recently lost a child only a few months old. Perhaps grief was a factor in her anger. Who knew, though, what connections any of them had to Letty or the Whitehearts.

"When are you going to resign?" Letty shouted at the Ranger. "Haven't you and the whites you serve done enough damage to this people?"

"I don't serve any one group of people. I serve the law."

"The laws are written by the whites for the whites," one of Letty's young cousins shouted.

"I'm not talking about human written laws," Concho replied. "I'm talking about the greater laws, the laws almost all peoples have about theft, and rape, and murder. The most damage that can be done to the Kickapoo people right now is when one of *us* commits such acts against our own. And when that happens, I'm not going to let it stand!"

"Tallulah Whiteheart is innocent!" a voice shouted from the crowd.

The lawman shook his head. "Every one of you knows that isn't true."

"Liar!" voices shouted, striving to drown him out.

"Corruption!" others yelled.

"Killer," Letty screamed.

"Enough!" Concho roared.

The Ranger's voice was as big as he was. It cut through the din and closed every mouth. His dark eyes glared at the crowd, challenging. Then he shook his head. He spoke again into the quiet, in a softer voice. He wasn't speaking to Letty or her closest allies. Nothing would get through to them. He was speaking to the others, those who might have come along out of curiosity or for the excitement, or those who'd been paid. Those who could still be reached by reason.

"Look, we live in unsettled times. Things changing fast and

faster. But the Kickapoo have been living through those times for centuries now. We have a right to anger but it does no good to turn anger on the innocent, or on ourselves. Most of us. Most of *you*! We're doing our best to do the right thing. Defending someone who you *know* is a criminal just because they live on the reservation with you is not the right thing.

"Most of you sense that in your hearts. Perhaps some of you were even paid to be here. But you've all made your point and it's done now." He nodded toward the woman filming the encounter. "You've got your video and you'll edit it however you see fit. Go home. It's over."

Letty didn't speak but she nudged one of her young cousins with a shoulder. The man twitched, then reached down and grabbed up a rock. Concho caught the fellow's gaze as he straightened. Everything paused.

Ten-Wolves spoke softly again, his gaze directed at the man with the rock but with his words meant mainly for Letty. "If you throw that, I won't turn the other cheek."

The man's arm shook with tension as he started to raise the rock. He thought better of it and dropped the stone as he turned away. Letty made a face but, while the anger hadn't left her, the will to start trouble had dissipated. She turned away as well. In a few minutes, both pickups loaded up again and peeled away down the driveway.

One sign remained dropped in the yard, the one Nate Wronghorse had held. Ten-Wolves walked over and picked it up. In big white letters on a blue background, the front read, *Police Corruption Must Stop.*

On the back, handwritten in pencil by Nate no doubt, were the words. "I'm sorry."

CHAPTER EIGHTEEN

FRIDAY MORNING. KING MODINE SAT IN THE FRONT PEW OF THE small country church. He waited calmly enough, though patience was not something he practiced very often. The preacher had let him in the locked nave but gone on about other business; Modine sat alone for now.

The morning sun slanted through the windows. Dust motes danced in the light. The place smelled of wood wax and old perfumes. Modine prayed, and felt sure the prayers were being heard. Plenty of supposedly religious people had told him over the years he prayed for the wrong things, that God didn't honor needs based on rage rather than love. Some even told him he sinned. They were wrong. They didn't know God like King knew him.

The church doors opened behind him and footsteps sounded on the pine-wood floor. King stiffened in the pew but did not turn around. The steps stopped just behind his shoulder. He felt the weight of a presence and heard breathing. He heard the swish of clothing on wood as the stranger sat down in the next pew back. This meeting was the result of his recent calls.

"Your request has been heard," a man's voice spoke quietly into Modine's ear. "Help is on the way. He has your number and will be in touch. Explain to him precisely what you need. His name is Snow."

Modine nodded. "There's been one complication. I believe you'll recognize the name. The Texas Ranger, Concho Ten-Wolves, has taken an interest in the affair."

"Conch—" the man's voice grunted angrily before he recovered himself. "How did *he* find out about this?"

After King's son, Derrick, mentioned his confrontation with Ten-Wolves, King had gone back to his other two sons and asked them more about the "policeman" who'd interrupted their attempted deal with two Mexes for drugs and the Indian girl. They hadn't seen the fellow clearly but their overall description matched Ten-Wolves, as did the white Ford F-150 the man had driven. That was enough to clench if for King.

"I don't know exactly," Modine said to the man behind him, "but seems he's the one who rescued the girl initially from the gangbangers who had her. Maybe because she's Indian, too. Maybe they knew each other or something."

The speaker was still angry. "All the more reason to excise the girl quickly," he snapped.

"Yeah. And the remaining gangbanger. But what about Ten-Wolves?"

"Tell it to Snow when you speak to him. He'll want more money but I'll make sure you're reimbursed. That Ranger has a history of stumbling around poking his big nose into far too many places where it isn't wanted."

"From what I hear, the son of the devil is hard to kill. You sure this Snow can handle it?"

"I know Ten-Wolves. He *is* dangerous. But he's emotional and that's his weakness. Snow is cold as his name. He has over a hundred confirmed kills and he takes every job personally. If he can't do it, no one can."

"Good," King said. "But I want to meet Snow."

"Why?"

"Certain things I need to tell him about this contract that I don't want to put on a phone, even coded."

"All right, but you know the consequences if anything leaks."

"Yes."

"Is that all?"

"No. We're all getting restless. I appreciate you pulling me out of San Antonio when the Feds were closing in but we've been sitting on our hands ever since."

"You've been stockpiling resources and making money. Revolutions require both in abundance. They also require patience."

"I know. But if we could just make some kind of gesture. Something to show the mud people they can't be so complacent."

"We *want* them complacent! Unprepared. Look, we believe in the same goals. But changing the world is a big thing. You're not in a position to see the overall picture. I am. But I'm going to call on you and yours. It's only a matter of time. We start right here, with Ten-Wolves and this Indian woman."

"All right," King said. "I understand." He heard stirring behind him, followed by the echo of footsteps moving away toward the exit. He waited anyway, still without turning his head. For a few more minutes, he prayed to *his* God.

When he rose and turned, the church lay empty. As he started to leave, he noted an odd smell from the pew where the other man had been sitting. It was very faint, a kind of roux of sweet and musty at the same time. No one would wear a cologne like that. It must have been some lingering hint of the man's breath, though what could have caused it he had no idea.

Shrugging, he continued on his way. He was anxious for this Snow to call. Anxious to get the affair of Jane Doe and Ten-Wolves behind him so he could get back to real business. Money to be made, plans to be laid. Revolution to come.

———

THE WIDE TEXAS highway stretched out straight in front of Snow. The bike glided along the pavement. A warm wind flowed over him. With his feet up on the highway pegs, he rode comfortably. All of it together invited his mind to wander.

On a job, he kept his thoughts laser focused, but he didn't even know what this job was to be yet and wasn't going to waste energy in useless speculation. And so his mind tracked back to his last artwork, finished in the generator room beneath a Dallas industrial laundromat. A very pleasant memory.

"Please. Please!" the young police detective said. "You don't have to do this. I've given you everything you wanted. I'll tell you anything. Just ask me. Please!"

"Shh," Snow soothed. "We're almost done."

"You don't have to kill me. I'd never say anything about what happened here."

Snow allowed himself a frown, merely for the effect it would have on the young man. He glanced just to the fellow's right, where his partner hung tied to the same drainpipes as he. She had not been so cooperative. And now she made a pretty scene in scarlet.

He enjoyed killing both women and men but thought he liked the men better. They almost always tried the macho route first, to pretend they weren't afraid, that they were dangerous. They wanted you to believe that if they got a chance they'd tear you apart with their bare hands. It was laughable, but he wasn't ready to show this victim his laugh yet.

Hope makes loss ever more exquisite, he thought. If I were prone to cliché, I'd say it 'gilds the lily.'

But the policeman wouldn't understand such concepts. He was the tool of an artist, not the artist himself. Though he had his part to play. His role now was to hope.

"Not even if they question you about your partner there?" Snow asked, as if just the right answer might sway him.

"I...I'll tell them I didn't see it. Say I found her like this. That I don't know who could have done it."

Snow mused over the answer. Or, he appeared to. Seconds passed. Desperation grew even stronger in the young man's eyes. He started to speak and Snow held up a silencing finger, on the same hand that held a knife.

The assassin let almost a full minute pass before he spoke. "That's not very consistent with human nature. I'm afraid I don't believe you."

The man's whole body collapsed against his ropes. All hope fled. "Please!" he whispered. "I'm begging you! I've got a kid." Tears began to drip down his face. He was lost now, all his posturing finished.

Snow cut his throat.

The policeman's eyes grew impossibly wide. He strained against his bonds, trying to raise his hands, trying to throw them up to his throat to cram the blood back in as it pulsed out.

Snow laughed.

A tiny change in the engine noise of his Honda Magna caught Snow's attention, bringing him back from his memories. He glanced down. He was getting low on gas. Time to pull over and fill up.

CHAPTER NINETEEN

CONCHO TOOK A DEEP BREATH OF RELIEF AS THE TRUCKS OF
protestors disappeared back toward Kickapoo Village. Letty
Garcia was not the type to give up her hate so he doubted the
trouble was over, but at least for now peace had returned to his
trailer.

Stepping back inside, and hungry for more of what he hoped
would be good news, he called the hospital to check on Terrill
Hoight. Helen Riley, who'd been so helpful before, wasn't on
duty this morning but the lady who did pick up transferred him
to the intensive care unit.

"ICU," a nurse answered.

"Hi. I was calling to check on Terrill Hoight."

"Are you a family member?"

"No, I'm a friend but also a Texas Ranger who is investigating
Deputy Hoight's shooting. My name is Concho Ten-Wolves."

"Oh, yes, Mister Ten-Wolves. I've heard of you." She paused,
then continued. "Deputy Hoight is awake. We're not really
supposed to allow phone calls in here but I guess I can make an
exception. He has his cell but I'm not sure it's within easy reach
and I don't want him popping his sutures trying to find it. Does
he have your number in his phone?"

"I'm sure he does."

"OK, if you'll hang up, I'll go to his room and make sure he has his phone and I'll let him call you back. Is that adequate?"

"Perfectly, Ma'am, I appreciate it."

"OK, it'll be a moment." She hung up.

While he waited, Concho considered that maybe being a celebrity had a few perks to go along with its miseries, even if he was small time and probably about at the end of his fifteen minutes of fame. His phone rang; the caller ID said "Hoight."

He swiped to answer. "Darrell?"

"Ten-Wolves. Thanks for calling."

"You sound a little rough."

"Happens when you gargle on a bullet," Hoight said.

"I can imagine. How you doing overall, though?"

"They said I'm going to live, and I'll be able to return to duty."

"Take your time on that."

"I will."

"It hurt to talk?"

"Less than sitting here all alone thinking."

"Right. Brave thing you did. Throwing yourself in the way of a bullet. Maybe a little stupid, though."

"I never was exactly Mensa material."

Concho chuckled. "You and me both, brother."

"The girl OK?"

"She is. Sheriff Parkland has her in protective custody."

"Good. By the way, I've got something to tell you. Don't know if it means anything. Maybe not, but..."

"What is it?"

"After I was shot. I'd thrown the girl down. I think I was lying on top of her. She said something. With a Spanish accent. Very quiet but terrified like. I think it might have been 'angel.'"

"Angel?"

"Yeah, maybe."

"Thanks. I'll ask her about it."

Hoight coughed. A rattling of objects followed and the nurse's voice replaced the deputy's. "I'm afraid that's enough for now, Ranger Ten-Wolves. He needs to stop talking."

"Right. No problem. Tell him I'll come by to see him soon."

"I will."

"And thank you."

"Of course." The phone went silent.

Concho took a deep breath. "Angel," he muttered to himself. Could it mean anything? Probably just something the woman said in a moment of terror. But he'd ask her about it. After he did some more considering. He decided to take a run, which always helped him think. He hadn't been able to for several days.

After slipping into moccasins and cut-off shorts, he stepped out onto his back deck. Though it was still early, the sun had claimed the sky and hung there like a burnished medicine shield. The morning smell of prickly pear blooms tingled his nostrils. Some small bird trilled madly from the clump of junipers at the left side of his trailer.

Bird trills sounded a bit like a police whistle to Concho, and he knew of only three birds found around here that trilled— pine warblers, chipping sparrows, and the dark-eyed junco. The warbler was the most common and he looked for the flash of puffy yellow that might indicate one. No sign of it. And no repetition of the trill.

Turning his mind to his run, he thought of the opening scene of Navarre Scott Momaday's *House Made of Dawn*, which won the Pulitzer Prize and was one of the most beautifully written novels he'd ever read. He owned two copies, one signed by the author, who claimed Kiowa descent.

He quoted from the book now, as was his want. "There was a house made of dawn. It was made of pollen and of rain, and the land was very old and everlasting."

With those words lingering on his lips, he took off across the Rez. As with Abel, the protagonist of the book, he ran heavily and roughly at first, but soon regained his rhythm and his legs and arms and breath began to work in concert.

There had been snow in the book and there was no snow here. But the landscape was not otherwise dissimilar. Juniper and mesquite marked his path, and dust and rock. The sun glinted and sweat began to pour. While his body ran, his mind soared. It took him to...

Afghanistan, 2009.

Three weeks "In Country." With a squad of other Army Rangers around him, Ten-Wolves rode a Chinook transport helicopter into his first battle. The world roared at him, from the thrust of the chopper's twin rotors against the sky, to the hot wind rushing past the open door up front, to his heart hammering behind his ribs. An M16A4 rifle lay across his lap, his hands sweaty on the nylon stock. His mouth tasted of acid and brass.

The chopper came in to land through clouds of desert dust kicked up by previous Chinooks of the 75th Ranger Regiment. With hydraulics squealing, the rear ramp dropped and hit the ground.

"All out!" a staff sergeant shouted, and led the way.

Concho followed two other troopers out of the chopper. One was his buddy from ranger training school, Tommy Dougall. The other was Pitt Higgins, a fellow Texan, who shouted as his boots struck the ground, "Rangers lead the way," a quote from the Ranger Creed, which they'd all memorized.

More soldiers poured down the ramp. More Chinooks dropped down to land behind them. Other sergeants yelled; other squads of troopers piled out. Ahead, Concho could see the partially standing walls of a bombed-out Afghan village where rebels were rumored to be massing men and ordinance.

With their loads deployed, the Chinooks started to lift off again. Two Apache attack helicopters streaked between them, launching missiles from beneath their stubby wings. Explosions sent flames and smoke corkscrewing up from amid the ruins. More walls fell down.

An angry hornet buzzed past Concho's ears. A whipsnap slapped the lifting helicopter behind him. It took a second to realize he was under fire. He dove for the ground even as the staff sergeant yelled, "Down!"

More hornets buzzed overhead. Tommy Dougall didn't hit the ground. He shouted out, "Rangerssss!" and opened fire with his M16, with the selector set on three-round burst.

The sergeant chopped the big man behind the knee with his hand, collapsing him down. "Get your ass on the ground and hold your fire until you see something to shoot at you stupid hick!" the NCO yelled.

Tommy turned and growled at the sergeant. Concho grabbed his arm, seizing his friend's attention. More bullets whipped overhead and Tommy forgot about the sergeant. The crackle of small arms fire from the ruins began to grow. The air smelled of powder and lead, and the propellent from the Apaches' rockets. Ten-Wolves pushed himself a foot further ahead through the dirt until he reached a clump of torn up cobblestones and dead, dried grass.

The attack helicopters made another run, this time strafing the ruins with their machine guns. It looked like a small controlled rain striking the earth—a very hard rain. The gunfire from the ruins dropped off.

"Forward!" the staff sergeant yelled.

Other sergeants yelled the same and by squads the soldiers advanced. Concho rose to a crouch, charged forward. Tommy lumbered along behind him now. The sergeant was on one side, Pitt Higgins on the other. A flash of something white showed behind a broken stone wall fifty yards ahead. Concho and the sergeant fired at the same time, raking the rocks with .223 slugs. A man screamed in Dari. An Afghan, either hurt or dead.

The Apaches swung around one more time and pumped a concussion of machine gun fire into the ruins. Pulverized rocks sprayed stone splinters. Debris leaped and bounced in the that lead hail. Then the choppers peeled away as their own troops got too close for safe fire.

Concho reached the partial wall, which rose only about two feet high, and dove behind it. He immediately popped back up and fired ahead into more walls and pieces of walls. The sergeant dropped to a squat beside him but didn't rebuke him for shooting when he couldn't see a target. The NCO understood it was suppressing fire, to keep the enemy's heads down until the rest of the rangers reached cover.

A few feet ahead on the ground lay a dead man in red stained white. The Afghan's headwrap had tumbled off. An AK-47 lay just beyond his outstretched fingers. This was the man Concho had fired at, though whether it had been his or the sergeant's bullets that killed him, he couldn't say.

Nausea boiled up into Concho's throat. He spat and spat again. Tommy slammed down next to him, between his friend and the sarge. He panted for breath but saw the dead rebel and crowed.

"You got one, bro. Good shootin'."

Ten-Wolves wanted to punch him but merely growled, "Shut up!"

Tommy looked hurt. Concho ignored him. A concussion rocked the ground ahead, knocking dust from the wall down on the rangers. "Grenade!" the staff sergeant bellowed. "Keep your heads down!"

But the sergeant failed to take his own advice. He lifted his head just a little. Another grenade exploded and a hunk of whizzing shrapnel ripped through the left side of the NCO's face, tearing away most of the cheek and part of the eye. The man didn't even scream; the blow knocked him unconscious. He fell backward, blood spurting in an arc from his wound.

"God!" Tommy yelled. He recoiled instinctively from the injured man.

Concho dove past Tommy to land next to the sergeant. A pulse of blood sprayed across his face and chest. A chunk of meat had been torn out of the NCO's left cheek, leaving a gaping hole. A wide flap of skin hung loose. Concho dropped his rifle and grabbed the skin in his fingers. He folded it back over the wound and pressed hard with his big hands to stop the pulses of bright red.

"Medic!" Tommy screamed, his voice almost impossibly high pitched for such a giant of a man.

Within a minute, another soldier dropped down beside them, having risked his own life running to the scene. Modern combat medics seldom wore any clearly identifying symbols in battle; too many enemy fighters targeted them. But this one had been pointed out to Ten-Wolves, even though he didn't know the man's name.

The medic pulled gear from a bag between his legs and leaned forward to take over with the sarge. Concho slid backward on his knees. He grabbed up his M16. A bullet whined past his head. He didn't flinch, but returned fire, pumping shell after shell into a mound of rubble off to one side.

Tommy opened fire on the same mound. A frightened voice shouted in Dari from behind the mound. Another grenade came arching over the rubble, headed for where the two rangers and the medic squatted next to the wounded sergeant. Ten-Wolves snapped a shot that hit the grenade and sent it spinning to one side. It exploded, sketching smoke fingers in the air.

"Seems like he's got a ton of those grenades!" Tommy yelled. "He's gonna kill some more people!"

Acting on impulse, Concho threw himself over the short wall of stones in front of him. He hit the ground, rolled, came up in a crouch and charging. The Afghan behind the mound lifted his head. Concho sent a brace of bullets his direction and the man ducked again.

Concho reached the mound, circled it. The enemy fighter squatted behind the rubble pile. He swung his AK-47 toward the Ranger and Ten-Wolves kicked it out of his hands, hoping to take the fellow prisoner instead of killing him.

A small pile of American style grenades lay next to the Afghan. The fighter looked up in terror. He babbled something in Dari that might have meant "devil." Then he grabbed one of the grenades and sprang to his feet, yanking at the pin as he did so. Maybe he intended to sacrifice himself and take an American with him.

Concho didn't want to be taken anywhere. With no time for a capture now, he fired one .223 round between the dark eyes. The enemy fell back. The grenade dropped free of the dead hand, the pin coming loose.

Four to five seconds was the typical fuse delay on an American grenade. Concho moved like a striking adder, catching the grenade in his left hand before it hit the ground. He twisted his body, hurled the thing away while he counted in his head. He let himself fall forward on his face, grabbing for his helmet and yanking it down to cover the back of his skull.

With the crack of a wooden bat breaking, the grenade exploded. Hot metal blasted in every direction. Fragments whipped into the ground to Concho's left and right but nothing struck him.

He bounced back to his feet. Someone cheered. He turned to see Tommy Dougall lumbering toward him. Other rangers ran beside the big man. Ten-Wolves' ears told him the firefight was over. The cracking of shots was moving away to the north and falling off.

Tommy reached his friend and pounded him on the back. The Ranger tried to grin, mostly with relief, but his face must have looked ghastly because Tommy stopped what he was doing and shook his head.

"Don't make that face," the big man said. "You look like Old Scratch himself."

A strange chill prismed down Concho's spine at the words, which were so similar to those of the Afghani he'd shot.

"It's the blood," he replied. "I guess."

"You look like you're wearing red warpaint," Tommy added.

"It's a war isn't it?"

A new voice interrupted their conversation, a familiar one. He turned his head to see a different kind of soldier among his fellow rangers. This one wore the insignia of a Green Beret.

Concho blinked, then saluted. "Captain Jack Travers," he said. "Sir, what are you doing here?"

Travers, who he and Tommy had met in the Staghorn bar outside Fort Benning a few weeks earlier, stared at him with a straight face. "Observing, son. Just observing. What you did. That was both brave and stupid."

"Good thing I didn't think about it too much then."

"Yeah, good thing."

"Shoot!" Tommy said. "Your first battle and you're probably gonna get a medal."

"I hope not," Concho said, glancing at Tommy.

By the time he turned back toward Travers, the captain had gone. The dead Afghani wasn't gone, though, and this time there was no doubt whose bullet did the killing. The nausea he'd felt before didn't return, but the world felt hollow. He'd taken a human life. It was nothing to celebrate.

CHAPTER TWENTY

A QUICK SPASM OF PAIN IN CONCHO'S LOWER BACK BROUGHT HIS run to a halt. He slowed to a walk, reaching back to massage the tender spot. It hurt right where he'd been stabbed with a hunting knife some eleven months ago. The wound healed but he was starting to realize that the burden of repeated injuries accumulated over time. He didn't like it but there was nothing he could do. Soon he'd be thirty-five and he wasn't ever going to start getting younger.

Glancing around, he realized he'd covered a couple of miles from his house, some of it on the Rez, some of it off in the surrounding wild lands. He knew this area. A spring burbled to the surface nearby, with water that was always cold. As a kid, back when he'd thought he might become an ornithologist like John James Audubon, who he much admired, he'd visited this place frequently to sketch the birds that drank here.

A sip of cool water sounded inviting so he turned toward the spring, moving softly on his moccasins to keep from startling any creatures who might be hanging out there. Slipping past a grove of juniper, he saw the spring ahead, the water nestled in a hole in the earth surrounded by willows and oaks and various other trees.

The pool was stained black with tannins, dark as cream-less coffee. He knew from experience the water would have a tangy taste, but it wasn't harmful to drink. Most people hated the taste and aftertaste; he didn't mind it. However, he couldn't approach quite yet. Through the drooping limbs of a willow he could see other visitors to the pool—a whitetail doe and her fawn.

The fawn was small and big-eared, with white spots daubed along its sides like spattered paint. In early summer, those spots should have been fading, but this little one must have been a late birth.

The man watched the pair with pleasure. Deer were sacred to the Kickapoo. Pasheekashee, as they were named. For many years, Ten-Wolves generally pushed away the mystical and spiritual aspects of tribal life. He no longer did so, although he still questioned meanings and symbols. But the deer... They meant something to him despite his rationalistic training. So, he watched, and as he watched he spotted something that electrified his senses.

To the right of the drinking whitetails, behind a deadfall of trees, he saw a smooth expanse of tawny color. Not a tree, or leaves, or grass. And then it twitched and revealed its nature.

Puma!

He did not see them often here, but sometimes they crossed from Mexico. And they hunted deer. All things had to eat. The big cat was only doing what nature had built it to do. But at this moment, on this day, almost without thought, Concho intervened. He leaped from behind his tree, throwing up his hands and shouting, "Hiyee!"

The mother whitetail spun on her rear hooves and lunged away. The fawn followed. The pair ran away from Concho, and thus away from the puma. The big tawny cat crashed from its hiding place to the water's edge but the deer had a big head start and it wouldn't catch them.

The beast turned in its crouch and glared across the dark water. It was a big male, maybe eight feet long and probably at least two hundred pounds. A shock travelled Concho's spine as the savage yellow eyes studied him. He didn't carry his guns with him on a run, though he had a hunting knife in a sheath at his belt. He didn't draw it yet.

Straightening, he squared his shoulders, increasing his own apparent size, which was already considerable, of course. He lifted and spread his hands. "I would apologize brother of the wild, for scaring away your dinner. But I'm afraid I'm not sorry. That little one deserves a bit of a better start in this world."

The puma snarled in disagreement but decided against making it an argument. It melted away into the brush, creating no more sound than a ghost as it went. The lawman relaxed. He considered what he'd done, and why. For some reason, thoughts of Jane Doe, came to him. He realized something about the young woman he should have realized before. The deer had told him and he'd almost failed to listen.

Pulling out his cell phone, he saw he had no service. Well, it wasn't an emergency. He started jogging toward home. No, not an emergency, but he had people to see and things to do before the morning drew to a close.

———

THE MAN CALLED Snow rode his motorcycle into Eagle Pass around 11:00 AM. He found a quiet place and made a call to the number he'd previously been sent. A man's voice answered and spoke a few words—"Kickapoo Lucky Eagle Casino and Hotel. Room 333"—before hanging up.

Snow considered. A face-to-face meeting wasn't usual in such matters but it wasn't unheard of. And his handler had indicated such a request might be forthcoming. He'd never been to Eagle Pass before but the casino was widely known and there were plenty of signs. He followed those to the parking lot at 794 Lucky Eagle Drive.

Leaning the Honda Magna on its kickstand, he entered

through the casino itself, knowing that crowds and noise could easily be made the friends of anyone who preferred to remain anonymous. The shrieks of winners and the low pitiful moans of losers mixed with the pinging and jingling and clatter of the slots. He passed it all unnoticed to the elevators, took an empty one to the third floor.

Room 333 was easy enough to find. He knocked on the door with his left hand, standing off to one side with his right hand under his leather jacket next to the Glock 19 Gen5 9mm in its shoulder holster.

The door opened. A big man with short-cropped, graying hair stood there. He was at least six two and probably weighed close to two fifty. He had a farmer's tan and wore an open necked blue work shirt revealing a thick mat of reddish-brown hair on his chest. He looked to be unarmed.

"Snow?" the older man asked.

Snow nodded.

"I'm King Modine. Folks mostly call me Pa." He stepped back and motioned Snow into the room.

The contract killer slipped warily past and stepped over to put a wall at his back. The bathroom stood wide open and didn't appear occupied. A mirror on the inside of that door reflected his own image. His blue-gray eyes looked sleepy, or maybe stoned. Both those things were lies. Every nerve was alert.

"You swept this room for bugs?" Snow asked.

"Same room I always use. It's swept."

Snow considered, and believed. He had a sensor on his phone that should have been squalling at any electronic surveillance devices in the room.

"OK, why the face to face?" Snow asked.

"Right to the point. I appreciate that," King Modine said. "I'm that kind of man myself. I'll tell you. I know who you work for and they hire the best. You've been vouched for. It happens I occasionally find myself in need of that kind of reliability."

"You want me to work for *you*?"

Modine spread his hands. "Not full time, of course. But on occasion. And I figured neither of us would agree to that kind of thing without meeting the other."

"No, I don't suppose we would. But my other employer might not like me...going off the reservation, so to speak."

"Why would they need to know? And, of course, their work would take precedence. But I'm assuming your job is not twenty-four-seven."

"There are down times."

"So, what about it?"

"Too early to decide. This job first."

Modine smiled broadly. "I like it."

"Tell me."

"First we have a gangbanger. Hispanic. Named Martino Salas. He may not know much of anything but I don't want to take the chance."

"Where?"

"The Eagle Pass Correctional Facility. It's at 742 Texas Hwy 131."

"Not easy to get at someone in jail."

"I'm working through some go-betweens to get him out on bail. Of find some other way to make him vulnerable. Something to give you a chance."

"If you know my employer, talk to him. He might be able to help."

"Good idea. I will."

"No picture?"

King shook his head. "Afraid not."

"What else?"

Modine walked over to a small table in the room and tapped his finger on a set of photos. Snow joined him. He still wore his thin leather riding gloves and picked up the pictures to shuffle through them. They all showed a young Native American woman of about twenty or so. Exotic looking and pretty but showing signs of partial drug sedation. She'd been posed for the camera to emphasis her sexuality.

"Location?" Snow asked.

"A problem at the moment," Modine replied. "She's in protective custody in the Maverick County Sheriff's Office. Same address but she won't be in a jail cell. Rumor is they have some separate rooms for protective custody. However, I believe she'll be walking pretty soon. She's a *victim*. They won't be charging her with a crime and they won't be able to hold her against her will."

"Unless she decides to stay for protection."

"She won't. She's got a reason to get out."

"What reason?"

Pa chuckled. "Something she really values. It's at 1224 Mesa Street right here in Eagle Pass. That'll be a good place to start watchin' for her."

Snow realized he might need to know more about the woman's *reason* in the future. But not right now. "Pa" seemed to want to keep that information close to his vest and Snow wasn't going to argue. He memorized the contours of the woman's face. The next time he saw her, she wouldn't be made up to look glamorous. She'd likely be dirty and scared. But the eyes, the cheekbones, the mouth, the chin, those wouldn't change.

As the killer's mind began clicking over possibilities, he glanced at King Modine and realized there was still more. "OK," he said. "What else?"

Modine nodded. "You're good. There *is* more. A third contract. I already ran it by your employer and he approves."

"Tell."

"His name is Concho Ten-Wolves. He lives right here on the reservation. Comes into this casino fairly often. The only problem is, he's a Texas Ranger."

Modine turned toward the single bed in the room and picked up a magazine lying on it. He placed it down on the table in front of Snow and opened it to a photo and accompanying article about Ten-Wolves.

"He's got a hat on in the photo but hardly ever wears it in real life," Modine said. "He's...well, a bit of a celebrity in local circles. I imagine that complicates things so I'm willing to pay more."

"*Texas Monthly*," Snow said. "I read the article. A hard ass."

Modine chuckled. "Some people even claim he's magic. Nonsense, of course, but he is a tough target. How much do you want?"

A feeling of excitement fluttered in Snow's stomach, surprising him. It had been a long time since he'd taken a job that challenged. This could offer an opportunity for a real work of art. But it wasn't good business to kill for free.

"Two hundred K. To start. More, depending on how much trouble it is."

"All right. That's three hundred up front. For all three."

Snow pulled a small white card, about the size of a business card, out of the inside pocket of his jacket. He handed this across. It was blank and King Modine looked at it curiously.

"Heat it," Snow said. "Gently at first. Then fry it."

Modine nodded. "Gotcha. That'll be the routing number for your bank."

"It's also got a number for a burner phone in case you need to contact me."

"Good idea." King offered his hand.

Snow stared at the proffered handshake. "Not yet," he said.

Modine nodded and let his hand drop. Snow turned and left the room, his mind already working on the job he'd just contracted for. First, he needed to find a place to stay. But not on the reservation where Ten-Wolves lived. And then he wanted to check out Mesa Street.

CHAPTER TWENTY-ONE

Concho's phone pinged. He pulled it out of his pocket, saw he had cell service again and had missed two calls—both from Isaac Parkland, Sheriff of Maverick County. It was 11:37 AM and the calls had come in over the last half hour, with the latest only ten minutes ago. A feeling of foreboding took a bite out of him and he quickly swiped to return the calls.

"Ten-Wolves," Parkland answered. "Glad you got back to me."

"What's up?"

"The girl. She's going wild. She's demanding to be released. I think she may have remembered something but she won't tell any of us. She's asked for you several times."

Concho could see his trailer half a mile ahead, with his truck in the driveway. "OK. Tell her I'll be there as quick as I can. Half an hour or a little more."

"Hope it calms her down."

"Listen, one thing. I'm pretty sure there's a reason why she's so upset and wanting out. She's worried about someone."

"What makes you think that?"

"Too complicated to go into now. Tell you later."

"All right, hurry."

But Concho had already swiped off and launched into a dead run for home. Only a little while earlier this morning, he'd decided the situation with Jane Doe wasn't an immediate emergency. Maybe he'd been wrong.

———

AT 12:14 PM, Concho strode through the glass doors into the Maverick County Sheriff's Office. He'd taken a four-minute shower and dressed in less. He'd run his siren part of the way on the trip in to clear the way—though he'd turned it off once to make a phone call that had been very informative.

The officer at the front desk was clearly expecting him. She waved him past without asking him to sign in. "The Sheriff is in his office," she said.

Ten-Wolves strode down a corridor past the desk and turned in at the first door he came to. Isaac Parkland had heard the exchange outside and was already rising from his chair. Parkland was in his late fifties, short and a little on the heavy side. He wore his usual white shirt with a silver star pinned to it but had taken off his ten-gallon hat. The few strands of hair on his head gleamed with sweat.

"Glad you're here," Parkland said. "Let's go talk to her."

The Sheriff grabbed his hat off his work desk and crushed it down on his head, then led the way toward the same set of special cells where the Ranger visited Jane Doe before. On the way, he shared a bit of new information.

"We got the tox screen report back from the hospital. She was dosed with Rohypnol. Repeatedly. At high doses. Might explain her memory loss."

Concho knew a little about Rohypnol, one of a class of drugs sometimes called "date rape" drugs. It basically produced a kind of drunkenness and had strong amnesic effects, but those effects wouldn't completely explain the woman's reported experience.

"It might be why she didn't remember her abduction,"

Concho replied, "but it shouldn't have erased her identity. That's something else."

"Psychological trauma?" Parkland asked curiously.

"Or she's lying."

Parkland had no time to say anything more. They reached a familiar corridor. Kerry Keegan was on duty again and opened the outside door for Parkland and Ten-Wolves. They stepped through.

The woman paced back and forth in her cell. She turned as she heard them enter and rushed to the Plexiglass partition. Desperation had aged her face since the Ranger's last visit. Her gaze passed over Parkland and focused on Concho.

"You've got to let me out of here. I need to be out of here."

"What's going on?" Ten-Wolves asked.

"It's...it's nothing particularly. I just can't stand to be in here anymore. You can't hold me. I've done nothing wrong."

Concho decided it was time to stop coddling her. "You're lying to officers of the law," he snapped. "Not exactly an endearing trait."

The woman blinked as if slapped. "What? I don't—I'm not lying."

"We know you were dosed with Rohypnol. So that certainly explains some of your memory loss. But it wouldn't have made you forget your name. Or your *family*."

The woman blinked again. She took a step back from the partition. "You don't know. You're not a doctor."

"I've got a good friend who is. Earl Blake. I just spoke to him on the phone."

Both Jane and Parkland looked at Concho with confusion.

"I spoke to Earl about memory loss," Ten-Wolves continued. "Rohypnol came up. Other drugs, too. They can create short-term amnesia. Physiological. But they don't erase whole identities. You know who you are. You're hiding your name for some reason. And I'm wondering if it has to do with the child you're not telling us about."

———

AFTER THE MEETING WITH SNOW, King "Pa" Modine returned to his farm. He'd already made a call to Snow's "employer," as the assassin had suggested. The man agreed to look into it but gave no guarantees. It occurred to King on the drive home that if he could get Martino Salas injured in jail, the man would have to be taken to the hospital, which would give Snow a chance to get at him.

He was still mulling over that idea when he stepped into his house and realized immediately something was wrong. Of all things, he smelled *baby powder*. It had been a long time since there'd been a baby in this house.

His oldest son, Derrick, still wasn't home, but the two younger boys, Taylor and Justin, should be here. He called out to them as he stalked to investigate the smell. He didn't have to investigate much. A kid began to wail from the back of the house. King tore off down the hallway, saw the door at the end of the hall open and Taylor step out.

"Boy!" he shouted. "What in tarnation are you doing?"

Taylor startled. He seemed to consider darting back into the room he'd just exited but thought better of it. King reached his son and shoved him aside to step past into the old bedroom beyond. They used this room mostly to store coats and junk but there was still a twin bed in it. His youngest boy, Justin, stood beside the bed looking all kinds of discombobulated. Lying *on* the bed was a squalling kid.

King had absolutely no idea for a moment what he was seeing. Then he realized who the kid must be—the lost woman's baby, the one the Mexes had been holding over her head as a final piece of insurance. Though why his stupid, stupid sons would have kidnapped the child and brought it here, he could not discern.

He came closer to cursing in that instant than since he'd first married his dearly departed wife, Scarlett. Somehow, he swallowed it back. The child was a girl, he realized, not even half a year old, and wearing a pink nightdress with roses on it. She apparently possessed a good set of lungs.

"Are you boys brain damaged or are you just idiots?" he shouted. "Why did you ever bring that kid here?"

Taylor answered. "We thought you'd be happy, Pa. Now we've got the kid and the Injun girl will have to do what we say."

King threw up his hands. "I've raised morons. If I'd wanted the kid taken I'd of said so. I wanted it exactly where it was so when the woman came to get it we'd have someone waiting to take care of her."

"We didn't know, Pa!" Justin said.

Pa threw up his hands again. "You didn't *need* to know. You just needed to sit on your hind ends and eat chili until I told you what to do."

"We're sorry, Pa," Taylor said. "You want us to get rid of it?"

King sighed and shook his head. "There you go trying to think again. You're going to take care of the kid and make sure no harm whatsoever comes to it. I'm going to have to cogitate on our next step but maybe there's some way we can salvage this. And you need to figure out how to shut it up." He raised his voice. "*Without* hurting it! Do I make myself clear?"

"Yes, Pa," both brothers said.

"I don't reckon you left the woman alive who was keeping it?"

"No, Pa," Taylor said, not quite sure if that had been the right thing to do or not. "There were two women there. One tried to shoot at us so we had no choice. And we didn't want no witnesses left behind."

"So, you did the right thing by accident," King said. He shook his head. "Well, even a blind hog finds an acorn once in a while."

"Thanks, Pa," Taylor said.

King rolled his eyes and turned to leave the room. "Pa," Justin said.

"What?"

"I think...I think the kid's cryin' because it needs changing. Sure smells like it."

"Then change it!"

"We don't know how," Justin protested. "We don't even have any diapers." The two brothers exchanged glances that held a hint of terror in them.

Pa snorted a laugh that grew slowly into a guffaw. He finally recovered enough to say, "Then I reckon you two geniuses better figure it out. You wanted to get your hands dirty. Here's your chance."

He slammed the door shut behind him and stalked off down the hallway, leaving his sons to their fears of a dirty diaper. He did take a moment to call Snow on a burner phone and report the recent deaths and kidnapping on Mesa Street. That information would soon get back to the assassin's handler/employer and might offer a fresh way to get Martino Salas released from jail so he could be killed.

Maybe old King could still spin dirty straw into gold.

CHAPTER TWENTY-TWO

"YOU'RE HIDING YOUR NAME FOR SOME REASON," CONCHO SAID TO Jane Doe. "And I'm wondering if it has to do with the child you're not telling us about."

While Isaac Parkland frowned, Jane stepped back from the front of her cell. Her left hand fluttered to her face. "How did you—" She froze in midsentence, realizing she'd given herself away. Abruptly she deflated. Her shoulders sank.

"Who told you?" she asked.

"Let's just say a *deer* friend."

Parkland had no idea what that phrase meant, but Jane Doe —or whatever her real name—was Native American. She understood.

"You had a vision," she said.

Concho felt his face heating. For a moment, he felt almost embarrassed. Then he rejected that feeling. He didn't know what had happened exactly when he'd seen the mother white-tail and her fawn. His rational mind told him he'd already noted other cues hinting at Jane Doe's child and that sight of the deer just coalesced those thoughts. Meskwaa would have rejected such an explanation and called it a "knowing." Not quite a vision but something more than an educated guess.

Perhaps it was the "vision" aspect that cemented Jane's next decision. She straightened her shoulders though her body thrummed with tension. "All right," she said. "If you take me to her now, I'll answer every question I can. I don't remember everything that happened but you're right, I haven't forgotten... who I am."

Concho exchanged glances with Isaac Parkland. The Sheriff nodded.

"Please!" Jane begged. "I'm worried. I think something's wrong. Please!"

Parkland unlocked the cell. Concho opened the outside door. Jane followed him through it, with Parkland on her heels.

"Kerry," the Sheriff said to the deputy on duty, "you accompany Ten-Wolves and the young lady. I'll follow."

They rushed through the building toward the parking lot. In moments, they were on their way, Concho leading in his F-150 with Parkland following in a police SUV. Deputy Keegan rode in the passenger seat with Ten-Wolves while Jane Doe sat in the extended cab area.

"Where we going?" Concho asked.

"1224 Mesa Street," Jane replied. "Please hurry."

Concho flipped the switch to activate his lights and sirens. Sheriff Parkland followed suit. They raced into Eagle Pass through the blazing sun of early afternoon.

"Why do you think something's wrong?" Concho demanded from Jane.

"Just a feeling. It started last night. That's...I was asking them to let me out. I felt like I needed to check on her."

"What's her name?"

Jane blinked in the rear-view mirror. "Winona," she said.

Concho knew enough Navajo to translate the name as "first born daughter."

"You call her 'Angel' sometimes?"

Jane startled. "How did you...?"

"When you were shot at and Terrill Hoight took the bullet, he told me later you gasped out the word 'angel.'"

"I don't remember but it could be. I was thinking about her, wondering how she'd be if I died. If she would have any memory of me."

"How old is she?"

"Just four months."

Concho kept his gas pedal to the floor. Most cars pulled over for the sirens but he had to steer around the occasional clueless driver. He still possessed the focus to ask one more question.

"What's *your* name? I'm tired of calling you Jane."

"My parents weren't traditionalists," she replied. "They left the reservation before I was born. Said they wanted me to live like "normal" people. I guess they meant "white" people. They even changed their last name to Green. They called me Heather. So, I'm Heather Green. Too bad they couldn't change my face and skin and hair."

Concho didn't reply. They were getting close to Mesa Street. He flipped off his sirens and lights. Parkland did the same behind them. They turned onto Mesa, into a typical suburban neighborhood in Eagle Pass, although on the poor side of suburban. Ten-Wolves looked for house numbers."

"Down there," Heather Green said. "Twelve houses. On the left."

"Whose place?" Concho asked as he accelerated again.

"My best friend, Tamara Salas. She's keeping Winona for me. Her and her mother, Henrietta."

"They speak English?"

"Tamara does. Her mother understands some."

Concho wheeled into the driveway of 1224 Mesa Street, parking behind an old blue Chevrolet Impala. He and Keegan both bailed out as Isaac Parkland squealed up along the curb. Heather tried to follow Concho out of the Ford but he pushed the seat back to constrain her and ordered her sternly to, "Stay put!"

The Ranger motioned for Keegan to head around the back while he rushed toward the front door. The house was built of brown brick with faux rust-red shutters bracketing the windows. A dry flower bed with a few wilted blooms decorated the front. Concho rang the doorbell. No answer.

He rang again, then pounded his big fist on the door. "Senora Salas! Por favor! Abierto! Senora Salas! Policía"

No answer.

Heather Green hadn't stayed where she'd been ordered. She came running, yelling, "Tamara! It's Heather. Where are you? I brought the police but they're OK."

Parkland had climbed out of his car. He caught the young woman's arm and held her still.

"Around here!" Keegan shouted from behind the house, his voice pitched high with excitement. "Looks like a break in."

"Get her back!" Concho shouted to Parkland as he rushed toward Keegan's voice. He drew his right-hand Colt.

A rickety wooden fence enclosed the Salas's back yard but the gate stood open. Concho could see the porch with the screen door hanging askew. He proceeded with more caution, the pistol in his hand up and ready to fire. Keegan followed.

The back door to the house stood ajar, with a small glass panel removed from the lower right-hand corner of it. The intruder or intruders must have pulled out that panel and reached through to unlock the door from inside. If they'd used something to hold the glass with, like a suction cup, the break-in wouldn't have made much noise.

Concho eased the door open and stepped inside, into a hallway. He knew instantly something was wrong. He could hear it, the buzz of flies that emphasized the profound silence of the rest of the house. He could smell it, death in the form of released bodily fluids.

A small, crumpled shape lay at the end of the hall. He recognized it as a body, though whose he could not yet tell. A doorway to his right showed a short hallway and an open bathroom and laundry room. Empty, it seemed. A little farther ahead lay a door off the left side of the hall. That one was closed.

Ten-Wolves pushed ahead, toward the as yet unexplored room. He motioned to Keegan behind him to check the bathroom area. Stopping beside the closed room, Concho took a moment to study the body at the end of the hall more closely. An elderly woman, with gray hair in disarray around her flyspeckled face. A pool of dried blood had formed a kind of gelatin around her upper body. A shotgun lay on the floor against the wall. This must be Henrietta Salas. She'd tried to fight, without success.

There remained Tamara Salas, Heather Green's friend. And the child, Winona. Concho took hold of the doorknob to the room next to him and twisted it open, hoping he wouldn't find Tamara or Winona inside, because that would certainly mean they were dead.

That hope shattered as the door swung open and the smell of blood stung his nostrils. In a crouch, he stepped quickly into the room, his gun swinging left and right to cover any danger. There wasn't any.

He straightened slowly, with a sigh. He stood in a small bedroom. Heavy curtains hung over the windows and the room was only dimly lit by a pink nightlight. Only a few flies had gotten in so far, probably under the door. Against the wall to his left stood a crib. Empty, though it still carried the faint scent of baby powder.

To his right lay a twin bed and another corpse. This one must be Tamara. He stepped around her, looking for any sign of a child's body. He couldn't see any, and a faint flicker of relief crossed his thoughts. Maybe the little one was still alive.

Then he noticed a scrawl of vermillion on the whitewashed wall above the bed where Tamara Salas lay ruined.

CHAPTER TWENTY-THREE

AFTER GETTING SETTLED IN AT A LOCAL MOTEL, SNOW CHECKED his burner phone and found a message from King Modine. He noted the information and used the same phone to text a thumbs up response. Pulling out the phone's SIM card, he crushed and flushed it, then replaced it with another card so the phone could be reused.

After that, he called his handler on his own phone, which couldn't be traced, to report it—both as an update on the job and a potential opportunity for intervention. Finally, he used MapQuest to show him the way to Mesa Street.

He tooled slowly down that direction on his bike for a reconnoiter. Two police vehicles were parked in front of 1224 Mesa. An older officer wearing a white, ten-gallon hat stood outside holding onto the arm of a young woman who Snow immediately recognized. He knew her as "Jane Doe."

A grin crossed Snow's face. *Talk about luck!* But this was not the place for taking action. There'd be more cops around, probably in the house. And plenty more likely on the way. At least two dozen potential civilian witnesses lined the sidewalks on both sides of the street as they rubbernecked the affair.

Snow cruised by, looking at the scene no more and no less

than anyone else. A hundred yards down, he found a vacant lot and turned and parked. Time to wait. Until a plan came to him. Or until opportunity knocked.

"RANGER?" Kerry Keegan called from outside the bedroom where Concho stood staring at the death scene of Tamara Salas.

"Yes?" he asked heavily.

"Rest of the house is clear. No sign of the kid. How about you?"

"The child was in here. She's gone now."

Keegan came through the door. The deputy saw the crib and shook his head, then noticed the direction of the Ranger's stare. He winced at sight of the dead body. A frown covered his face as he saw the image scrawled on the wall.

"What? What is that?" Keegan asked.

"It's a straight razor," Concho said. "Half open. Drawn in the blood of the dead woman." He pointed toward a hairbrush lying on the bed, its bristles clotted with crimson. "He used that to do it."

"What does it mean?"

Concho sighed. He pointed to three dimly visible words beneath the image. They'd been quickly and clumsily done, with blood that left smeared and distorted lines.

"America," Keegan read. "I can't...make out the rest."

"Is ours," Concho said. "America is ours."

Keegan made a face. "White supremacists, you're thinking?"

"Or meant to make us believe so."

"Because the dead are both Hispanic?"

"Yeah, but whoever did this didn't come here to kill Hispanics. They came for the child."

"Then why the razor?"

"I've seen it before. Engraved on a shell casing. And as a

tattoo. But the meaning..." He shook his head back and forth. "It reminds me of something."

Concho turned and looked at Keegan. "Start getting some photos of the crime scene with your phone. Turn on the lights if you need to. I've got to report to Sheriff Parkland."

"And figure out what to tell the child's mother," Keegan commiserated.

"That, too."

Walking as if weights dragged at his boots, Ten-Wolves left the house by the same door he'd come in and circled around to the front. Heather Green saw him coming. She jerked free of Isaac Parkland's grip and ran to the Ranger. As soon as she got close enough to see his face, she staggered and cried out. He caught her and held her upright.

The Ranger was aware of the onlookers, a mixed crowd of the white and Hispanic homeowners along Mesa Street, but he spared them no attention. "I think she's alive," he said to Heather. "I think your daughter is alive. Whoever did this took her. They wouldn't have if she..."

Heather trembled as she cried on his shoulder. "She's so little. Small for her age. Oh my God! Who could have taken her?"

"I'll find her. I'll find them."

Heather hiccupped, like a crying child herself. "What about...what about Tamara? And her mother?"

Concho squeezed the woman a little harder as he answered. "I'm afraid they're both dead. Shot."

Heather's sobs turned to a long moan. She seemed to liquify in his arms, as if all she wanted to do was fall. He held her for a moment, then gently lowered her to a sitting position in the yard. He stayed leaning over, one hand on her shoulder. A large form blocked the sun and Concho looked up at Sheriff Isaac Parkland's stricken face.

"I heard," Parkland said.

"Keegan is taking photos of the scene. But we need—"

"I'll call it in," Parkland said quickly. He hurried toward his SUV, as if happy to be doing anything other than sharing Heather Green's despair.

Concho folded himself into a sitting position beside the woman. She gave a loud sob, paused for a breath, loosed another sob. Rage swirled around inside the Ranger like water around a clogged drain. He wanted to get his hands on whoever had killed the two women inside and stolen a small child. But right now he had to be here, sitting in the dirt beside a heart-broken woman.

For an instant, a cloud darkened the sun, chilling him. But when he glanced up there were no clouds, only an infinite blue. Where had the shadow come from then? He looked around. At least two dozen onlookers watched them with faces upon which many emotions danced—fear, surprise, anger, melancholy, curiosity, glee, doubt, hope, hopelessness.

None of those things had chilled him. Something else. Something he couldn't see but which could see him. He was being watched by cold eyes.

CHAPTER TWENTY-FOUR

AN AMBULANCE ARRIVED AT 1224 MESA STREET. A PARAMEDIC examined Heather Green and gave her something to calm her down. She stopped crying. Mostly she stared into space in shock. Concho had seen the look plenty of times in Afghanistan. Soldiers sometimes called it the "thousand-yard stare."

More cops had arrived as well and a steady stream of people moved in and out of the house where the murders and kidnapping had taken place. The crowd of onlookers had thinned and swelled as some folks left and others arrived. A KVAW— Channel 16—news crew showed up but were being held back with the crowds by the police.

"What do we do with the girl?" Isaac Parkland asked Concho.

The Ranger sat wearily on the tailgate of his truck in the driveway. "She's got things she needs to tell us, and we need to know them if we're going to have any chance of finding her daughter."

"You want me to try and get a statement from her?"

"No, it's my job."

Ten-Wolves pushed himself upright and strode toward the cab of his truck where Heather Green now sat. She'd been too much in the open in the house's front yard where she'd collapsed after learning of the horror at 1224 Mesa. He'd moved her here, where cops walked back and forth past her the whole time. He'd also had her put on an extra Kevlar vest Parkland carried in his vehicle, along with a blue windbreaker to go over it.

The paramedic working with the woman nodded at him and moved away. Heather sat slouched in the passenger seat and Concho leaned against the cab beside her and waited for her to look in his direction. She blinked slowly, then finally did so.

"I need to know everything," he said.

She nodded. "I was...I met Diego Cabello at Tamara's church. I usually went with her on Sundays. He was interested in Tamara. And Martino—Tamara's brother—was interested in me. She wouldn't go out with Diego. But sometimes I talked to them after church. They told me they could get me a job. Making real money. I only had a part-time job at the 7-Eleven so I needed it. For Winona. And so I wouldn't have to scrounge off Tamara and her mother as much."

"What kind of job?"

She looked away from him. "Porn," she said, her voice flat. "They...well, Diego said he knew some local guys trying to make a film. They had actors but needed...an actress."

"You agreed?"

She nodded. "Diego said it wasn't going to be anything too... bad. And it wasn't like I was a virgin anyway. But there wasn't any film. Or at least I don't think there was. They picked me up after work one day. Diego and Martino. I'd told Tamara and her mother I'd be gone a few days. I didn't tell them where. They agreed to look after Winona. Martino poured me a drink in the car. He said it would relax me. I remember laughing about something he said, but I don't really remember anything else until when you found me in the trunk."

"You were drugged with Rohypnol. That's what your blood test showed. It's a drug that causes amnesia."

"I've heard of it. Even the memories of you finding me are... vague. I can see you looking down on me in the trunk. But afterward...I know something happened. A police officer got shot. But I don't really remember much until sometime after I was in that...cell at the sheriff's office."

"I'm sure you still had the drug in your system."

She nodded. "When I started thinking normally again, that's when I got the feeling Winona was in danger and I...I tried to get them to let me go."

She sobbed, then fought the tears back down.

"I think Diego and Martino were going to deliver you to two men in a Jeep," Concho told her. "Along with some cocaine. Those men ran when I confronted them and I couldn't go after them because I was being shot at. But I think they're likely the ones who took your daughter. I just don't know why. You have any idea?"

Heather shook her head but gave a response anyway. "I remember something Diego said. He was talking so slowly, though. I thought maybe it was a dream."

"What?"

"He said they were going to...sell me to someone."

Something clicked in the lawman's mind. *Sell her to someone.* He thought suddenly of the tattooed man at the bus station, the one who'd pretended to be homeless but almost surely wasn't. The man had been hanging around the station? Why? To meet some arrival? Or to pick up someone vulnerable?

Could there have *been* a pornographic film? One where they did things to women that no one would agree to? Afterwards, of course, those actresses would disappear. He didn't say any of this to the grieving young woman by his side.

"Look," Heather said suddenly. "Maybe if I could get a note pad and a pen. Maybe if I wrote things down I could make sense of it. Remember things a little better."

"That's a good idea," the Ranger said. "We can go back to the police station with Sheriff Parkland? He can get you the supplies you need. And from there I have to go talk to Martino Salas."

Heather's mouth twisted into anger at mention of Martino's name, but she couldn't sustain the emotion and her body slumped even further. "OK," she said, in a small voice.

Concho motioned Isaac Parkland over and explained their plan. The Sheriff agreed. But a fresh arrival at the scene changed everything. A dark blue SUV pulled in behind Isaac Parkland's car. The logo on the side read, in big white letters: FBI.

Bihn Bui, a Vietnamese agent who Concho had met several times and liked, climbed out of the driver's side. He wore his usual starched shirt and tie, white and blue respectively. He nodded at the Ranger, who nodded back.

The passenger side of the SUV disgorged a very different type of agent—Special Agent Della Rice, who came striding purposefully toward Concho wearing a black pantsuit over a white silk blouse. She was a tall woman, nearly six feet, with wavy hair cut to shoulder length. A once broken nose, with its faint crook to the right, toughened her already sharply defined features. Rice was in charge of the local FBI contingent. She and Ten-Wolves had a complicated history, though *mostly* they seemed to be on the same side.

Rice glanced at Sheriff Parkland and gave him the "yes I acknowledge the presence of another officer of the law" smile before turning her dark-eyed stare on Concho and saying, "Kidnapping? Tell me everything."

"I put it in the report I filed to you," Concho said softly.

Rice's gaze flicked over the scene where they stood now. "And obviously more has happened, so spill."

On occasion, Concho found Della Rice irritating. This was such an occasion. Maybe because of his emotional exhaustion. He took a faintly perverse pleasure in playing obtuse. "How do you know this is connected?"

Rice stared. "Get up on the wrong side of your kennel this

morning, Ten-Wolves? I've already heard the radio chatter. There's a child missing. That's FBI territory."

Concho took a deliberate glance toward Heather Green, who sat within easy hearing range of the conversation. Della Rice saw the glance and had the decency to flush faintly, indicated only by a slight deepening of the color over her cheekbones.

Heather chose that moment to speak. "I want to get going. Get started making those notes."

"Right," Ten-Wolves said. He hesitated.

"I can take her," Parkland added. "You'll need to orient Special Agent Rice here."

Rice acknowledged Heather and Parkland with nods, then cut back to Concho with her main point. "Yes, I want everything you've got. And to see what's here. I've been out of town so I need to get caught up."

"All right," the Ranger said. He glanced at Parkland. "Make sure you ride with backup, though."

"Of course. I'll take deputy Keegan. No one's going to attack a couple of armed cops on the road."

Concho glanced at Heather. She looked scared. He felt a little of that himself.

CHAPTER TWENTY-FIVE

CONCHO WATCHED ISAAC PARKLAND LEAVE WITH HEATHER GREEN.
Kerry Keegan drove the Sheriff's vehicle. They had a short trip
back to the station. Not much time for anything to happen. It
shouldn't have worried him but it did. He'd feel much better if
he was driving the young woman. But...

"Let's take the tour," Della Rice said.

Concho nodded and led the way to the house while he
started to explain what he knew and surmised about the case.
Still, some part of his mind rode with Parkland and Keegan and
Heather Green. He remembered the feeling from a little while
ago of cold eyes watching them. That feeling had faded but the
unease it generated had not.

After fighting the unease for a few moments, the Ranger
paused the tour and pulled out his cell phone. "I have to make a
call," he told Della Rice. The woman shrugged.

Concho dialed deputy Roland Turner. Turner answered
promptly.

"You at the station?" Ten-Wolves asked without preamble.

"Yeah. What's up?"

"Parkland and Keegan are on their way with the woman you

know as Jane Doe. They'll take 2nd Street. Will you meet them, escort them the rest of the way in?"

"Is something wrong?"

"I'm not sure. Maybe. Will you do it?"

"On my way," Turner said.

Concho swiped off the call. Agent Rice was staring at him. "What's that all about?" she asked.

"An irrational precaution," he said to her. To himself, he thought, *I hope!*

————

THEY WERE COMING DOWN 2nd Street toward the Maverick County Sheriff's Office when the irrational happened. Kerry Keegan drove. Isaac Parkland sat in the passenger seat with Heather in the back. A few scattered buildings marked the boundaries of the highway but it was mostly open fields to either side, defined by dirt, dry grasses, and the dark, almost rubbery green of mesquite bushes.

They passed Legacy Boulevard, with the Claymex Brick and Tile building just ahead on their left. A motorcycle sitting at the junction with Legacy waited for them to go by, then pulled out and sped up behind them. No other vehicles were on the road.

Keegan noticed the bike in his rearview mirror. He frowned when the rider accelerated and switched lanes as if to go around. Most people didn't pass cops even when the officer wasn't doing the speed limit, which he was.

With his muscles tightening slightly, Keegan glanced out his side window. The biker wore a full-face helm that left his features hidden. A leather jacket hung open from his shoulders, the bottom of it whipping back in the wind.

Keegan started to let off the gas to allow the biker to pass when the rider reached down to the left side of his bike and yanked out a sawed-off shotgun. In the half second before

Keegan could react, the man fired the weapon twice into the driver's side window.

Heavy pellets of double-ought buckshot smashed through the glass like a wrecking ball and punched into Keegan's head above the shoulders. The deputy died instantly with most of his skull and brain turned into a white and red ruin.

The last reflexive act by Keegan had been to jerk the steering wheel to the right to avoid the attack. The SUV swerved hard across the road toward the ditch. From Isaac Parkland's point of view, the roar of the shotgun blasts came as a complete shock. Shattered glass sprayed him, along with wet daubs and strands of flesh and blood. He cried out while Heather Green screamed in the back seat.

Parkland grabbed for the steering wheel and got hit by the nearly headless body of Kerry Keegan being thrown into his lap. The SUV wheeled like a juggernaut of steel into the shallow ditch and slammed into the barbed wire fence lining the field next to the highway. The top strands of wire parted; the bottom ones held. The SUV flipped over the fence and came down on its roof. Window glass exploded like a bomb.

Parkland found himself hanging upside down from his seat belt. The pain of twisted muscles and joints stabbed through him but his instinct as a law officer took over. He grabbed for the latch, twisted it. The belt released and he crashed a foot down onto his shoulders. Something popped and agony blasted through his upper left side. He couldn't be sure he hadn't cracked his collarbone.

The sound of a motorcycle engine whined in his ears; the shooter was coming back. The passenger side window had been smashed out. Parkland squirmed through it. It was a tight fit. His shirt caught and tore. Glass and sharp metal edges gouged his skin, drawing blood, but he found himself free on his belly in the dirt. Everything hurt.

Grass pollen and dust clogged his mouth and nostrils and made him sneeze, but he pushed himself to his knees, drawing the four-inch barrel Colt Trooper .357 riding high in a holster on his right hip. A moan from the SUV's backseat drew his gaze. Heather was conscious but obviously hurting. She'd unlocked her own seatbelt and lay flat against the new "floor" of the vehicle.

"Stay down!" he ordered her.

Parkland was fifty-seven years old and not in the best shape. But he was Sheriff of Maverick County and he wouldn't forget that. He'd been elected to protect people like Heather Green and he *couldn't* forget that. On trembling legs and favoring his left side, he forced himself to his feet and brought his pistol across the bottom of the SUV behind the front tire, taking a shooter's stance against whoever might be coming for the woman.

CHAPTER TWENTY-SIX

On his Honda Magna, Snow watched the police SUV careen into the ditch and hit the fence. He saw it flip as he zipped past it on the empty highway. Slamming the shotgun into the scabbard he'd made for it under his left leg, he grabbed the clutch and stomped the rear brake on the motorcycle, leaning low toward the left side of the bike as he twisted the handlebars slightly. The cycle skidded sideways to a stop, the rear tire pouring up smoke and burning rubber.

Expertly, Snow brought the bike back upright and toed the gear shift, dropping the big 750 into low. He cranked the throttle. The two V-4 engines screamed; the bike leaped forward, back down the street toward the overturned SUV. The driver was dead. He'd seen the head explode like a watermelon hit by a baseball bat. The other officer in the car was an old man. And then there was the woman he needed to kill.

Working both brakes, Snow brought the bike to a sliding stop on the roadside shoulder. He kicked the stand down to hold the bike upright and flipped the faceplate of his helmet up so he could see better. Dismounting and leaving the engine running in neutral, he drew the Dan Wesson 10mm semi-automatic holstered at his right hip. The 10mm made a good cartridge for hunting deer. Humans were about deer sized.

A balding, sweat-dappled head popped out from behind the front tire of the overturned SUV. The Sheriff, with a short-barreled revolver. Snow snapped a shot and the man ducked back down. Snow couldn't see the girl. Maybe she'd been killed in the wreck but he doubted it. People didn't die easily. He stalked toward the vehicle. He'd have to make sure.

The Sheriff popped up again and blasted two quick shots. They whizzed past Snow. He didn't flinch. All he could see of the man now was a shoulder, with everything else hidden behind the tire. He fired, saw crimson spurt as the Sheriff cried out. But it was barely a flesh wound. Skin and blood and nothing vital.

Snow moved to his left, intending to circle the SUV and take out the Sheriff first. As he did so, the woman exploded into a run from her hiding spot, darting into the field behind the wrecked vehicle. That field was mostly open, though dotted here and there with mesquite bushes. A newish apartment complex rose on the other side of the field, maybe two hundred yards away. She seemed headed for that imaginary shelter.

The woman's flight caught Snow by surprise. He was out of position, without a clear shot. Apparently the girl's action startled the Sheriff, too. The older man shouted at her to, "Get down!"

She didn't, and—in a desperation move—the Sheriff risked his own life for hers. He stepped out from behind the tire to take aim at Snow. With a clear shot, Snow took a half second to aim. The Sheriff fired first. One bullet buried itself in the ground just in front of him. Number two struck center of mass, right in his chest.

Snow pulled the trigger on his 10mm but the blow he'd taken ruined his aim and the slug that would have gone straight between the Sheriff's eyes went wild instead. He staggered back, feeling anger erupt inside for the first time. He straightened, brought his pistol to bear.

The Sheriff's eyes widened even further. He started to duck. From down the road came the sudden blare of sirens. Snow made a choice. The woman still fled, getting farther away every second. He swung his gun away from the Sheriff toward the woman. She ran flat out, like an athlete who knows how to move. He placed the red bead at the end of his pistol sight on her back.

The Sheriff aborted his attempt to duck and snapped a desperate shot at Snow's helmeted head. The bullet whined past like a hornet. Snow didn't flinch. He fired. The woman was running across uneven ground, her body moving up and down, swaying from side to side. A difficult shot, but he got a hit. She threw up her arms and stumbled forward to fall behind the broad limbs of a low growing mesquite bush.

The sirens raced closer. Snow shook his head. He slapped his pistol back into its holster and ran for his bike. Mounting up, he toed the Magna into gear and left rubber behind him as he peeled away down the road. His bullet had struck the woman. But whether it killed her or not, he couldn't be sure.

If not, there'd be another time.

———

DEPUTY ROLAND TURNER brought his prowl car squealing to a halt on the shoulder of the road next to the overturned SUV of his sheriff. He piled out of the vehicle, leaving the sirens shrieking as he drew his pistol. He'd seen a rider on a motorcycle speed away from the scene but still didn't know what he might face. A moan and a voice from behind the wrecked SUV pulled him into a run.

"Here," the voice called.

Turner recognized Isaac Parkland. He circled the upside-down vehicle and leaped across two twisted strands of barbed wire. Parkland sat heavily on the ground just beyond, reloading his revolver with one hand. His left arm hung limp at his side and blood trickled down from a nasty gouge across the biceps. It also looked as if the shoulder had been twisted out of its socket.

The Sheriff had other injuries, though Turner wasn't sure the man was aware of them. Cuts across his face leaked reddish tears. A piece of glass was embedded in his nose and another in his left cheek. His white shirt hung shredded on the left side where more cuts and gouges trickled a crimson rheum.

"Help me up!" Parkland said.

The chief lawman switched the reloaded pistol to his left hand, though the fingers hardly seemed to grip it, and held up his right arm. Turner obeyed his commander instinctively, grabbing the Sheriff's hand and heaving upward. Parkland reached his feet and switched the gun back to his right hand.

"The girl," Parkland said, turning toward the field. "We've got to find her. She was running and he shot at her. I couldn't see if he hit her."

The Sheriff started toward the field, limping, and Turner grabbed his good arm. "Call it in, Boss," he said. "I'll check on the girl. I can see the trail she left through the grass."

Parkland coughed, then nodded. "Yeah, you can move faster. Go!"

Turner took off at a trot. He saw where running feet had scraped through bare patches of dirt. Weeds had been stomped down. He reached a wide spreading mesquite bush about forty yards from the road. The dry grass in a kind of hollow behind the bush lay smashed flat, with seed pods scattered like tatters of wild confetti.

He saw blood and dropped into a crouch to examine it. Three small spots, nickel and dime sized. The woman might have been hit but it didn't look too bad. Handprints in a patch of crusty soil showed where she'd pushed back to her feet.

Turner followed, until he reached the parking lot of a big apartment complex across the field. He found another dollop of blood behind a trash bin but nothing more. And he couldn't even tell if it was from the woman he searched for.

There was no sight of her but there were plenty of cars in the parking lot to hide behind. Or she might have gone into the building, or just kept running. Before he could decide what to check first, his cell rang. He saw Isaac Parkland's name pop up on the screen and answered.

"You all right?" Parkland asked.

"Yeah, Boss. The girl doesn't seem to be hurt too bad. I found little spots of blood but not much. She made it to the apartment complex over here but I can't see her."

"Her real name's Heather Green. Maybe try calling her name. She was cooperating with us before this shooter came along."

"Right," Turner said. "But how are you?"

A thick cough wracked Parkland before he spoke again. "Ambulance on the way. And backup. I'll send them your way. We need to find the girl before the shooter does."

"I'll keep looking, Sheriff."

Parkland sighed. "And I'll phone Ten-Wolves."

"Don't envy you that job."

"That's why I make the big bucks." He swiped off the call.

CHAPTER TWENTY-SEVEN

SPECIAL AGENT DELLA RICE AND CONCHO TEN-WOLVES STOOD IN the hallway of the home near where Henrietta Salas had been murdered. Her body had been removed but the blood stains made a gory reminder of the casual savagery of the shooting.

"You thinking human traffickers?" Rice asked as Ten-Wolves finished telling and showing her what he knew about the Heather Green case.

"That's a possibility but I think it's more complicated. You saw the symbol on the wall in the baby's room. That's not traffickers. Whatever the answer, it worries me that they've got a child in their hands now."

Rice shook her head back and forth. "I'll talk to my boss. Get as much help as I can in here."

"Thanks," Concho replied. His phone rang and he pulled it out of his pocket. When he saw Isaac Parkland's name he immediately swiped to answer, feeling a fresh chill of apprehension slither down his back.

"Sheriff! You home yet?"

"Not exactly," Parkland answered. His voice sounded phlegmy and weak.

"You OK? What happened?"

"Ambushed. A biker. Keegan is dead."

Keegan, Concho thought. He'd liked the man; there'd been promise there. He forced himself to remain calm as he said to Parkland, "You sound hurt yourself. Ambulance on the way?"

"I'm all right. Roland Turner came along at just the right moment. The biker took off. The girl ran. I just spoke to Turner. He went after the girl. He thinks she's not hurt too bad but she's hiding. Somewhere around that newish apartment complex on 2nd Street. Over by the Claymex Brick and Tile building."

"I know it. I'm on my way."

"See you."

Concho swiped off the call, still trying to maintain his calm. Rice was staring at him as if he weren't being completely successful. He explained. "Isaac Parkland was ambushed with the girl. They're both alive but the girl ran. I'm headed over there."

"I'll ride with you."

Concho didn't argue. He rushed for his truck. Rice followed, yelling for Bihn Bui to trail them in the FBI's vehicle. Reporters yelled questions at the officers as they emerged from the Salas home but were ignored. The doors on Concho's F-150 opened and slammed again. Ten-Wolves wheeled across the Salas's front yard to reach the street and accelerated quickly toward the mayhem on 2nd Street.

———

Concho beat the ambulance to the scene and pulled up on the shoulder behind Isaac Parkland's overturned SUV.

"Damn!" Della Rice murmured.

Concho didn't respond. He exited the truck and strode past the wreck to Roland Turner's cruiser. Parkland sat in the driver's side seat, with the door open and his feet flat on the highway. The man looked completely drained and was spackled with blood. All of it his.

Parkland lifted his right hand a few inches as he saw Ten-Wolves, then let it drop. "Sorry," he said.

"You gave your blood. Can't give more than that."

Parkland shook his head. "Keegan gave more."

The Ranger huffed a sigh. "Yeah. I think he'd have been a great officer."

"I think so, too. You know, I haven't lost a deputy to anything other than retirement in ten years. And in just a few days I've lost one forever and have another laid up in the hospital."

"My turn to say I'm sorry."

Parkland frowned. "For what?"

"I brought the problem to you that started it all."

"Hazards of our job," Parkland said. "No one's fault but the criminals."

The sound of sirens came from back toward Eagle Pass and Concho turned to see the ambulance arriving. An Eagle Pass police car followed it, and a brood of blue lights were turning into the apartment complex where the search would continue for Heather Green. He wanted to be there but needed to make sure Parkland was OK first, and find out what the Sheriff knew.

Two paramedics bailed out of their vehicle and rushed toward Parkland and Concho. Ten-Wolves stepped aside and gestured toward the other man. One quickly bent to work, cleaning the law officer's wounds while the other went to inspect the overturned vehicle.

"Be careful," Parkland called to the latter. "There's a dead officer in there."

The man hesitated, but then dropped down on all fours to peer through the broken-out window on the wreck. In the next instant he bounced back to his feet, gagging and turning away.

The paramedic working on Isaac Parkland plucked a piece of glass out of the man's nose with tweezers. The Sheriff winced.

"You're going to need that shoulder popped back into its socket," the paramedic said. "And stitches in the left arm wound."

"Then do it," Parkland said.

"We'll get you to the hospital and—"

"Just do it here," Parkland snapped.

The paramedic stopped working and gave him a glare. "Texas isn't the wild west anymore, Sheriff. I don't have any leather for you to bite down on while I sew you up, or whiskey to sterilize your bullet hole."

Parkland sighed. "Sorry. But you can still do it here. And if you'd seen what happened a few minutes ago you wouldn't be so quick to claim that Texas isn't the wild west anymore."

"What *did* happen?" Concho asked.

"Fellow on a motorcycle," Parkland explained. "He pulled up beside us. Fired a shotgun through the driver's side window. Keegan got hit. He fell across me as I tried to grab for the wheel. Kind of jumbled after that. The SUV flipped. The man came back to finish the job. The girl ran. He shot at her while I was shooting at him. Then Turner came riding to the rescue."

"Anything you can tell me about the shooter?"

Parkland shook his head. "Not much. He wore a helmet with a face shield. Long white hair hanging out from under it. Had on a leather jacket. I tell you, he was one cool customer. He walked straight at me. Like he didn't have any fear."

"Meth head?" Ten-Wolves asked.

"Not on your life. A pro."

The paramedic injected Parkland's upper arm with a local anesthetic and started stitching his bicep wound where a bullet had gouged away flesh. The Sheriff gritted his teeth but managed to provide a little more information.

"The bike was one of those cruiser types. Not a sport bike. It was like purple, or black, or both."

"Lot of bikes like that around."

"Tell me about it." The Sheriff paused, then added. "Another thing."

"What?"

"I hit him with one shot. A .38 Special. Straight to the chest."

"And?"

"He shrugged it off."

"Special is a hot load. He must have been wearing a vest."

"I guess. But his jacket was open. He wore a blue T-shirt with something written on it I couldn't read. The vest would have had to have been under that."

"Not the usual way of wearing one but I don't see any other explanation."

Parkland's voice seemed noncommittal as he said, "No, I reckon not."

"I'm going to snap your shoulder back into its socket," the paramedic said. "It's gonna hurt. A lot."

"Do it!" Parkland said.

The paramedic "did it" before Parkland finished speaking. Concho winced at the cracking sound and the Sheriff gave a long, low groan as he closed his eyes to take the pain.

"I don't recommend that," Parkland said when he opened his eyes again.

"I'll try to remember," the Ranger replied. He gestured across the field toward the apartment complex where blue light blazed. "I'm going to head over there. If she's there, maybe she'll trust me enough to show herself."

"Right," Parkland said. "Be cautious."

"The time for that may be over!"

CHAPTER TWENTY-EIGHT

SNOW'S MOTEL HAD A SMALL COURTYARD. THOUGH HE WASN'T supposed to, he parked his Honda there where it wouldn't be easily seen from the street. The manager wasn't likely to say anything about it. She'd made her interest in Snow apparent from the moment he'd checked in. He'd given her a smile and a little hope for just such reasons.

The assassin's room lay on the ground floor, at the far end of a row of rooms whose backs faced an open field. Carrying his shotgun and saddlebags, which were loaded with other weapons and supplies, he strode down a concrete walk between the rooms and a laundry area. With it being just after mid-afternoon, no one was around.

Entering his room, Snow tossed his equipment on the bed and stripped off his jacket. The T-shirt underneath had a hole in the chest, almost right over the sternum. He shook his head. This was his favorite tee. That Sheriff owed him for this.

He pulled the shirt over his head and dropped it on the bed, then stepped into the bathroom to examine himself in the mirror. Covering his chest from neck to waist, and then tucked into his jeans, he wore what looked like a densely interwoven spider web. It glistened even in the dim daylight that filtered through the curtained window.

He ran his fingers over the front of it, where the slug had struck. The material felt cool to the touch, despite lying right against his warm skin. And there was no marring to indicate where the actual bullet hit. He could feel some bruising beginning at the point of impact but not nearly as much as with Kevlar. This was the best bullet proof vest money couldn't yet buy. Compliments of his employer.

Taking off the vest and the rest of his clothes, he showered, then checked, cleaned and reloaded the guns he'd used, the shotgun and the 10mm semi-automatic. A quick message to his handler updated the situation and he got an almost immediate response about target 2.

T2 will be freed soon.

Good. If he'd gotten lucky with the girl, this could all be over soon. He slipped on fresh jeans and pulled on his vest, dragging a new T-shirt over the top of it. This one was gray and had an image of Cthulhu on the front with letters below it reading: *Property of Miskatonic University.*

Checking himself in the mirror, he murmured a little poetry to the world. "A saber smile. A memory of ancient knights. Who guards the abyss when the devil dwells on earth?"

He grabbed his saddlebags and headed for his bike. Back to work.

———

THE SUNRISE APARTMENT Complex stood in an area of Eagle Pass unused to criminal investigations. Numerous folks dotted the balconies of their apartments as they watched the blue lights and the parade of police officers in their parking lot below. Concho drove in with Della Rice still riding shotgun. He saw Roland Turner at the center of the uniformed chaos and pulled up beside him.

Turner glanced at Concho and shook his head. "No sign of her," he said. "I've got people going door to door but I'm not confident of getting anything. I think she kept running after she reached here. No way to know where, though. I took a quick turn around the building but there are a bunch of streets, apartments, and neighborhoods back of here."

"Guess she's afraid the police can't protect her," Della Rice of the FBI said from her side of the truck.

"Sheriff Parkland did his best," Turner snapped back hotly. "And a deputy gave his life protecting her."

"I didn't mean." Rice started, then stopped and merely shook her head.

Concho pushed open his door and stepped out. "I'm gonna make a try," he said. "Not that I'm likely to have any more luck."

Turner nodded. "No harm."

Concho reached back into the Ford and flipped a switch on his dash. His police radio had a built-in megaphone. He pulled up the mic and spoke into it. His amplified voice echoed across the landscape.

"Heather! If you can hear me, it's Concho Ten-Wolves. You know I'll do my best to protect you. Come out to the front parking lot. I'm right here and I'll take you to safety myself. I guarantee it."

No response. He repeated his appeal, and added, "If you're here, I need your help to find out who took Winona and hurt your friends. Please!"

The parking lot had mostly fallen quiet, with police officers pausing in their movements and all the onlookers observing the affair as if attending a funeral. And still no response came from Heather. Only a deafening silence.

———

AFTER HALF AN HOUR more of fruitless searching, a dejected Concho climbed back into his truck. Heather Green must have kept running past the Sunshine Apartments. She was free but alone in Eagle Pass, a small town, a small hunting ground for the motorcycle shooter. She had no one she felt she could trust. Her friends were murdered and her daughter missing. He couldn't imagine how hard she must be grieving, and how much fear must be twisting her guts.

And then there was Kerry Keegan, dead and gone. Barely into his twenties. Ten-Wolves had only just met the man but liked him. He wondered if he had a family. Probably. Most cops did. Which meant more grieving, a world too full of it right now.

Realizing that Della Rice was staring at him, he asked, "What?"

"I can read everything you're feeling on your face," she answered. "You keep hurting yourself this way and you'll never last in this business."

"I hate this business."

"No, you don't. Or you wouldn't still be in it. Someone has to do what we do. But you don't have to crucify yourself every time someone else's choices put them in danger or get them hurt."

"If I knew how to do it differently, I would."

"You better learn." She puffed out a breath of air and opened the passenger side door. "I'll head back to the office with Bihn. See what resources I can bring to bear on *our* problem."

"Thanks."

She didn't answer but slipped out of the Ford. Concho's cell phone pinged, signaling a message. He swiped it on, hoping it might be Heather texting him. It wasn't. The text came from Earl Blake, the county coroner.

"I've got info on your case if you stop by. Be aware, I've got a new secretary. She bites."

CHAPTER TWENTY-NINE

It was almost 3:00 in the afternoon when Concho arrived at the Maverick County Coroner's Office, which was staffed primarily by Doctor Earl Blake, and apparently by a new secretary with teeth. Concho entered the one story, L-shaped building at 1995 Williams Street in Eagle Pass rather cautiously.

A woman he did not recognize sat behind the front desk. She looked to be in her fifties, with gray hair piled on top of her head in an old-fashioned puff-ball bun. In contrast to the hair, she wore a smart-looking woman's businesses suit in blue pinstripes. She looked up at him instantly as he entered, focusing on him intently with the kind of gray eyes the novelists call "steely" and "icy." He felt reminded of the way a cobra stares at a mouse it's about to eat.

"Ma'am," he said, almost wishing he'd worn his hat so he could doff it.

"How can I help you?"

"I'm here to see Doctor Blake."

"Name?"

"Concho Ten-Wolves."

"Have a seat."

"Doctor Blake is expecting me. He sent me a text to come over."

"Have a seat."

"Maybe if you—"

"Is it your intention, Sir, to waste the rest of my day trying to subvert protocol? I'm afraid I cannot tolerate that."

Concho opened his mouth, closed it. He found a chair and squeezed into it, though it made a tight fit for his six four frame.

The gray-haired woman pressed a button on the intercom on her desk and spoke through it. "Dr. Blake, a man named Concho Ten-Wolves is here to see you. Is this a good time?"

Blake's voice came quickly back. "Send him in."

Now, the woman smiled at the Ranger. "You can go on back. Do you know where Dr. Blake's office is?"

"Yes, Ma'am."

She gestured. "Then please."

Concho stepped past the woman down the single hallway leading into the interior of the building. He turned right at the first door and peeked in. Earl Blake sat behind a computer screen, tapping slowly on the keys. Blake was in his late fifties, a heavy-set man, though of late he seemed to have gone on a diet and lost some weight. He was mostly bald. He gestured for Ten-Wolves to enter.

"Close the door," Blake said.

The lawman did so, then sat in the extra-large chair across from the coroner.

"What did you think of Ms. Linseed?" Blake asked.

"I think she scares me."

Blake chuckled. "Good, she's supposed to."

"What's the deal?"

Blake stopped typing and pushed back in his chair. "Remember a few weeks ago when I got tazered in the lab and some evidence was stolen?"

"I was just testifying in that case a couple of days ago. How did that lead to Ms. Linseed?"

"The State decided I needed some protection here."

Concho so wanted to arch an eyebrow but did not possess the physiology for it. "She's your...bodyguard?"

"Ex-military. And armed to the teeth."

Ten-Wolves nodded. "All right, good to know. Guess I won't have to worry about your health anymore." He grinned. "Unless you piss off Ms. Linseed that is."

Blake gave a mock shudder. "If you find me dead at my desk one day you'll know who to investigate."

"So, what kind of information do you have for me on my current case?"

Blake grunted. He shifted some papers around on his desk until he came up with a notepad full of handwritten scrawls. "I'm still typing up my report but thought you might appreciate a preview."

"I would."

"Diego Guzman Cabello," Blake read off his notes. "Hispanic male. Thirty years old. Death by gunshot. One .45 slug to the chest."

"Yes. Drug dealer and kidnapper. And I shot him. What about him don't I know?"

"He had a little coke in his system."

"Not surprising."

"Also, we can say he's a rapist."

"Heather Green?"

Blake frowned. "Who?"

Concho shook his head. "Sorry, when I spoke to you on the phone before I called her Jane Doe. We've learned her real name now. Heather."

"Aww, then yes. I managed to finagle the rape kit on Jane... Heather, from the hospital. She'd had intercourse with three men in the past few days. Diego was one. And one of the memory loss drugs you wondered about was in her system. She'd been given several very high doses of Rohypnol. Enough to incapacitate her for a while. And it was present at the same time as the sex, meaning it would be rape by definition."

"I'd gotten a report about the Rohypnol. But not about when it was in her system. What about the other two men?"

"One remains unidentified, but the hospital also took a blood sample on..." Blake consulted his notes, "one Martino Salas. I ran his DNA. He's the second man."

Concho took a deep breath. "I'd kind of expected it but knowing for sure will be useful. Interrogating Salas is next on my list of things to do today."

"There's more."

"What?"

"About a month ago, a young woman's body was brought in. African American. Somebody tried to sink her in a pond but she floated to the shore and was found pretty quickly." Blake gave a long sigh and shook his head. "She'd also been raped. Much more brutally."

A frisson tightened Concho's scalp. "Don't tell me..."

"Cabello and Salas's DNA was present."

"Not the third man?"

"Not this time."

The law officer sagged in his chair. "So, they've done it before?"

"Looks like it."

"And probably more than twice."

"Probably. I'm going to examine more kits as I get a chance."

"Not a pleasant chore," Concho commiserated.

"But one that needs doing."

Both men sat quietly for a moment. Blake sighed. Concho made a conscious effort to short circuit the despair that clawed at him when he considered how inhumane humans could be to each other. That wouldn't help him help Heather Green now.

"What made you look into it?" he asked. "Some kind of hunch?"

Blake shrugged. "It's a puzzle. Just...one with some very unpleasant associations."

"Maybe you have a knack for detective work."

"Maybe I read a lot of mysteries. Been thinking of writing one myself."

"Oh?"

"Yeah." Blake lifted his hands and spread them apart as if seeing his name up in lights. "Coroner solves crimes and becomes famous," he said. "Probably a movie in it. Or a popular TV series."

"I think they had that. The TV series."

"Oh yeah?"

"Yeah, they called it *Quincy*."

"Never heard of her."

CHAPTER THIRTY

After leaving Earl Blake's office, Concho took a spin through the McDonald's drive-thru and picked up a twenty-piece chicken nugget box. He hadn't eaten since breakfast and it was almost 5:00 o'clock now. His stomach was ticked off and mad about it. He inhaled the nuggets, and as he pulled into the parking lot of the Eagle Pass Correctional Facility at 742 Texas Highway 131, his fingers explored around in the box hoping for one more nug. They found only disappointment.

The Eagle Pass jail was operated by the Maverick County Sheriff's office but also housed inmates from some other local communities, as well as for the Eagle Pass police department. It held mostly prisoners awaiting arraignment, trial, or sentencing.

Concho found a space in the crowded parking lot and proceeded inside. A small foyer greeted him. The smell of cleaning agents couldn't hide an underlying sour smell of sweat and grime. To the right, blocking off the end of the foyer, stood a long check-in desk. Only one guard stood behind the desk, protected by a shield of bullet-proof glass. The fellow stared steadily at his phone as the Ranger approached and only looked up when he cleared his throat.

"Yes," the man said. He sounded irritated until he noticed

who awaited on the other side of the glass. Then he became all smiles. "Ranger Ten-Wolves! I just read a piece on you in the paper. What can I do to help you?"

The perks and perils of celebrity, Concho thought. He wasn't sure whether to appreciate it or hate it. To the guard, he said, "I believe Sheriff Parkland sent through permission for me to interrogate one of your inmates. Martino Salas."

The guard's smile faded into a frown. "Did you say Salas?"

"Yes. Martino. Is there a problem?"

"Well, you...I mean, Martino Salas was released about an hour ago."

"Released? How could he be released? He hasn't even had a bond hearing yet!"

"We got orders. I...well, a bail order came through for him. And then his lawyer came and bailed him out."

"Orders? Signed by a judge?"

"Yes, Sir!"

"What judge?"

"Uhm, it was..." The man tapped at the keyboard of the computer in front of him. "It was Janet Peregrino."

Concho frowned. He knew Janet Peregrino. Sort of. She was the judge he'd just testified before in the Tallulah Whiteheart case.

"And you verified this with the judge's office?"

"Of course, Sir. Anytime something irregular like this happens, we check it out."

"And?"

"The judge's office confirmed it."

Concho shook his head. What in the world was going on? "What about the lawyer who bailed him out?"

The guard tapped at his keyboard again. "Manny Freed."

Concho had heard of Freed. Most of it not good. He turned and walked out.

———

Pa Modine's oldest son, Derrick, finally arrived home. Pa was glad to see him, and so were his younger brothers, Taylor and Justin. Derrick had a kid, though he wasn't living with the boy or the mother at present. Still, he knew more about taking care of babies than Taylor or Justin did, and Pa took pity on them and let them off child duty after Derrick agreed to babysit for a while.

Taylor and Justin fled the house for the front yard, where they stood talking and smoking and drinking beer. Justin cursed angrily where his father wasn't around to hear him. "I'm getting tired of this," he said.

"Tired of what?"

"Of the way Pa treats us. He runs us like we're jigs."

"Well," Taylor said. "Seems like he did have some reasons for wanting the kid left alone."

"Then he shoulda told us! That's all it woulda took."

Taylor nodded and took another swig of beer. "It's like he don't trust us."

"Exactly," Justin seconded.

"Nothing we can do about it, I guess."

Justin's eyes glittered as he dropped his cigarette butt and toed it out in the dirt. "Maybe there is."

Taylor shook his head. "Don't even think about it. Look how much trouble we got in for last time."

Justin smirked. "If you ain't got the cojones, that's fine. I'll do it myself."

Taylor flicked away his own cigarette. He sighed. "What?"

Concho googled "Manny Freed" and got a quick address on the lawyer's office. 314 Cooper Street. It was almost 5:00 PM so Ten-Wolves ran his pickup hard to get there before closing time.

He got lucky. A man stood locking the front door of the building as he arrived. The shiny dress shoes, dark blue suit, and powder blue tie suggested a lawyer. And when the fellow turned toward him, Concho recognized him from the advertising billboards he'd seen standing tall around Eagle Pass.

Freed's office was in a small, square building sandwiched between a hardware store and a bank. There were four parking spaces, one of which held a new looking white Lexus ES. Given that the ES series started at about forty thousand dollars, business must be descent. Concho parked and stepped out of his truck. Freed watched him approach.

"Mister Freed," the Ranger said.

Freed offered a broad and practiced smile in return, but his brown eyes glittered with caution and speculation. As a criminal defense lawyer, he probably didn't experience a lot of friendly encounters with law officers, and it was clear he recognized Concho and probably knew his reputation.

"Ranger Ten-Wolves," Freed said. He held out his hand for a shake. "I'm glad to get a chance to meet you. I've heard a lot of complimentary things about your work."

Concho took the proffered hand. Not quite time yet to become adversarial.

"What can I do for you?" Freed asked.

"A few minutes of your time. For a talk."

"Concerning?"

"It might be better inside."

Freed considered. His smile flickered off, and back on. "Of course," he said. He turned and unlocked the door he'd just bolted, then stepped inside and held it open. Concho followed into a short hallway with a bathroom at the end. An office stood on either side, each with its door closed. The brown carpet on the floor had seen better days and the walls could use a fresh coat of the pale yellow paint they'd been coated with.

Maybe Freed's business was not quite as good as the Lexus made it seem, Concho thought.

"This way," Freed said, unlocking the door on the left and passing through. As he flipped on the lights inside he said, "I'm afraid my secretary is already gone so it'll just be us. I could get you a soda if you'd like. Or a spring water?"

"No thanks."

Freed nodded and walked around behind a large, polished desk and seated himself. He motioned to a chair across from him, one big and sturdy enough to suit Ten-Wolves. The Ranger stood for a moment longer, examining the office without appearing to do so. The blinds were drawn; the usual law books were in evidence. Nothing personal anywhere on the desk or the walls. No art. Not even the smells possessed any character. They were antiseptic and bland.

Freed himself was of medium height and slender, with brown hair cut stylishly. He was neither handsome nor ugly. If he could be described as anything, it would be "bland," like his office decor. But Concho felt pretty sure both were disguises for whatever lived inside the man. Maybe just an opportunist. Maybe a predator. Ten-Wolves sat down, and waited.

Freed waited, too. Seconds ticked by. The lawyer's fingers began to tap on the desk. Finally, he spoke. "What did you want to see me about?"

"So, Manny Freed is a sort of stage name right?"

"Excuse me?"

"Many... Freed. With an extra 'n.' Great moniker for a lawyer but surely that's not your real name."

A quick tic of irritation twisted Freed's face, then dissipated like frost in a desert dawn. He leaned back in his chair and laughed. "Good, good," he said. "Took me a second to catch on."

"Oh?"

"Throw 'em off balance with a non-sequitur. Then go in for the kill. Standard courtroom technique. You were a little obvious but with some practice you could handle a cross-examination just fine. Sure you're not a lawyer yourself?"

Concho smiled faintly. Time now to be adversarial. "No, I like to be able to look at myself in a mirror."

Freed's casual face disappeared. "You seem to want to make this personal, Ranger. I'm wondering why?"

"Because it is personal. A little over an hour ago, you got Martino Salas released from jail. And Salas is a big flight risk because he's a kidnapper and rapist."

"I believe you mean *alleged* kidnapper and rapist."

"Nope. This isn't court so I'll speak plainly rather than obfuscate."

Freed picked up a slim black pen lying on his desk and began tapping it against his free hand. "Unless the state of Texas is lying to me, my client stands accused of kidnapping and possession of cocaine with intent to deliver. Not rape."

"The rape charges are recent," Concho conceded, "but substantial."

Freed shrugged. "I'll have to see the evidence for myself. Personally, I think you're bluffing."

"Let's hope you get to find out in court."

"Mister Salas will be there when it's time."

"I doubt it."

Freed rose from his chair. "I believe we're done here."

Concho stood up, too. He towered over Freed, who was maybe five nine in his shoes. "Not just yet. In order to protect an innocent's life, I need to know who hired you to bail out Salas."

"Mister Salas himself hired me."

"That's a lie."

Freed's lips tightened into a thin line. He started toward the door to his office and Concho stepped in his way. "This is getting pretty close to assault," Freed snapped.

"Not even. You'll know when I cross that line."

"I know your reputation for brutality, Officer Ten-Wolves. But I'm not a helpless poor person you've accused of some crime. I can and will sue you."

"Because of Martino Salas, a four-month-old child is in danger. I'm not going to let that go. I'm pretty sure Judge Janet Peregrino is involved somehow. I'm thinking she's the one who contacted you about Salas. But I don't know if she understood who Salas was or if she were just doing a favor for someone else without questioning it. I also don't know who put up the money behind it all. That's where the primary blame lies."

Freed didn't bat an eye when Concho mentioned Peregrino, but that didn't clear the man.

"Slandering a judge," Freed said. "I'm used to it myself but I suspect Peregrino wouldn't be so quick to forgive. Isn't she presiding over one of your cases right now?"

Concho let his shark smile show through. "I plan to tell her myself as soon as I get a chance."

"Good luck with that."

Freed started around Concho again and this time he let the man go. He walked out behind the lawyer, and through the outside door the man did *not* hold open for him.

"Call your client," Concho said. "For his own good. Tell him he'd better spill."

Freed said nothing. The Ranger stepped over to his Ford. In another moment, he wheeled onto the road and sped away. He hadn't expected to learn much from the encounter with Freed, and hadn't, other than the lawyer made a skilled and unscrupulous opponent who should not be underestimated.

But, Freed would likely contact whoever had retained him in the Salas case and the trees would have been shaken. He'd see what fell out.

CHAPTER THIRTY-ONE

MARTINO SALAS WAS SCARED. A LAWYER WHO HE DIDN'T HIRE AND had never seen had bailed him out of jail, even though he'd not even had a hearing yet. With Diego Cabello dead, Martino had no friends or contacts close enough to put up the money for him. And neither his mother nor his sister even knew he was in jail. They wouldn't have any money to spare for bail anyway.

So, who'd gotten him out of jail? And why? The only good reason he could think of was to shut him up, to make sure he didn't spill any sensitive information about the kidnapping case he'd been arrested for. He understood what "shut him up," meant.

Kill him.

He wanted to run but the only way to disappear off the grid was to have plenty of cash. He could access some of that kind of money, but it was hidden and to get it would be risky. He could also use a gun but the only gun he knew of was secreted with the cash. He had to figure out how to get to both without dying.

He found a place to hide in a culvert and pulled the cheap cell phone the lawyer had left for him at the jail out of his pocket. A single number was preprogrammed into the device, under the name Manny Freed. But he didn't call it yet. He wasn't sure he could trust the lawyer. He wasn't sure he could trust anyone.

Well, maybe his mother and sister. He punched in his home number. The phone rang and rang. He frowned, and the frown turned to concern, and to terror. His mother was always home. She was old school and answered every call she got. She still had a landline for goodness' sake.

The phone kept ringing. Twelve times. Fifteen. He hung up. What had happened to his mother and sister? Maybe they'd gone to the store. Maybe the little kid had gotten sick and they'd taken it to the doctor.

None of those things sounded right to him. It felt like they were in trouble. And if they were, he was. And his troubles were worse. But he couldn't do anything about it without money and a gun.

He climbed out of the culvert and began to jog toward Diego Cabello's apartment, where he'd find everything he needed.

———

WHILE STILL STANDING in the parking space in front of his office, Manny Freed made a phone call. A voice picked up he didn't know. He reported the incident with Concho Ten-Wolves. He got instructions, hung up, and immediately made another call. As he was ordered to do. He didn't like it and wished he'd never taken the money for bailing Martino Salas out of jail. He'd needed it, though, and there was no going back.

Climbing in his Lexus, he pulled out on the highway and headed toward his next meeting. It was early so he took the long way, partly to pass time, and partly to see if he was being followed. The big Texas Ranger had driven off in the opposite direction but Manny was a suspicious man by nature and wanted to make sure he hadn't picked up a tail.

Convinced after twenty minutes that he was safe, he sped up and turned his ES coupe toward the Kickapoo reservation and the Lucky Eagle Casino which stood on the Rez. He parked among a crowd of other cars and went inside. At 6:00 in the evening, the place roared.

Breaking a fifty-dollar bill for change, he joined the addicted gamblers, the bored wives, the philandering husbands, and the sensation seekers at the slot machines. He played along a row of quarter slots with images of diamonds and gold bars and wheels of fortune on them. Mostly he lost, but at one machine he got lucky.

While he counted the thirty-dollar jackpot he'd just won, a man sat down at the machine on his left. Manny's groin tightened and contracted. He stopped counting as his mouth went dry. This was it, the contact he was supposed to meet. He couldn't help but glance over and quickly glance away. The man had long, white-blond hair, which he wore in a ponytail. His upper body appeared lean yet muscled beneath the leather motorcycle jacket he wore.

"Could I borrow your cell phone?" the man asked quietly. "I'm afraid mine has a dead battery and it's kind of an emergency."

The voice, though soft, contained a hint of razor in its tones. Freed licked his lips. He glanced around, and knew he was behaving suspiciously. He fought to control his impulse to either pee or run, or both.

"Sure," he said, pleased his voice sounded pretty much normal.

Fishing his phone out of the inside pocket of his dress jacket, he passed it over to the man, who'd turned toward him. The fellow's bluish gray eyes looked sleepy, except for a faint glitter in their depths. Manny's urge to pee intensified.

The fellow smiled and said "Thank you." He swiped for the phone's keypad and pressed a few numbers, then held the cell to his ear. Only a few seconds went by before the man swiped the phone back to its home screen and passed it back to Manny.

"Much appreciated," he said, as he rose and moved away.

Manny took a few quick breaths and tried to relax. He quickly scooped the rest of his small jackpot into the plastic bucket he'd been supplied by the casino and headed for the bathroom.

He still needed to urinate.

———

AS SNOW LEFT THE CASINO, a young woman in a tight, red cotton dress smiled at him. He smiled back but did nothing else about the clear invitation for a connection. Not when he was working.

As he stepped outside under the darkening sky to walk toward his bike, he pulled out his own cell phone and called up a special app provided to him by his employer. He tapped in the information he'd gotten from the lawyer's phone and activated the app. While it did its thing, he unlocked his helmet from his bike.

"Got a light?" the woman in the red dress asked.

Snow smiled. He'd heard her approaching and now he turned. He slid a hand into his jeans and pulled out the lighter he always carried, though he didn't smoke himself. Stepping toward the woman, he flicked the lighter on and held it to the cigarette that dangled from the woman's lipsticked mouth.

"Filthy habit," he said, though he kept his voice soft and easy.

The woman stared at him challengingly, then pulled the freshly lit cigarette from between her lips and exhaled a puff of smoke. Her breath smelled of liquor. "I've got lots of filthy habits," she said. "Bet you do, too."

"Only those who wallow in rot can ever truly be cleansed."

The woman blinked her hazel eyes. "Is that like...Shakespeare?"

Snow shook his head. "No, much more contemporary."

The woman nodded. She started to take another puff but thought better of it. She just stood hip-shot, with the cigarette hanging between two fingers of her right hand. "I'm...I'm not a pro," she said, blushing. "I just saw you and thought you looked interesting."

"No. You thought I looked dangerous. And it made your panties wet."

The woman recoiled. She had started to sober up from the fresh air, and the surge of adrenaline that coursed through her at Snow's words helped the process along. She looked around. A few people moved to-and-fro across the parking lot but none were close enough to save her if he decided to attack her.

"I...guess I made a mistake."

The gentleness left Snow's voice as he said, "You did. And if I wasn't busy already I'd show you just how bad of a mistake."

The woman bit at her upper lip. She dropped the cigarette and walked swiftly away, her heels clicking on the asphalt.

Snow watched her go. The cigarette she'd dropped smoldered in the parking lot. He reached down and picked it up, staring at the smear of crimson lipstick across the brown filter. He brought the cylinder to his lips, not to puff but to taste the smear. It tasted red, like blood.

CHAPTER THIRTY-TWO

Almost 6:00 PM now and Judge Janet Peregrino would be long gone from work. Her home address and phone number were unlisted but, as a Texas Ranger, Concho had access to information sources a regular citizen did not. He found both the address and phone number. The address was 111 Rio Grande Drive, in a very exclusive Eagle Pass neighborhood. He drove over.

Peregrino lived in a gated community. Concho pulled up to the gate guard, who sat in what had to be described as a small, brick, sentry post. The fellow manning the post wore a uniform and looked young and healthy and competent.

"I'm here to see Judge Peregrino," Concho said.

"Is she expecting you?"

"Afraid not, but I still need to see her."

"Your name?"

"Concho Ten-Wolves. Texas Ranger."

The guard didn't blink. He pressed a button on the console in front of him, which Concho couldn't see very much of, then spoke through an intercom system. "Judge, I'm sorry to disturb you but a man named Concho Ten-Wolves is here wishing to see you."

"Ten-Wolves?" the woman's voice at the other end of the intercom said. "I can't speak to him. He's a witness in a trial I'm sitting on right now."

"She says—" the sentry started to say.

"I heard," Concho interrupted. He leaned his head out the window of his pickup toward the guard. "Hold that button down and I'll talk loudly enough for her to hear."

The guard hesitated, then pushed something. "Go ahead."

"Judge Peregrino. This is Ten-Wolves. What I need to talk to you about is not related to the Whiteheart case. It's about an active investigation involving Martino Salas."

No response at first. Then, "I didn't think you had anything to do with Salas."

"Salas and Diego Cabello and Manny Freed. And a dead officer named Kerry Keegan, as well as a wounded officer currently in the hospital."

Again, a pause. Longer this time. "Send him in," Peregrino said. The intercom went silent.

The guard shrugged and pressed a different button. The steel bar across the driveway began to lift. As soon as it was out of the way, Concho pulled through.

Rio Grande Drive was the highest point in Eagle Pass, which wasn't very high. It was little more than a ridge running generally east and west along the curve of the Rio Grande River. A single row of large, expensive homes sat along the ridge, with big yards separating one house from the other.

Parts of the river itself could be seen between the houses. It was fairly wide here, and deep enough so it couldn't just be waded across. The water looked dark as blued steel in the gathering evening but would be a muddy yellow brown in brighter light. You'd be able to smell the wet muck and reeds if the wind blew right.

Off to the east stretched the span of the Eagle Pass International Bridge. A golf course lay between the bridge and the ridge, its greens still faintly gleaming in the late light. A few players tooled along its trails in carts or stood on the greens making their final putts of the day.

As Concho passed along the street, he saw two men in black suits standing beside a black Chevy Tahoe SUV with no markings on the sides. Both men were armed, with shoulder holsters bulging under their suit jackets. Private security. And watching him.

He ignored them as he pulled into the driveway of 111 Rio Grande Drive. He didn't know much about architecture. The house was big. Two stories. Though of what style, he couldn't say. The walls were painted to look like adobe though he was quite sure it wasn't. The roof was of Spanish tile, more orange than red.

A small, neatly trimmed hedge grew along the front and two jacaranda trees framed the small front porch and double doors. The jacaranda were in bloom. Concho stepped out of his truck to glance up at the brilliant purple blossoms on the trees, which hung overhead like puffs of cloud. The scent overwhelmed.

A red brick walkway, scattered with purple petals, led him to the front door. He rang the bell and it opened immediately. Janet Peregrino herself stood just inside. She wasn't smiling, but—come to think of it—he'd never seen her smile. Judges weren't usually touted for their friendly demeanor.

The woman, in her mid-forties, was neither tall, nor short. She wore a long blue cotton dress reaching her ankles. Her auburn hair hung down around her shoulders instead of being knotted on top of her head as per her usual in court. She reminded him a little of Captain Kathryn Janeway from the TV series *Star Trek Voyager*.

"You shouldn't be here," she said.

"I wouldn't be if it wasn't necessary."

Janet shook her head slightly but held the door open wider and gestured him in. He stepped past her into a long hallway and waited. After closing and locking the door, she led him along the hall. Rooms opened on either side but he had no time to examine them. Peregrino walked fast.

They reached a large study. Two walls stood full of bookshelves. The shelves were stuffed. And not just with law books. He caught a few titles shining in gilt on the leather spines of collectible hardbacks. *The Three Musketeers* and *The Count of Monte Cristo* by Alexander Dumas, *Treasure Island* by Robert Louis Stevenson, *The Adventures of Tom Sawyer* by Mark Twain, *Old Yeller* by Fred Gipson. The collection was well maintained; he could smell the leather polish used on them.

A third wall boasted a fireplace, cold now and maybe never used. He couldn't smell any smokey residue permeating the atmosphere of the room. The fourth wall was mostly windows that provided a view out into a big fenced in backyard. The tall wooden fence looked new and probably was. What might have once been a tranquil view of the flowing river was more likely now to feature Nicaraguan and Guatemalan migrants swimming across the Grande with their few belongs held over their heads.

"What's this all about?" Peregrino asked, distracting Concho from his thoughts.

"You signed a bail order for Martino Salas."

"Yes. A few hours ago."

"Why?"

Peregrino bristled. "Because I decided to on the merits of the case."

"The case hadn't even been called for a bail hearing yet."

"I know my job, Ranger Ten-Wolves. You don't need to tell it to me."

"Did you know Salas is a suspect in at least two rapes, a kidnapping, and a murder?"

Thin lines appeared around the woman's eyes as she frowned. Her voice became gravelly in response. "There was no mention of murder or rape in the file."

"It's a recent discovery. Salas's semen was found inside the body of the woman he helped kidnap. She was drugged at the time, making it a rape. It was also found in a murdered rape victim from several weeks ago."

"This is news to me. Why is it just coming to light? I should have been given complete information on the investigation."

"Don't tell me my job, Judge Peregrino. We're still discovering the evidence."

For a moment, the woman seemed taken aback. Then a tiny ghost of a smile crossed her lips. That quickly faded into a look of irritation. "What I was given," the woman said, "was a record completely clean of any criminal behavior. Not even a traffic ticket. And I was informed that Martino Sala's mother and sister were murdered earlier in the day and no other relative was available to take care of their arrangements."

It was Concho's turn to frown. "Not many people knew about those murders," he said. "And no one who would have gone looking for a judge to sign a release based on the man's personal hardship."

"Obviously, you're mistaken. It was in the file."

"Who gave you that file?"

"I'm not going to tell you."

"It was favor for a friend then?"

"You're free to think what you want. I assure you I'll check with that individual concerning what was in the file."

"And what got left out?"

"That, too."

"How did Manny Freed get involved?"

"I didn't realize he was. How *is* he involved?"

"He paid the bail. I figured you'd put him onto it."

"I didn't."

"I don't suppose you'll tell me who you gave the bail order to."

"Not at present."

"Whoever it was, they must have contacted Freed."

"Have you talked to him?"

"I have. He was less forthcoming than you've been."

"You mentioned two officers who'd been hurt. Tell me about them."

"Kerry Keegan, one of Isaac Parkland's deputies, was killed by an unknown assailant while driving Salas's kidnap victim to the Sheriff's office."

Peregrino winced, and it didn't look practiced.

"Another of Parkland's deputies, Terrill Hoight, is in the hospital. He was shot by someone trying to kill the same woman."

"You don't suspect Salas in either of these shootings do you?"

"No. He was still in jail when Keegan got killed. And hand-cuffed by me just before Hoight got shot. I do suspect, however, that whoever is trying to kill the woman would be happy to kill Salas, too. And that might be the reason they finagled his release."

Janet Peregrino stiffened. Her gaze shifted quickly toward a writing desk in the corner where a cell phone lay. "That...," she started, and paused. "I think it's time for you to leave, Mister Ten-Wolves. You know the way."

Concho puffed out a breath. He started toward the front door, then paused and looked back. "I'm going to be honest with you, Judge. I came in here suspecting you'd been compromised. But now I think you've been duped. Whoever convinced you to sign that bail order is not your friend."

Janet Peregrino had gained complete control of herself again. "I asked you to leave. I won't repeat myself."

Concho nodded. He left her with a few final words, "I think you've got my number. If you need me, call. I'll answer."

CHAPTER THIRTY-THREE

As Ten-Wolves drove away from 111 Rio Grande Drive, he considered his meeting with Janet Peregrino. He'd gone in expecting her to have been complicit in some kind of plot to get Martino Salas out of jail and exposed to an assassin. He no longer believed that.

The judge had been used. And from the look on her face at the end of their conversation, she knew it and was going to call someone on it. He needed to know who that someone was, but he didn't have the authority to try and force it out of her. He'd have to hope she volunteered the information to him later.

Darkness had arrived. He flipped on his lights. The SUV with the two private security guards was no longer parked along the road but he gave it little thought. He pulled up to the exit gate from the community. The gate stayed down. A man came out of the sentry box carrying a wrench. It wasn't the same man who'd been there when he went in.

"The gate's malfunctioning," the man called to Concho. "Give me a sec and I'll have it open."

Concho's windows were down and a warm breeze trickled into the Ford. He could smell the Rio Grande and a closer scent of soil and freshly mown grass. The security guard leaned over the steel gate and tapped it with his two-foot-long pipe wrench. Nothing happened. And a pipe wrench didn't seem the right kind of tool for this task.

The Ranger's heart sped a few beats. He shifted into reverse. The black SUV from before—a Chevy Tahoe—pulled in behind him, blocking any retreat. So now he knew what was coming. He shifted back into park and did the unexpected, pushing his door open and stepping out onto the tarmac.

The guard with the wrench looked up, startled as Concho started toward him. The man's pupils dilated. He panicked and swung the wrench hard at the Ranger's head. Ten-Wolves was already too close. He blocked the man's arm in mid swing and punched him in the face. The man wilted and fell, his back striking the gate and the wrench clanging to the ground.

Concho spun, palming both .45s. The two private security guards had exited their vehicle but froze at the threat of the Colt semi-automatics. Neither one had drawn their own gun; those weapons remained holstered under their jackets, out of easy reach. But each had a weapon in hand, a pair of brass knuckles for the passenger, a lead-filled sap for the driver. The driver was at least six-two, the passenger shorter. Both wore crewcuts and looked like ex-military.

"What's it all about?" Concho demanded.

"We're supposed to teach you a lesson," the driver said.

"Looks like you're the ones who got schooled. Who hired you? Not Judge Peregrino. She wouldn't have had time to set this up."

The driver smirked. "You don't seriously expect us to tell you."

Concho smiled. He holstered his Colts and snapped the straps down to hold them in place. "I hope not. That would take away all the fun of beating it out of you."

———

NIGHT NOW. Martino Salas lay behind a long unused watering trough for cattle and gazed at the small ranch house ahead of him. A few dim lights burned in the downstairs but the rest of the house loomed dark.

The house still lay technically within the boundaries of Eagle Pass, although right on the line. A row of tract houses ran about a quarter of a mile behind him but nothing stood very close to this house. It had been a perfect hideaway for Diego, who'd lived in a small apartment over the garage.

The two older ladies who owned the house had needed money and let Diego live in the apartment for cash rent without asking any questions. Diego said they were dykes but Martino thought they were probably just spinsters or widows. Not that it mattered. They were too old to interest him in other ways.

Rising from behind the trough, Martino darted through the darkness to the bottom of the stairs leading up to Diego's place. He took the steps carefully. He'd been here enough times to know which ones creaked. The door was locked but he had the key. He'd spent quite a bit of time here with Diego, smoking and toking and sniffing and sipping.

Opening the door gently, he stepped inside. Diego always kept the curtains drawn and it was black as a crow inside. Martino shut the door, then fished the loaner cell phone out of his pocket. Pressing the button on the side produced a faint bluish glow, and by that light he found his way into the kitchen.

One particular kitchen drawer beckoned him. He pulled it back and took out a small stubby candle and a lighter. Soon, a faint yellow gleam of candleflame lit his immediate surroundings. He doubted any sign of it could be seen from outside through the thick, fake velvet curtains.

Turning to the refrigerator, he opened the freezer and began pulling out Hungry Man TV dinners, a couple of containers of Mrs. Paul's Fish Sticks, and a single package of hamburger meat. Beneath those, covered in frost, sat a box labeled Omaha Steaks. He dragged this out and sat it on the counter.

Pulling a kitchen knife out of a block holder on the counter, he slit the tape sealing the box closed and pulled back the lid. A plastic wrapped bundle of greenbacks lay inside, along with a small baggy of white, crystalline powder, and a larger baggy holding a two-inch barrel Smith & Wesson .38 revolver.

He picked up the baggy of cocaine and a flood of saliva burst ripe in his mouth. His hands shook, but he forced himself to put it down on the counter and reach for the gun. He'd have a toot of the coke before he left, but the weapon first. He began tearing at the plastic covering the pistol.

The small flame of the candle guttered. Martino started to turn and the barrel of another gun pressed into his right ear. He froze.

"Put it down," a soft voice said.

Martino obeyed, laying the Smith back on the counter and placing both hands where the gunman could see them. "Who... who are you?" he asked.

The man with the easy voice grasped the plastic wrapped pistol with a gloved hand and slid it along the counter out of reach. He chuckled. "You really want me to tell you?"

Martino thought better of his question. "No, no, just take the stuff. It's yours."

"I will. But first a few questions. If I get good answers I'll have no reason to kill you."

"OK."

"You are Martino Salas?"

"Ye...s."

"Now, Martino, the woman you and your partner kidnapped. What's her name?"

If Martino had imagined his captor was a cop, he'd have tried to bluff. But this man was no cop. His nature was clear. Martino spoke very carefully, in perfect English so couldn't be misunderstood. "Heather...It's Heather Green."

"You still have her ID?"

Martino started to shake his head and decided not to. "No, we...burned it. All her stuff."

"Does she have any family?"

Now, Martino paused. Heather Green had a baby but it was staying with his mother and sister, and he dared not send this man to them. "Not, not around here. I think her parents might be alive. But they're in California from what I understand." He added, "I didn't really know her well."

"Hum," the gunman said, and Martino's heart quailed.

"One last question, you have any idea where she might be?"

"I thought she was in jail. Protective custody at least."

"No, she isn't."

"I'm sorry then, but I'd have no idea where she would be."

"All right, Martino. Not so hard, was it?"

"You're going to let me go?"

"Why not."

Martino took a breath. His mouth felt like back-alley concrete, and tasted worse. He licked his lips. "Thank...s."

"I'll even give *you* a bit of information," the soft-voiced gunman added. "Fair exchange."

"What's...that?"

"The mother and sister you neglected to tell me about. The ones who are keeping Heather Green's baby. They're both dead."

Martino's spine and legs weakened. He moaned. Part of his pain came from the almost surprising spasm of grief that struck him over his mother's death. Most came from terror for himself. His mother always warned him the devil would get him for his actions. And now the devil was here. Who would have imagined he'd speak so gently?

"Please," Martino begged. He sank slowly to his knees, his hands still clinging to the edge of the counter. "Pleaseeee."

In that moment of Martino's greatest despair, Snow put a bullet in the back of his head.

CHAPTER THIRTY-FOUR

"THAT WOULD TAKE AWAY ALL THE FUN OF BEATING IT OUT OF you," Concho said to the two private security guards who faced him.

The biggest of the two, the driver of the SUV, grinned. Despite Concho's size, the man apparently felt confident with the lead filled sap in his hand. His partner, the SUV passenger with the brass knuckles, didn't look so happy. "Top," he said to the driver. "He's a Texas Ranger. Maybe we should think about—"

"Less thinking and more hitting, Bo," the one called Top interrupted.

He started forward, the sap bouncing in his right hand. Concho moved to meet him. Quick as a striking cobra, Top lunged low and swung the sap toward the Ranger's left knee, hoping to surprise him and bring him down.

Faster than a cobra, Concho dodged. He lashed out with a boot, which connected with Top's shoulder as he was rising, sending him rolling but doing little damage. Before he could follow up the kick, Bo charged, swinging lefts and rights.

Concho swayed right, swayed left. He had longer reach than Bo and a left arm jab stung the man in the mouth. Bo's adrenaline pumped now, though. He shook his head, came wading in with both fists popping. A right hand caromed off the lawman's left arm and Ten-Wolves snapped out a right jab in response that did more than sting his opponent.

Bo staggered. Concho moved in for the finish. But Top had regained his feet. He swung hard with the sap at the Ranger's head and Concho dodged back to avoid the blow.

Bo recovered. The two men stepped in. Concho backed up toward his opponents' black SUV, avoiding shots, looking for an opening. Top took a swing with the sap. Missed. Concho kicked him between the legs. The man cried out and grabbed for his crotch as he bent over. Concho measured his next kick to put Top down, but again Bo saved his partner.

A powerful right slammed into the Ranger's left bicep, the brass knuckles digging deep. The arm went numb below the shoulder. Concho threw a right that popped Bo's lower lip and sprayed blood. He swept the man's legs with his boot and Bo fell heavily.

It might have been over right then but the man with the pipe wrench, who Concho had knocked out with his first punch, rejoined the fight. The lawman heard him charging, slid to his left just as the man swung his wrench. The heavy tool clanged into the SUV's hood, gouging a big dent in the metal.

Concho slapped his right hand down on the wrench, pinning it to the hood. The numbness in his left arm was fading. He grabbed the man by the collar with his left hand and used all his strength to swing the man around and crash him into the side of the SUV. The back of the fellow's head struck the driver's side window with stunning force, starring the glass. Lights out!

In the meantime, though, Top straightened and Bo climbed to his feet. Ten-Wolves took the attack to them, his fists and feet flashing. The blows connected, thudding into flesh.

Top slashed desperately with his sap. Concho spun away from it, coming around with a kick that put his boot up alongside Top's right cheek. The blow knocked the man sideways. His sap fell from nerveless fingers and he collapsed.

Bo swung a right. Concho blocked and levered a fist into the man's gut. He spewed vomit over the hood of the black Tahoe. Ten-Wolves avoided the spew and grabbed Bo by the back of his suit jacket. He slammed him face first into the hood, though not as hard as he could. He didn't want him unconscious. Pulling him back up, Concho sought the man's gaze. The eyes were unfocused, glazed. A cut on his forehead wept blood.

"Who paid you?" the Ranger demanded.

"Screw you!"

Concho slammed his face into the hood again, pulled him back up. "Who paid you?"

"I'm not tell—"

Blam. Again into the SUV. And back up.

"Who?"

"Manny Freed!" Bo yelled.

Concho let him sink to the ground. He walked through the carnage to the gate house and reached in to push the button to raise the metal rail blocking his exit. Climbing back in his truck, he drove through.

———

SNOW UNSCREWED the silencer from his Dan Wesson 10mm semi-automatic and holstered the weapon. He searched Martino Salas's body, finding only the cell phone Manny Freed had given him. This he tucked into his pocket for later discard. Salas should never have kept that phone. It had been preloaded with a tracker app that allowed Snow to zero the man's location. Without it, he might have still been alive.

Checking out the package Salas had removed from the freezer, Snow shoved the two-inch barrel Smith & Wesson aside as of no use to him. He made a face at the baggy of cocaine and carried it over to the sink to dump it and wash the coke away.

Next, he examined the package of money. Nice crisp fifties and hundreds. He estimated sixty thousand and it never hurt to have extra cash on hand. He tucked the package inside his leather jacket and zipped up.

Blowing out the candle and locking the door behind him, Snow slipped out of the apartment. He left the corpse behind to eventually be found. It probably wouldn't be soon, though he didn't much care. On the way to his bike, he broke Salas's cell phone and tossed the pieces into a small pond.

After reaching the bike, he used his own phone to text a coded message to his handler giving him Jane Doe's real name of Heather Green, which was the only useful piece of information he'd gotten from Salas. It was beginning to look like the shot he'd hit her with during the ambush hadn't been fatal. Else, his employer would likely have heard about her death and already informed him.

Soon, the assassin was on his way to his motel room. *One of three contracts fulfilled*, he thought. *Two to go*. Heather Green and Concho Ten-Wolves. The girl would be the hardest to find and he wasn't sure where to begin. He figured to save the lawman for last, unless a particularly good opportunity presented itself. And then.... Maybe he'd go back to the Lucky Eagle casino and find that woman in the red dress.

CHAPTER THIRTY-FIVE

HEATHER GREEN LAY HIDDEN AND WEEPING IN AN OVERGROWN field a few miles from where she and the two lawmen had been ambushed. She'd run from there and kept on running, panic stricken and stopping for nothing as she fled. She'd seen one of the officers dead. Maybe the other was, too. She'd almost been dead herself. The silver haired killer on the motorcycle had shot her.

A small part of the reason she wept was because of that pain. The bullet hit her in the upper back but hadn't penetrated the vest she'd been given. It still hurt. She could feel the impact site with every breath she took.

Physical suffering was the least of her pains, though. Far worse were the emotional agonies, mainly her fears for her daughter. Winona was just over four months. She was small for her age, a quiet child. But smart. She'd learned to recognize her own name. She understood the meaning of "mama," though he couldn't speak yet. She had big, solemn eyes and a heartbreak-ingly elven face. She didn't cry often but when she did it felt like the end of the world.

Heather thought of the mistakes she'd made in her own short life. A legion of them. But Winona had never been a mistake. And now the girl was in danger, in the hands of those who'd proven brutal in their wanton murders of the first surrogate family Heather had ever known. Probably in the hands of men who'd wanted to *buy* Heather for savage purposes. How could a child be safe in such hands? But she had no idea where Winona might be, or where to start to look.

She felt helpless, with no one she could trust and no one who cared what happened to her except for how they might use her. She couldn't even be sure of Ten-Wolves. The man radiated confidence and strength. But it was clear he doubted aspects of her story. Perhaps rightly so in that she *had* lied to him about some things. But couldn't he see she'd lied to protect her daughter and those who'd been taking care of her?

Not that she'd been *able* to protect any of them, she scourged herself. Her mistakes had gotten her friends killed and her daughter stolen. They'd sent her fleeing to this field, left her hiding under a mesquite bush while she cried out her eyes. Maybe she should just lie down here and die. She'd be better. The world would be better.

What about Winona? the question came from deep inside. *Will you leave your daughter to pay for* your *sins?*

The questions evoked anger. She dashed her hands against her eyes, swiping away tears. She forced a deep breath in and out. This was a mistake, too, letting her emotions blind her to the work she needed to do to find Winona.

Wiping her face, she rose to her feet. She must do something but she couldn't do it alone. A chance had to be taken to trust someone, and there was only one person she could think of.

Through the darkness, she began walking, heading west toward the Kickapoo Reservation. It was miles away and she needed to make it before morning light revealed her to the world with all its dangers. She started to hurry.

———

MANNY FREED'S home address wasn't listed on the search engines but Concho located it through his Texas Ranger connections. He drove by the place but found the windows dark and Manny's car gone. Parking along the curb, he waited. But by 9:00 PM the lawyer still hadn't shown.

Feeling both exhausted and restless, Concho drove back to the Rez and to his trailer. The entire local law enforcement community sought Heather Green and her kidnapped daughter. A new APB had been released on Martino Salas, though Concho suspected the man was already in Mexico. There was not much personally he could add to any of those searches right now.

He ate a can of chili from his pantry and paired it with a hunk of buttered bread. Then fell into bed. His dreams were of:

Afghanistan, 2009

A child wailed in the distance under a blazing noonday sun. Concho paused. He was almost a month into his first tour of duty. Elements of his regiment—the 75th Ranger—were moving into the outskirts of Kajaki, a village in south central Afghanistan. They'd met resistance, street to street fighting with rebels armed with AK-47s and LAWS anti-tank rockets, as well as captured US arms. The wailing was the first sign Ten-Wolves had of the presence of non-combatants in the area.

The alley where he stood ran between walls of rammed earth, with buildings of mud brick on either side. It was narrow enough to be shaded even at this time of day, though the shade didn't do much against the heat that rose out of the very soil. He almost felt he could smell it.

The child's cry died away. Concho eased forward again. Sweat dripped down his body under his fatigues. His longer than regulation hair hung soaking wet. In the alleys and streets to either side, he could hear the whispers and clankings of other rangers moving ahead, stalking and being stalked.

A figure wearing a white turban darted across a gap in front of Concho. He glimpsed the rifle in the figure's hands and fired a three-round burst from his M16A4. The bullets slammed into the mud walls, shattering fragments of brick. The enemy had already disappeared.

A voice from somewhere shouted. Not in English. Concho couldn't catch the words. He darted forward to duck beneath a wooden overhang. Rebel gunfire erupted from his right, where an even smaller alley connected this one to the next street over. Ten-Wolves couldn't see the shooters but heard the big voice of Tommy Dougall shouting. American M16s answered the rebel fire. A man cried out in Dari for god.

"Shit!" Tommy Dougall yelled.

The flat crack of an explosion rocketed down the side alley. Dust followed, boiling along the ground. A terrible fear clutched at Concho's heart. He darted into the alley, beating his way through the dust.

Coughing, he surged out into a wider street, his rifle slick in his fists. The street was clear of inhabitants except for one ranger. Tommy lay on his back, and for an instant Concho couldn't make sense of the scene. Then he did and wished he hadn't.

His friend had stepped on an IED. His legs were gone to above the knees, except for shreds of flesh and bone. The big arteries pumped out crimson fluid in pulsing streams, spraying it into the air and spackling the dirt with red.

Bile burst into Concho's mouth and stung his nostrils. He ran toward his friend, slinging his rifle over his shoulder. As he dropped down beside his fellow ranger, blood-filled soil squelched under his knees.

"Tommy! Tommy!"

"That was stupid," Tommy said, his voice normal, even casual. His gaze met his friend's. "Stupid!" he said again.

"Medic!" Concho bellowed. "Medic!" He gazed frantically around for anything to use as a tourniquet. The smell of blood hung nauseatingly in the air. He could taste it on his lips.

Tommy's M16 lay next to the big man. It had an adjustable rifle sling for ease of carrying. Concho unhooked the sling and immediately twisted it around the stumps of Tommy's legs. He cinched it tight, as tight as all his strength could muster. And still he called, "Medic! Medic! Medic!"

"Ouch," Tommy said.

Concho stopped yelling for help and looked at his friend. "You idiot!" he said softly. "Now I'm gonna have to carry you home."

Tommy looked down at his missing legs and bellowed a strangled laugh. "At least I don't weigh as much as I used to," he said.

A wetness ripped at Concho's eyes as Tommy Dougall slipped away.

CHAPTER THIRTY-SIX

1:00 AM. SATURDAY MORNING. PA MODINE WOKE TO THE SOUND of the Peterbilt tractor trailer rig starting up in the front yard of the farmhouse. He leaped to his feet. His first thought was that someone was stealing the truck and had to be stopped.

Running down the hallway and into the kitchen in his long johns, he found his oldest son, Derrick, sitting calmly in the kitchen holding the sleeping Indian baby in one arm while he drank coffee with his free hand.

"What...what's going on?" Pa sputtered. "Who's takin' the rig?"

"Just Taylor and Justin," Derrick said.

"Why?"

"Said something about fueling it up." Derrick grinned. "Figured to let 'em do something useful that won't get 'em into trouble."

Pa opened his mouth, then snapped it shut. He walked to the window and looked out. The big truck was just pulling out of the driveway and turning onto the highway toward Eagle Pass. "Why so early?" he asked.

Derrick shrugged. "Said they were going to take it to that new truck stop over on 277. You can get a wash there, too. Shoot, they been seeming pretty antsy, though. Maybe they're gonna look up some lot lizard. Get their rocks off."

"Why wouldn't they just go to the Red House?"

"That's the same old, same old, Pa. Could be they're lookin' for some strange."

Pa shook his head. "They'll probably screw that up, too."

"Stupid is as stupid does."

Pa snorted a chuckle and went to pour himself a cup of coffee now that he was up. "Well at least they can't foul up my plans while they're out getting their ashes hauled," he said.

"Nope," Derrick agreed.

———

SNOW NEVER SLEPT MORE than a few hours a night. By 5:00 AM he was up and on the road. He'd made a decision about how to search for Heather Green. He'd follow Ten-Wolves, and when Ten-Wolves found the girl or she found him, Snow would be there to take them both.

He dared not go onto the Kickapoo reservation itself, though. He'd be too easily spotted. He located a hidden spot along the road leading into—and out of—the Rez and parked to wait for the lawman to come to him.

"Sleep the last warm sleep, Ranger," he muttered. "Before the dirt nap. Before the winter sleep. For the earth is cold beneath the stones."

———

CONCHO WOKE EARLY, at a little after 5:00 AM. His eyes felt heavy, his chest hollow. He knew it was from the results of the dream, which he recalled in every detail. His best friend at the time, Tommy Dougall, had died that day. He remembered the aftermath of Tommy's death. And so close was he still to sleep that he found himself caught up in a waking dream of those next few minutes.

The smell of blood and explosives beneath the hammer of the sun. The still body of a friend who'd been alive seconds before. The grief and rage and awful realization of a world emptied of something important.

Concho lunged to his feet, swinging his rifle down from his shoulder into his hands. Adrenaline poured into his blood-stream. The air glittered; sound belled. He charged down the street, searching for an enemy.

A five-foot-high barricade of tires blocked the way. The house to the right of the barricade stood open; the dead body of an Afghan lay across the threshold. With all his senses height-ened, Concho saw the almost invisible wire running from beneath the corpse back into the house.

Booby trapped!

With one hand, the Ranger began yanking furiously at a single stack of tires, pulling them down, throwing them away. He stepped through the gap. The street lay empty ahead. But he turned back, stuck just his rifle through the gap and fired a quick burst into the dead body.

The rest of the tires protected Concho from the explosion that followed. Shrapnel shrieked and thudded into the pile from the other side but nothing penetrated. He stepped back through the gap. The booby-trapped body had disintegrated. The front wall of the house lay ripped open.

Dust hung like a fog, but through it he could see two men inside the house, bent over, coughing and hacking. Both carried weapons. The explosion had been directed away from them— leaving them unharmed—but the dust billowed back upon them.

Ten-Wolves opened fire with his M16. The men cried out as lead punched into their bodies and they were thrown back-

ward. *The Ranger leaped through the torn open doorway. The men he'd shot lay dead, their epitaphs written in gore on the plastered wall behind them.*

Another foe still lived, though. He didn't have a gun, only a machete. He charged the American. Concho swung his M16 across to block the attack. The machete's edge cracked across the steel barrel of the rifle and glanced away. Concho twisted the rifle's muzzle upward. At point blank range, he fired a three-round burst into his attacker's skull. The head exploded as the .223 slugs ripped through.

The house had two stories. A fourth rebel, dressed all in black, raced up the stairs. The American fired toward him. The slugs tore up splinters of wood but the man disappeared. Concho followed.

A single gunshot rang out. Concho flung himself forward onto the floor of the second story, his M16 thrust out in front of him. It was a single large room. Two men occupied it. One in black lay writhing on the floor. Standing over him was an American soldier in army fatigues. In one hand the soldier held a government issue Colt .45, its barrel still smoking. In the other he swung a glittering blade, either a stiletto or a razor, which instantly disappeared into a pocket of his BDUs.

"Soldier, hold your fire!" a voice shouted from behind the Ranger.

Concho turned his head. Jack Travers of the Green Beret stood three-quarters of the way up the stairs. Ten-Wolves glanced from Travers back toward the other soldier, who'd holstered his pistol.

Concho rose slowly to his feet. Travers came the rest of the way up the stairs and shouldered past the big Ranger. The second soldier bent down to handcuff the Afghani, ignoring the man's screams as his bullet-holed arm was yanked behind him.

"We've been looking for this one," Travers said, gesturing at the prisoner. We appreciate your help in apprehending him."

Concho took a deep breath; the berserk that had overcome

him in the wake of Tommy Dougall's death had burned itself out. "Who is he?" he asked.

The second soldier spoke for the first time, and he didn't look friendly. "You don't need to know that, grunt."

Ten-Wolves bristled. There was something he didn't like about this fellow.

Jack Travers intervened. "It's all right. I'll tell you when I can tell you. But right now we've got to keep his identity quiet."

Concho nodded, but his gaze never left the other soldier. "So who are you?" he demanded.

The man grinned; it mimicked friendly but the predator stared like a skull from underneath.

"Let me introduce you," Travers said. "This is Hieronymus Gall."

The phone rang. Concho came fully awake and sat up in bed. He had a feeling something important had been about to be revealed in his waking dream. It was gone now. He clawed at the bedside table and scooped up his cell. The caller ID read "Isaac Parkland."

"Yes," he answered.

"Sorry to bother you but I figured you'd want to know."

"What?"

"Martino Salas has been found."

"Where?"

"Dead on a floor. With a bullet in the back of his head."

"An execution?"

"It looks that way."

"When?"

"It'll take the coroner to tell us for sure but it looks like early last night. Maybe ten or eleven."

"Where's the body now?"

"The Eagle Pass police took the report. The body has already been transported. But if you swing by later, I'll take you to the site. If you want. An older woman called it in. Apparently Salas's buddy, Diego, had been renting from her. Off the books, so to speak."

"You working Saturday's these days?" Concho asked.

"Until we find the woman and her kid."

"Yeah. I'll be over to see you in a few hours. I want to stop by Manny Freed's place first."

"Freed? What's he got to do with this?"

"He's the one bailed Salas out. You know him?"

"A scum bucket lawyer. He sure loves the criminals."

"Or their money anyway."

"Right."

"It's not much of a lead but I'm pretty much empty everywhere else. See you soon."

Concho hung up and went to take a shower, though his thoughts kept drifting back to the day Tommy Dougall had been killed in Afghanistan. He wasn't sure why.

————

"Something ain't right," Pa Modine said to his son Derrick over the breakfast table.

Derrick paused in the act of shoveling cereal into his mouth. "What?"

"Your brothers. Taylor and Justin. They shoulda been back by now from fueling up the Peterbilt."

Derrick shrugged. "Like you said, maybe they're getting' their ashes hauled."

Pa shook his head. "That ain't it. They're up to something. And it's probably stupid."

"What can we do about it?"

Pa pulled his cell phone out of the pocket of his overalls and swiped up a number. He pressed send and let it ring. After ten times it went to phone mail. A computerized voice informed him the mailbox was full. He tried a second number. More ringing, no more answering. He slammed the phone down on the table hard enough to make Derrick wince.

"Go find 'em," Pa ordered.

"How am I supposed to do that?"

"There's a GPS on the Peterbilt, remember?"

"Oh, right." Derrick drank the sugary milk left in his bowl and pushed up from the table, wiping his mouth on a hand towel he generally used as a napkin. "You gonna be OK with the Indian baby?"

Pa made a face. "I raised you three boys all the way from peeing your diapers to peeing on the floor *next* to the toilet, I reckon I can handle one girl child."

Derrick nodded and headed for his truck. It was almost 6:00 AM.

CHAPTER THIRTY-SEVEN

AFTER A HOT SHOWER AND A BIG BREAKFAST OF EGGS, BACON, AND toast to fuel his body, Concho climbed in his Ford pickup and headed off the Rez. As Isaac Parkland had said for himself, there'd be no true rest for Ten-Wolves until he found Heather Green again and solved the mystery of her daughter's kidnapping.

He had two very slender leads to follow: Manny Freed, who'd hired three men to beat him up for unknown reasons, and Martino Salas's dead body, along with the site where he'd been executed. He couldn't be sure any of those things were tied to the kidnapping but he suspected so, and he had no other place to start. He decided on Freed first. Salas wasn't going anywhere.

Gathered clouds kept the morning gloomy even after the sun started to rise. A light rain fell. The lawman rode with his windows up, with his windshield wipers beating a steady rhythm. He headed up Tierra Soberana Boulevard toward FM 1021, which would take him into Eagle Pass.

As he turned left onto 1021, he noticed a green Jeep Wrangler 2-Door Sport 4X4 parked at the Shell station on the corner. He did a double take. The vehicle looked familiar, much like the one that had escaped up the creek on the day he'd found Heather Green locked in the trunk of a Monte Carlo.

Of course, there must be more than one such Jeep around Eagle Pass, but Concho was used to playing hunches and having them pay off. He pulled a U-turn and headed back toward the gas station.

The Jeep must have been sitting with its engine running, with the driver inside. It immediately wheeled out onto 1021 and accelerated away from Eagle Pass at a high rate of speed.

Still acting under the spur of impulse, Concho hit his lights and sirens and punched the gas on his F-150. He roared after the Jeep and the vehicle's driver accelerated even more. They clearly weren't going to stop. Now it was a car chase and Ten-Wolves felt an exhilaration speed his heart, too. He was onto something or the Jeep wouldn't have run.

Traffic was sparse on 1021 at this time of the morning. The few cars on the road began to pull onto the shoulders as the Ford's siren startled them. Concho whipped around any slow ones. The Jeep was fast but the modified Ford pickup was faster. He began to gain and started to look for a chance to use the pit maneuver to ram the fleeing vehicle off the road. The rain-slick roads should make that easier.

Most of the cars in the left lane pulled over but a red-cabbed Peterbilt semi kept coming. It traveled fast, maybe a driver on a delivery deadline. Concho couldn't get room to pit the Jeep with the big rig in the way. He blinked his lights at it, trying to get the driver's attention. No response.

The Jeep's driver stomped his brakes. Concho stomped his an instant later. The smoke of burning rubber corkscrewed heavenward. The squeal of brakes and the shriek of tires shattered the morning.

Concho's focus was intent on the Jeep in front of him. It looked like he was going to hit it and he had to control that impact. And while his attention was focused away from the semi, the driver of the rig yanked his air-horn, adding to the cacophony.

At the same moment, the Peterbilt swerved around the back end of the Jeep into Concho's lane. The Ranger had a half second to see it coming and realize he'd been ambushed. He yanked hard on the steering wheel, knowing the ditch was his only chance to escape a head on collision that would kill him.

His quick reflexes saved him from the head-on but he didn't escape scot-free. As his hands clamped like vises onto the steering wheel in preparation for the blow, the massive grill of the Peterbilt smashed into his Ford just behind the cab. It felt like he'd been hit by Ahab's raging whale.

Metal crunched, glass webbed and exploded. Everything in the Ford shifted to the right, including—it seemed—the bones and organs inside his body. The rear end of the pickup slewed around, the tires shredding. It came up on two wheels and Concho knew it was going over.

The bed of the pickup had been half ripped away from the cab. Wet wind from outside pummeled the Ranger as the vehicle went airborne and flipped. With no time for thoughts, Concho hung on as the truck slammed down on its hood and rolled again.

Pavement and sky and grass. Something pounded into the top of Concho's head. His whole body went numb. The Ford caromed into the ditch and flipped back upright, slewing to a stop on its ruined wheels.

Get out! a voice shouted at Concho. *Get out if you wanna live!* It was his own mind yelling. Whoever wanted him dead wasn't going to stop. They'd be coming.

He let go of the steering wheel, which was bent inward. He fumbled for the lock on his seat belt. His fingers felt like sausages. Blood sheeted his face, blocking the vision in his left eye. His nose clogged with more blood. He moved in slow motion.

The seat belt came loose and whipped across his chest. He

slapped at the door handle. The crash had silenced his sirens but the blue lights strobed off and on. The door still worked. Somehow. He pushed it open. It took all his strength.

His legs felt as heavy as cement. He swung them out of the truck but they wouldn't support his weight. He fell forward into the ditch, landing in a half inch of mud and water. The rain misting his face felt cold.

With the sirens dead, he could hear steam hissing from his radiator and the shouts of people in the distance. Closer, running footsteps sounded. He glanced up. A man with short brown hair raced toward him, holding a submachine gun in his hands. Ten-Wolves grabbed for his right-hand Colt. It was still in its holster but held fast by the restraining strap.

He wasn't going to get it loose in time.

———

SNOW WATCHED the morning's events unfold. He'd been sitting on his motorcycle in the parking lot of the Shell gas station when Concho Ten-Wolves drove by in his F-150. He'd seen the truck before, of course, at the Salas home, and a quick internet search had shown him the route vehicles coming from the Kickapoo Reservation would take into Eagle Pass. Since Ten-Wolves was his best lead to the woman he needed to kill, he'd decided to trail the Texas Ranger.

But then Ten-Wolves made a U-turn and took off after a green Jeep that pulled out of the same Shell lot. Curious, he kept watching. He saw the Ranger's sirens and lights go on and immediately kicked his bike into gear to follow, to see the end of it. So, he had a perfect vantage point to catch the wreck as a tractor trailer rig deliberately swerved into the lawman's lane and rammed his truck off the road.

An ambush. Nicely done. Even he might have fallen for it.

Snow whipped his bike onto the shoulder of the road and came to a sliding stop. Ten-Wolves' pickup flipped twice and came back up on its wheels. The top was caved in, the windshield hanging in pieces, the hood mangled, the bed half torn away from the cab.

The Ford wasn't the only vehicle out of commission. The semi had jackknifed. Its engine still roared. He couldn't see if anyone had climbed out of it, but thirty yards beyond the wreck, the Jeep that initiated it all came to a screeching halt. A man swung out with a short-barreled rifle in his hands. Some kind of SMG.

Snow glanced back toward Ten-Wolves' truck. It sat still, though steam rose from the front end. The driver's side window lay shattered. He could see the dark bulk of someone inside but no movement at first. *Dead man in a tin can*, he thought.

Then the Ranger twitched. His door screeched open and he fell out of the cab. His face was painted with blood but his hand reached for the gun at his hip. Raindrops speckled Snow's face mask and he swiped them away with a hand. The man with the SMG charged toward Ten-Wolves, his intent clear. And the Ranger's weapon was strapped in its holster. He made a little more than a target.

Snow reached beneath his leather jacket and pulled his own pistol.

CHAPTER THIRTY-EIGHT

CONCHO LAY ALMOST FLAT IN THE DITCH. RAIN AND BLOOD smeared his vision. The man running toward him with a gun was little more than a blur. The Ranger's right thumb plucked loose the strap holding his Colt in its holster. His hand fisted around the gun butt and he drew the weapon. The barrel scraped through the mud as he dragged it forward. But he was slow, far too slow.

The running man paused and threw up his rifle to fire. He stood no more than fifteen feet away. Suddenly, he staggered, as if punched. From somewhere off to the left came the sound of a single shot. Who could have fired it? Was there another cop on the scene? Or a bystander trying to do the right thing?

The Ranger had no time to look. The gunman had been hit in the side but was clearly wearing a bullet proof vest. He'd staggered but wasn't seriously hurt. With a wild shout, he swung his rifle around again, but the respite gave Concho the time he needed. He pulled the trigger on the .45 Double Eagle.

The heavy slug punched into the gunman's right thigh below the edge of the vest. Blood and meat sprayed. The outlaw dropped to his knees, screaming in pain and rage. He yanked the trigger of his own weapon but his aim was off. Bullets spattered against the highway and ricocheted away into the brush.

Concho lifted the barrel of his Colt, sighting along it with his one good eye. He had time for a single shot. He fired. The bullet impacted the right side of the gunman's forehead and punched through. The man's head flung to one side. His gun dropped to the ground; his body followed.

There were two, Concho's mind told him.

The one he'd shot had been driving the Jeep. But what about the tractor trailer rig? Using every ounce of strength he could muster, Ten-Wolves pushed himself to his knees, groaning. Electric shocks darted up and down his limbs as the numbness in his body seemed to flicker off and on. The blow to his skull. He must have a concussion.

The driver of the semi must still be inside the cab, Concho thought. He heard the gears grinding on the big rig. He tried to force himself to his feet and couldn't. The Peterbilt lurched backward. The gears shrieked. It lurched forward. The front wheels straightened and it powered into a forward roll. But only the cab portion. The trailer stayed where it was; the driver must have unhooked it.

Again the rig's driver shifted gears. The engine roared. The vehicle lunged toward the Ranger and a chill swept his whole body. The man planned on running him down. That threat galvanized him. He still couldn't get his feet under him but threw himself to the side, off his knees, landing on his stomach and sliding on the rain-slicked pavement. The semi-automatic in his right hand hit the hard ground and went flying.

The Peterbilt barreled over the spot where Ten-Wolves had knelt an instant before, missing his legs by inches. The big rig smashed into the ditch and rammed into Concho's already destroyed truck. Its front wheels bounced as it climbed up and over the smaller pickup with the vicious sound of rending metal.

Ten-Wolves rolled over, groaning again as he tried to make

his twisted muscles obey his brain's commands. The semi's driver cut the wheel and fed the big diesel fuel, but his tires remained caught in the wreckage of the F-150. The rig lurched a few feet and ground to a halt.

"Get up!" Concho ordered himself. "Get up now!"

The door of the semi flew open. A big man, a wild man, leaped down into the ditch, his hands holding a long shotgun. He shouted a name, "Justin!" At the same instant, Concho found himself on his feet. His left hand dropped to his second pistol and yanked at it hard enough to break the snap holding it in the holster.

The wild man swung his shotgun to bear. Concho palmed his Colt and double actioned the trigger. The shot struck the man in the chest, knocking him back against his own rig. He didn't go down. The Kevlar vest he wore took the impact.

Concho fired twice more into the vest. He didn't want to kill the man. He wanted him to drop the shotgun and stay down. He needed to know if Heather Green's daughter was alive and where she might be. This man could be the only one who knew.

The man slid to his knees, gasping for breath, but he still held the shotgun. He started to lift it. The lawman fired again, aiming for the vest one more time. His hand shook. The bullet struck high, cutting through the man's chin and ripping into the throat behind it.

The man sagged back against his truck. The shotgun fell barrel-first into the mud. Concho staggered toward him, still trying to regain his normal balance. The dying man looked up. His irises were brown. He tried to talk. His mouth worked but no words came out, only blood. Concho's last bullet must have cut through the vocal cords.

Ten-Wolves cursed. He sagged against the truck himself, then turned and slid down to a seated position against the front tire. With a last burst of strength, the wounded outlaw grabbed the lawman's arm with his right hand.

The Ranger didn't bother to shake it off. The grip weakened on its own. The man slumped into death. His arm remained stretched out toward Concho. It was thickly covered with reddish brown hair. On the back of the grasping hand, just behind the thumb, was a tattoo of a half open straight razor.

———

ONE SHOT and Snow smoothly reholstered the pistol under his jacket. There weren't many bystanders this early in the morning and he doubted anyone had seen his quick action. He hadn't shot to kill. He'd deliberately fired into the running gunman's bullet-proof vest, and not specifically to save the life of Ten-Wolves, but to give the Ranger one chance of surviving on his own.

And the Ranger lived. Snow had watched the whole thing. The lawman was clearly hurt but hurts could heal. Snow took off his helmet and hung it from the mirror of his bike. After zipping his leather jacket up so no one would see the holstered pistol beneath it, Snow walked toward Concho, his motorcycle boots clicking on the pavement.

The Ranger noticed him coming and lifted his Colt. Snow held both his hands out, palms up to show he meant peace. The pistol dropped back down into the lawman's lap. Snow squatted in front of him.

"You're one tough hombre," the assassin said. "Hard to believe you're going to walk away from this one."

The Ranger's voice croaked hoarsely. "Who are you?"

"I'm a writer," Snow said. "Poet mostly. But I'm working on a longer story even as we speak."

"I wanted your name?"

Snow shrugged. "I'm not well known at present. You wouldn't recognize it. But maybe when this story is done."

"Did you...see?"

"Most of it."

"Who shot..." Concho gestured toward the first gunman he'd killed.

"That I didn't see." He smiled. "Providence arrives on strange arrows. Maybe it was God."

Concho shook his head very slightly. "More likely the Devil."

Snow chuckled, and rose to his feet. "You take care, Ranger. Until next time."

"You need to tell the police what you saw," Concho replied quickly.

"You can do it. Only the living tell tales." He walked away, climbed on his motorcycle. In another moment he was gone.

———

HEATHER GREEN HAD JUST REACHED FM Road 1021 when she heard the sirens through the rain. She immediately ducked down in the ditch. She saw a truck go by with blue lights raging and recognized it. Concho Ten-Wolves' F-150.

She leaped to her feet but there was no chance to catch the Ranger's attention. He was after someone. Then she saw the wreck unfold. Again, she dropped down in the ditch. Her heart beat frantically in her chest as she watched the ensuing gunfight. And she prayed, desperately, to any god who might be listening. She prayed for Ten-Wolves to live.

It seemed, though, as if only the Devil answered. A motorcyclist standing and observing the events took off his helmet. Heather saw the snow-white hair drawn back in a ponytail. The fear that lodged in her throat felt like vomit. This was the man who'd shot her, who'd tried to kill her.

She pushed herself as low into the dirt as she could get. She kept on praying, for herself now. She even closed her eyes. When she opened them again and dared take a look, the motorcyclist and his bike had disappeared. She could see a shape she thought to be Concho sitting with his back to the wheel of a semi. She couldn't tell if he lived.

She wanted to go to him, to see. But more sirens and flashing blue and red lights shattered the rainy morning. Too much of a gauntlet for her to dare when she didn't know where the biker had gone. *If* he was gone.

CHAPTER THIRTY-NINE

CONCHO CONSIDERED THE STRANGENESS OF HIS CONVERSATION with the motorcyclist bystander. The whole interaction had been surreal. Or maybe it was just his own confusion. Had it even happened?

The sound of sirens coming distracted him from that line of thought. He started to get up, then gave it up as too much effort. He'd figured someone would call the police. They'd come to him; he didn't have to go to them.

The rain had stopped for the moment. The air tasted fresh and cool. He sucked in a grateful breath. He still held one of his Colts and he reloaded and holstered it. He couldn't see where the other one might have gotten to. He was fond of it and didn't want to lose it, but it seemed like an awfully lot of work to search for it now.

The first policeman on the scene was an Eagle Pass officer, not one of Isaac Parkland's men. His eyes were huge as his head swiveled back and forth taking in the carnage.

"You OK?" he asked Concho.

"Not feeling particularly pert."

"I...I guess not."

Concho held out his arm and the policeman grabbed it

reflexively, then helped heave the Texas Ranger to his feet. Concho groaned and swayed, putting his hand against the wrecked semi to steady himself.

"These men," he said, gesturing at the two dead gunmen. "We need to find out who they are right away. If you'd take some photos with your phone. We can send them to the Rangers. Get those names. Get pictures of the vehicles and license plates, too. And the one over toward the Jeep, check to see if he has any visible tattoos. Particularly on the hands."

"Right," the officer said. He pulled a cell phone out of his pocket and moved away.

"Oh, and if you see Colt .45 Double Eagle lying anywhere, it's mine."

The officer nodded.

An ambulance worked its way along the shoulder and the two paramedics piled out. Seeing the blood on Concho's face, one of the two came immediately to him. The other went to examine the dead.

"You shouldn't be standing up with that head wound," the medic said immediately.

"Head wound?"

The man nodded. "Stay here. I'll get the stretcher."

"I can walk."

The medic pursed his lips but merely took Ten-Wolves by the arm and started leading him toward the ambulance. Concho let himself be led, then sat down on the back of the vehicle where the medic pointed.

The man began using gauze and swabs to clean Concho's face.

"How bad is it?" Ten-Wolves asked.

"Gotta get the blood away before I can see it clearly. Gonna need some stitches, though. How are you feeling?"

"Weak and woozy."

"You've got a concussion. Do you remember what happened here?"

"Every detail."

"Well, that's a good sign. What about the rest of you? Muscles? Joints?"

"Everything feels out of place and doesn't want to move the way I tell it to move."

"You were in the truck that flipped?"

"Yes."

"Then that's to be expected. Open your mouth."

Concho did so and the man peered inside. "No sign of internal bleeding," he said. "Another good sign. How's your breathing?"

"Chest hurts but it's like pulled muscles. I've had them before."

The paramedic nodded. He finished cleaning Concho's face, removing blood and bits of embedded dirt and glass. "The eye is OK," he said.

"Glad to hear it."

The medic started cleaning the scalp. It hurt and Ten-Wolves winced.

"Sorry," the man said. "You're going to need at least six stitches."

"Not the first time."

"The biggest issue is the concussion. We'll need to take you to the hospital. They may want to keep you overnight."

"Can't spare that kind of time."

"You'll have to argue it with the doctors. I just work here."

The police officer taking pictures of the dead returned to the Ranger. He handed him a muddy Colt .45, which Ten-Wolves slipped into the empty holster at his right side. Then the officer showed him the pictures he'd taken. The first perpetrator's face was distorted by a bullet hole in the forehead but might still be identifiable. The second perp was clearer. The vehicles could be clearly seen, and the license plates were there, too, but something was off about them. The biggest tell, though, was the straight razor tats on the back of both men's hands.

Taking the cop's phone, Concho sent the best pictures to his own cell before forwarding them to his buddy, Raul Molina, at Ranger headquarters. An accompanying text contained details and a request to expedite identification.

Another ambulance and more police vehicles arrived. Isaac Parkland and Roland Turner climbed out of a Maverick County SUV and approached. Parkland still wore the bandages from his own wreck.

"What in God's name?" the Sheriff asked.

"Long story," Concho replied.

"Connected to the Heather Green case, you think?"

"Absolutely."

"We need to compare notes."

"Not now," the paramedic said. "We're leaving for the hospital."

"Can't you forget me or something?" Concho asked.

"Not and keep my job," the medic replied. "Besides," he gestured toward what remained of the lawman's pickup crushed under the bulk of the Peterbilt cab, "you gonna walk home?"

Ten-Wolves glanced over at his Ford and puffed out a slow breath. "I see your point. Guess I do need a ride." He glanced at Parkland. "Join me and we can talk on the way."

The paramedic started to protest, then clicked his mouth shut. He climbed up into the rear of the ambulance. "All right," he said. "Let's get you aboard." He grasped Concho's arm to give him a pull while Isaac Parkland pushed from behind. Working together, the three got Ten-Wolves up and in. The paramedic patted a stretcher as an indication for him to lie down.

"Not gonna fit," Concho replied. He found a seat against the left side of the ambulance and slumped there.

Parkland climbed in and took a seat on the opposite side after indicating for his deputy, Roland Turner, to come pick them up at the hospital.

"Destroyed yet another truck," Parkland said, shaking his

head. "You're awfully hard on equipment, Ten-Wolves. Guess you're gonna want to borrow a vehicle from me again?"

"I promise not to get a scratch on it. Indian scout's honor."

"Liar."

———

THE CROWD around the wreck site began to grow. Heather Green moved back from the road into the field, hiding herself behind a wide spreading juniper tree. She was wet and filthy and would attract far too much attention if anyone got a good look at her. She felt pretty sure the motorcyclist assassin had ridden off. But how far had he gone? And would he return? He'd probably shoot her in front of a hundred witnesses if he found her.

She'd been glad to see that Ten-Wolves still lived, and when she saw Isaac Parkland join him at the back of an ambulance, she decided to take a chance. Ten-Wolves was an Indian, a man of her blood. Parkland had risked his life for her. She'd run to them. But just as she moved back toward the highway, the sound of a motorcycle engine sent her diving to the ground.

By the time she looked up again, the ambulance carrying both Ten-Wolves and Parkland had made a U-turn and headed for the hospital. The only one left who she'd had any interaction with was a black officer who seemed to be friends with Ten-Wolves. His name was "Turner," she believed.

But he was walking toward the SUV he'd arrived in, as if he, too, were preparing to leave. This might be her last chance to approach someone she could potentially trust. She had to take the risk, even though several men she didn't know loitered along the road near the deputy's vehicle.

She took off running along the fence row toward Turner, shouting his name. But the sirens and general cacophony must have masked the sound. He didn't hear her, didn't turn.

A barbed wire fence separated field from highway. She grabbed one strand of wire and pushed it down as she tried to slide through to reach the road. The back of her windbreaker snagged. She jerked; cloth tore but she still wasn't free. Frustration made her cry out.

A bystander with damp and tangled short black hair rushed to help. He pulled up on the offending strand of wire and twisted the barb free of the thin jacket. She slid between and straightened. The man grasped her arm to help her.

"Thank you," she said.

Deputy Turner began to climb into his SUV. She started toward him. But the man who'd helped her didn't let go of her arm and she jerked up short. She spun toward him.

Her mouth dropped open as she saw the hand that held her. Fear slammed her in the gut. A blue tattoo covered much of the back of the man's hand, a tattoo of a straight razor partially folded. A memory surfaced, like a shark hitting a kill.

The men that kidnapped and drugged her. Diego and Martino. They'd raped her. She knew already it had to have happened, but now she actually remembered it, felt it viscerally. She remembered being unable to move, numb and paralyzed as they took turns. And then they'd given her to a third man. This man, with this tattoo. And while he'd taken her he'd whispered in her ear, "Gonna buy you and loan you to all my friends."

CHAPTER FORTY

IT TOOK SEVEN STITCHES TO CLOSE THE GASH IN CONCHO'S SCALP. The doctors told him he had a concussion and wanted to keep him overnight for observation. He declined the invitation. They gave him pain pills. He didn't take them. They told him he needed to rest and take it easy. No physical or mental exertion for seventy-two hours. He told them he'd do just that. He was lying.

There was nothing he'd rather do than rest and relax but two lives were at stake, a woman's and a child's. And he had a lead to where one of them might be. A call came in from Raul Molina at Texas Ranger headquarters while Concho was being tended to.

"No hit on the perps," Molina said. "Neither of them is in our data base. And nothing on their tats. They may not have been clean before this but no one's painted any mud on them."

"What about the vehicles?"

"The license plates came back registered to clearly different people. So they stole a couple of plates to replace theirs before going after you."

"And the vehicles themselves?"

Concho could almost hear Raul grin over the phone.

"Nothing on the Jeep but I've got something on the tractor trailer."

"What? Tell me!"

"Since you said in your text that the Jeep might be the same one you had trouble with at Little Owl Creek Bridge, I went to your report on that incident. You mentioned the Jeep's driver seemed to know the area very well, which might mean he was from around there."

"True, too. But—"

"So, I went to Google Maps of the area. Satellite pictures. Nothing on the Jeep but I found what looks like the same Peterbilt semi parked in a ranch house yard less than fifteen miles from the bridge. Not absolutely sure but it looks like it. I'm texting you the address now."

"Molina...you're a genius. If you were here, I'd kiss you."

"Thank God I'm not there."

Concho laughed, although it pulled at his stitches. "You may have saved some lives, Raul!" he said seriously.

"Let's hope so."

————

HEATHER GREEN OPENED her mouth to scream and the man who held her arm pulled back his windbreaker to show her a gun holstered under his shoulder.

"Scream and I'll kill you and whoever intervenes," he said. "And that means you'll never see your daughter again."

Heather gasped. "Winona! Is she alive?"

"She is, and if you want to live to see her, keep your mouth shut."

Heather nodded. The man gave a tug on her arm and she fell in beside him as they moved toward a black Toyota pickup parked on the side of the road. She glanced only an instant toward the oblivious Deputy named Turner. He climbed into a Sheriff's Office SUV and drove away toward Eagle Pass.

Despair filled her. *Alone again*, she thought. Then she thought of her daughter. *Winona!* How she wanted to see her daughter again. Even if it killed her.

———

CONCHO TOLD Isaac Parkland what he'd learned from Raul Molina.

"Then we're on our way," Parkland said, excitedly. "Turner is already waiting in the parking lot. I'll call for backup."

"And I'll call the FBI."

"Right," Parkland said. "Della Rice?"

"Yep."

They rushed for the exit, both men on their phones. Concho didn't get Della. He got Bihn Bui and relayed everything he knew. Bihn promised to tell her immediately and they'd call to coordinate the strike on the target farm.

Turner started the SUV when he saw them coming. Concho slid in the back and Turner peeled out as Parkland relayed the address.

"Not too far from Owl Creek Bridge," Turner said. "I know the way."

"Good," Concho replied. Then he noticed the materials piled in the back seat with him. A deer rifle, a bow and arrows, extra ammunition, an oversized Kevlar vest, and a small possibles bag. All of it belonged to him but had been left behind in the back seat of his F-150 at the wreck site.

"You got my stuff," he said to Turner with surprise.

Roland glanced over his shoulder and grinned. "Thought you might want it."

"That's a 10-4."

Concho immediately opened the possibles bag and pulled out a gray chamois cloth, which he used to clean the Colt Double Eagle he'd lost in the mud. He oiled the actions on both pistols and reloaded.

He pulled one more thing out of the bag, a small yellow tin. He screwed off the lid to reveal the contents—red ocher. Reaching in, he scooped up two fingerfuls and smeared jagged lines beneath his right eye, then repeated the same action beneath his left. Resealing the tin, he wiped his fingers on the cloth.

Isaac Parkland had turned slightly in his seat to watch him. Their gazes met and both men nodded. Parkland turned back forward. Tension and adrenaline crackled in the air inside the SUV at the prospect of action. Parkland spoke to Roland Turner, who was focused on his driving as they left Eagle Pass at speed.

"Ten-Wolves put on his warpaint," Parkland said. Then, maybe to ease the tension, he made a joke, a Biblical reference to the four horsemen of the apocalypse. "I guess that makes him the rider on the red horse. I figure I'm on the white horse and you're on the black."

Turner laughed. "Sheriff, you might need some sensitivity training after this. White man on a white horse. Black man on a black horse. And an Indian on the red one."

Parkland cackled. "Never thought of it like that. Kinda funny."

"Seems like we're missing a horse, though," Turner said. "Weren't there four?"

"The pale horse," Parkland added. "Yeah." He quoted: "And he that sat upon him was named Death."

"Don't worry," Concho said, and his voice wasn't laughing. "That one's coming."

———

KING MODINE ANSWERED his cell phone when he saw the call was coming from his son, Derrick. "What's going on?"

"Pa! Pa! He killed them."

Derrick's voice was higher pitched than normal. He sounded scared, or angry, or both. King's stomach kicked acid up into his throat. Derrick was the calmest and most level-headed of his three boys. If he were upset then something bad had happened.

"Who?" he demanded. "Who killed who?"

"That Ranger. Ten-Wolves. He killed Taylor and Justin. Shot 'em down!"

The world seemed to kaleidoscope around King Modine's head. He couldn't process what his ears heard. "What? That can't be."

"He did, Pa. I can see their bodies. Both of 'em are dead. And that Ranger killed 'em."

King's confusion segued into growing anger. "How? Why didn't you intervene?"

"I got there when it was all over. They must a tried to take him out. Tried to run him over with the Peterbilt. They hurt him but he got 'em both."

"You should have killed him right there!" King raged into the phone.

"I couldn't it. It was like a pig farm already. Cops everywhere. An ambulance took Ten-Wolves away."

"Then he's at the hospital. I'll go—"

"Pa, I got the girl."

King blinked. "What girl?"

"The girl it all started with. The injun."

"How? Never mind. Bring her here. Now!"

"I'm on my way, Pa. But maybe we should get ready to move. They might figure out who Taylor and Justin are and find out where we live. They might be coming soon."

"You worry about gettin' here. I'll worry about that."

"Alright alright."

King hung up. For only a second, his legs felt weak. His two youngest boys were gone. But then rage strengthened him, a righteous rage. Maybe this was a sign. Time to stop hiding. Time to make a stand. Show the world what he stood for. If he had to be a martyr for the cause, so be it.

He began making phone calls to gather the troops. He wouldn't tell them he *hoped* for a showdown. Let them think it was just another practice run for something big. And then let the Texas Ranger come.

And die.

CHAPTER FORTY-ONE

A CALL CAME THROUGH FROM THE FBI. CONCHO ANSWERED.

"Rice here," Della said over the phone. "I'll have a copter in the air in ten minutes. We can be there via ground in forty. You sure these are the perps who kidnapped the child?"

"Gotta be. And the ones who had a hand in kidnapping Heather Green before."

"All right. How many men you got?"

"Three right here. Two more on the way."

"I'm bringing eight. You can be there in forty?"

"We can be there in fifteen."

"Well, hold off till we reach you."

"They could hurt the child in that time."

"Listen, Ten-Wolves. This is a kidnapping. The FBI has jurisdiction. If they were going to hurt the child they probably already have. I'm telling you to wait for us."

Concho felt his teeth grind together. "Make it faster than forty then," he snapped, and swiped off the call.

Roland Turner slowed the SUV. "Whatta we do?"

"We'll give them a little time. But I'm not waiting forty minutes. There's an old gas well about two klicks up this road. We can pull over there. Get on our vests and let the officers Parkland called catch up. Then we'll move. FBI or no."

"These guys are probably armed to the teeth," Parkland said.

"We'll have to pull those teeth."

———

DERRICK MODINE WHIPPED his black Toyota pickup into the driveway of the Modine farmhouse and slammed the brakes. The truck slid to a stop, spraying damp dirt from the rain shower that had passed over earlier this morning.

A car and a pickup he didn't recognize sat parked in front of the house. Derrick climbed out of his truck cautiously, his hand on the Glock semi-automatic he'd been carrying stuck between his legs all the way home. The farmhouse door opened. His Pa stepped outside onto the porch with another man. Derrick recognized him. He was on their side.

Taking a deep breath in relief, Derrick slid the Glock into his shoulder holster and went around the truck to open the passenger side door. Heather Green sat handcuffed to the seat. He released her, then grabbed her arm and jerked her out of the vehicle. Though she didn't resist him, he shoved her roughly toward his Pa and the other man.

He'd stripped her of her windbreaker and the bullet proof vest she'd worn, leaving her in the khaki shorts and white shirt she'd been wearing for the past three days. Both were splotched with mud, as were her bare legs and even her face. She stopped in front of Pa Modine, her look defiant.

Pa's companion whistled. "Quite a looker for an Injun. If you get her cleaned up. Don't suppose we have time..."

"Not right now," Pa snapped. "But maybe we'll send her to the Red House from here." To Derrick he said, "Take her inside and let her take care of the kid. But watch her. We might need 'em both for hostages before this thing is through."

"What thing is that, Pa?" Derrick asked.

"Payback for your brothers."

"We going after the Ranger?"

"Him and any other mud people get in our way."

———

TWO MORE MAVERICK COUNTY deputies joined them at the gas well, guided in by Roland Turner on the radio. The five of them geared up beneath a sky that darkened steadily with the threat of rain, slipping into their bullet-proof vests and making sure their weapons were loaded and ready to go. Concho strung his bow just in case, although if a fight came it would most likely be guns.

Bihn Bui called for Della Rice. "We're there in fifteen. If you're ready."

"We're ready," Ten-Wolves replied. "Let's do it."

Roland wheeled the SUV onto the main road and they tore out, running without sirens or lights so as not to give their targets any more warning than necessary. Twelve minutes down the road, they saw the isolated, single-story farmhouse they sought. Two unpainted barns flanked the structure. The front yard was nearly barren of grass and several vehicles were parked on the dirt. A welcoming party. Not likely a friendly one.

A short driveway turned into the yard. No gate blocked it. Roland headed for the drive but a blue SUV coming from the other direction and marked FBI reached it first. Turner followed; they jounced over ruts. Now everyone hit their lights and sirens. Shock and awe. The FBI vehicle went left. Turner went right. Both slid to a stop. The second Maverick County car and another FBI SUV flanked the driveway.

Concho bailed out of his seat, leaving his Colts in their holsters and catching up his 30-06 hunting rifle. He darted to his right, dropping down behind an old wooden watering trough for cover. Della Rice, Bihn Bui, and a third agent slid out the FBI vehicle and took cover at the back of it. The driver keyed the mic on a loudspeaker and made his demands.

"Everyone in the house. This is the FBI. Come out unarmed, with your hands up, and you won't be harmed!"

The sky answered with thunder and a few scattered drops of rain. But for a moment the house remained quiet. Then the front door opened. The shoulder of a man appeared in the gap. Something metallic and dull green perched on it.

"Rocket!" Concho shouted. He snapped his rifle up to fire but the man pulled the trigger on the launcher first.

Such shoulder held rocket launchers had been developed as anti-tank weapons. The FBI's SUV was probably armored but was no tank. The banshee-shrieking missile struck the front of the vehicle and exploded. A fireball ripped off most of the SUV's grill and front end, kicking the wheels up off the ground. The windshield slagged. The agent still inside the vehicle screamed and screamed as molten glass and fire engulfed him.

Concho pulled the trigger on his .30-06. The rifle bucked back against his shoulder. The man with the rocket launcher was slammed against the doorframe as the big bullet impacted. He cried out but wasn't dead. He fell back into the house and the door slammed shut.

Glass shattered in the front windows of the farmhouse. Gun barrels poked through and began to speak. Semi-automatics. Mostly AR-15s it looked like. The tak, tak, tak of three round bursts suggested that some of these people had military training.

Roland Turner and Isaac Parkland returned fire from behind the doors of their SUV. Parkland carried a shotgun. Della Rice had been knocked down by the concussion of the exploding rocket and Bihn Bui dragged her toward safety, if there *were* such a thing in a firefight. Concho emptied his .30-06 to provide cover, then lay down the rifle and drew his two Colts.

More Maverick County deputies and FBI agents worked their way forward, moving to surround the house. The FBI carried AR-15s of their own and that firepower began to tell as it drove the outlaw gunmen away from the front of the house. The barrel of a rocket launcher poked through a window but Concho blasted four shots at it. Whoever held it, ducked back.

The thwap thwap of helicopter rotors approached. This was no attack helicopter like those he'd seen in Afghanistan, but it still had a psychological effect on the perpetrators inside. As Concho darted from behind his water trough to the back of a red El Camino closer to the house, a side door opened and a man rushed through in a panic.

Ten-Wolves tracked the man with his pistols but the fellow threw away his gun and ran like devils dogged his heels. The lawman let him go. The helicopter would track him. He was thinking about Heather Green's daughter. She must be in the house. He needed to reach her.

Darting from the back of the El Camino to the corner of the house, the Ranger began easing along the wall toward the same side door the running man had just fled out of. A second man stepped out that door. This one still had his shotgun, and when he saw Concho his eyes widened and he swung the weapon around. No bullet-proof vest protected him.

Ten-Wolves put two .45 slugs in the fellow's chest. He fell back, his shotgun discharging but only blowing a hole in the dirt at his feet. Concho charged forward. Sudden lightning sizzled purple bolts across the darkening sky. Thunder crackled and the rain came hard, almost cold where it struck his heated body.

He yanked open the side door and peered through. A short hallway stretched into the interior, with paneled walls long out of style. He stepped over the dead man and inside, pistols ready. Steam rose off him from the rain. The place smelled mostly of men living alone. But there was something else, a hint, perhaps, of damp baby powder. It gave him hope.

A man stepped out of a side room into the hallway. Older. In his late fifties or early sixties. Graying. Concho had never seen him before but recognized a family resemblance with the two young men who'd tried to kill him on the highway early this morning. *Their father?*

A large frame Ruger Super Blackhawk .44. magnum swung in the man's right hand. His left hand locked a brutal grip on a young woman's arm. Heather Green. And she held a blanket wrapped bundle that had to be her daughter.

CHAPTER FORTY-TWO

THE MAN WHO HELD ONTO HEATHER'S ARM YANKED THE WOMAN IN front of him as a shield. "You!" he snarled at Concho. "You!"

The gunfire had died away at the front of the house. An injured man moaned loud enough to be heard over the rain drumming on the roof. Concho also heard the shouts of the agents and lawmen outside. They were moving in.

"Drop your weapon!" he ordered. "Release the woman. The FBI will be kicking in your front door any second. No need for you to die!"

"You!" the man said again. "You killed my boys." He swung the Blackhawk up to fire.

The man stood right behind Heather. Concho had no target. He threw himself to the floor, head down. The Ruger .44 sounded like an elephant gun discharging. The bullet whipped over Concho's scalp, skipped off the back of his bullet proof vest and slammed into the floor.

Heather screamed and twisted her body away from her captor. The man shouted angrily as he clamped down harder on her arm. But she no longer served to shield him. Recoil had kicked the big magnum revolver up in the air. He fought the barrel down.

Concho fired from the floor. The man wore a vest of his own. Ten-Wolves shot him in the right leg, through the meat of the thigh. The impact twisted the fellow to his right. The Ruger's second shot smacked into the wall to the left of the Ranger.

The gunman dropped to one knee but still didn't let go of Heather Green. Concho wanted a head shot; he took aim. Heather kicked the man in the back just as the Ranger fired. The .45 slug tore off most of the man's ear but didn't knock him out of the fight. And now, instead of blasting at the lawman again, he turned his weapon on Heather and shot her in the torso just below the breastbone.

"No!" Concho shouted. He fired both Colts. The top two inches of the man's head disintegrated. The magnum fell out of his hand to clunk on the floor. But the damage the gun had already done wasn't reversible.

Concho lunged to his feet and rushed to Heather Green. He still had his guns in his hands. She leaned heavily against the wall, holding her daughter. Gore scrawled the wallpaper behind her and more blood kept flowing. The bullet must have gone all the way through.

Little Winona screamed now. Heather was silent. Her gaze found Concho's. Then she looked down at her child. "The bullet didn't...hit her," she said. She started to slide down the wall and Concho caught her shoulders and eased her to the floor.

Running footsteps made Ten-Wolves look up. Bihn Bui stepped into the hallway, a Sig 9mm in his hands. He took in the scene instantly, holstered his pistol.

"Get an ambulance," Concho ordered. The man ran to obey.

"It won't matter," Heather said. "I can feel it. A big hole in my stomach. A big, big hole."

"Yeah," Concho said, his voice gone hoarse. He glanced at Winona.

"Take her!" Heather said. She lifted her arms slightly.

Concho holstered his Colts and took the baby. She wasn't much heavier than the guns. He pulled her close to his chest.

She stopped screaming, although her small body still rocked with sobs.

"You have to make sure," Heather said.

"Make sure of what?" Concho asked, though he was sure he knew.

"Make sure she's taken care of. Find someone to love her. Raise her."

"I don't..."

"Please. I trust you. You're the only one I can. Please!"

"All right."

A smile flickered across Heather's face. She turned her gaze toward her daughter. And the life froze and went out of her eyes.

Concho rose slowly to his feet. Winona stopped crying, though her face was still red and splotched. A pacifier had been pinned to the child's pink nightdress. Ten-Wolves offered it to the girl and she took it. He took a deep breath that shuddered in his chest.

———

AFTER SNOW SPOKE to Ten-Wolves directly at the wreck site, he knew the man would recognize him too easily in the future if he saw him on his motorcycle. He dropped by a car rental shop and picked up a nondescript gray Hyundai Elantra. He then rented an enclosed motorcycle trailer and loaded his bike in the back. Ten-Wolves was still his best lead to the woman he wanted to kill and a Hyundai pulling a trailer would be the last vehicle anyone would expect to be following them. He'd driven to the hospital and waited for the Ranger to emerge.

It wasn't long before Ten-Wolves obliged. He came out of the building in the company of a local sheriff. Both men appeared excited as they climbed into a police SUV and tore out. He followed them as best he could, but when they left Eagle Pass and headed down dirt roads with no traffic he had to drop far back to keep from being spotted.

By the time he'd sussed out the lawmen's destination, using tire tracks left in the wet roads by the police vehicles, the gunfight at the ranch house was over. He rolled slowly along the road as if he belonged there. A deputy waved him past but he slowed and stopped.

The deputy kept his hand on a gun as he approached the car and trailer, but relaxed slightly as he recognized that Snow was alone and that both hands were on the steering wheel where they could be seen. The assassin had also tucked his long hair up under a cowboy hat to make himself look more like a local.

"What's it all about, Officer?" Snow asked.

"This is a crime scene," the man replied. "You move along."

Snow offered up a hurt look. "I was just curious."

"Read the papers like everyone else. Move along or I'll arrest you for obstruction of justice."

Snow let off the brake and eased away, though he did a little neck craning to see what he could see. The deputy would expect it. He wasn't able to pick up much information other than there were FBI vehicles on the scene as well as Maverick County officers.

One thing the FBI investigated was kidnapping, and a kidnapping that King Modine and his bunch were involved in had set Snow's current assignment in motion. He'd never been told where Modine lived but was skeptical of coincidences.

Three quarters of a mile past the farmhouse, Snow pulled over to the side next to a tall oak tree. A hard burst of rain had muddied the ditches but had trailed past by now, leaving the skies gray. Taking a pair of binoculars with him, he climbed the wet oak and took a look back toward the site.

He immediately recognized the tall figure of Concho standing in the yard talking to several other law officers, including a tall black woman in an FBI windbreaker. Ten-Wolves held a blanket-wrapped bundle in his arms.

The bundle moved. It was alive, which made it likely to be a child. The woman—Heather Green—had a child. His handler had found that out and reported it to him. And Snow was pretty sure someone with the Modine faction had taken it from the people who'd been keeping it over on Mesa Street. He could see a couple of the perps from the house being shoved into the back of a police SUV. Neither of them was King Modine but he still had a good hunch the kid was Green's.

Letting the binoculars hang down around his neck, Snow pulled out his cell phone and called his handler. The man answered. "Is this important?"

"I'm watching a certain Texas Ranger holding a baby after a raid on an isolated farmhouse. Pretty sure it's Green's baby, which likely means the raid hit the Modines. I don't see King but he might be dead inside."

"Dammit!"

"I've been trying to use Ten-Wolves to lead me to the girl, but it's starting to look like a mistake to let him keep working this case."

The man on the other end of the line sighed. "Kill him! ASAP."

"And the girl?"

"The girl was a danger to the Modines. Not to me. I've got some calls to make. To find out if they *were* the ones hit. If so, and they're dead, we can forget the girl. I'll inform you either way."

"Right."

Snow hung up. He pushed the binoculars back up to his eyes and took a look through. A chill caressed him, though the day was warm enough. Ten-Wolves still stood in the yard. Momentarily alone. He certainly couldn't see Snow in his tree at this distance but stared in this direction as if realizing he was being observed.

Snow recalled a stray comment King Modine had made to him several days ago about Ten-Wolves. "Some people even claim he's magic."

"Just a man," Snow muttered to himself. "I'll prove it when I put him down."

CHAPTER FORTY-THREE

TEN-WOLVES WALKED AWAY FROM HEATHER GREEN'S BODY, UP the hallway and into a large living area on the left. He carried Winona with him and the child lay quiet. He could feel her heartbeat through the blankets, though, and the coal-heat of her little body. He wondered if she were hungry, or if she needed a diaper change. She wasn't squirming or crying so maybe she was OK on both counts for now.

The outlaws in the house had made their stand in the living room. Two bodies lay sprawled in death amid shattered furniture and other debris. The windows were broken out. Bullets had splintered the frames. A LAWS rocket launcher lay discarded on the floor.

Concho walked through it all and out the front door, which hung awry on its hinges. The hard shower of moments ago had already fallen away to a few scattered drops. An ambulance had arrived and two paramedics were looking for work. One approached Concho.

"Inside," he said, waving the man past him. "But I think they're all dead."

Della Rice and Bihn Bui stood together a dozen paces away from the back of their ruined SUV, which still held a murdered agent in the driver's seat. Both were damp from rain, though Bihn held a large umbrella over his boss that he'd gotten from somewhere.

Ten-Wolves could smell scorched metal and plastic, and another scent he recognized from Afghanistan as burnt flesh. He put his hand over Winona's mouth and nose to try and keep her from smelling the scent. He knew it would do no good but the baby already had too much experience with death.

Rice talked on the phone. Parkland and Turner leaned against their own vehicle. Their hats dripped rainwater. Both men drank from large plastic bottles of spring water. Concho joined them.

"Is that..." Parkland said, gesturing at the child.

"Winona Green. An orphan now."

Both Parkland and Turner winced. Turner plucked a water bottle out of the back seat of his SUV. He twisted off the cap and offered it to Concho, who took it and downed half of it in a couple of greedy gulps.

"You're bleeding again," Turner said. "Not as bad as before."

Concho became aware of the matted hair on the left side of his head. "Guess I tore a stitch or two."

Della Rice clicked off her phone call and walked over to the three officers, her hair gone frizzy in the dampness. Twin emotions of anger and upset shifted across her face. Bihn trailed her with the umbrella, his own face impassive.

"Well, that didn't go as planned," Rice said.

"Plans seldom survive first contact with the enemy," Concho said, his voice flat.

"Yeah," Rice said. "And we lost a man because of it. Mostly my fault."

"We saved a child," Turner countered, pointing to the baby in Concho's arms.

"Yes," Rice said. "And we did something else." She glanced at Ten-Wolves. "The gray-haired man you killed inside. Bihn showed me a picture. It's definitely King Modine. We've been looking for him for months."

"For what?" Concho asked.

"Terrorist. Of the homegrown variety. Did more than just talk about overthrowing the government. He was an organizer. And running drugs to finance his operations. Based originally in San Antonio. He disappeared right after Christmas. Apparently he's been hiding out here."

"He got any sons?" Concho asked.

"Three according to our records. All in their twenties. But they disappeared along with him. Apparently, his wife left him when he started getting caught up in conspiracy theories about ten years ago. She died shortly after. Under mysterious circumstances, I might add."

"Pretty sure two of the sons jumped me this morning along the highway."

"Ah," Rice said. "That where you got the souvenir?" She pointed to the stitched-up gash in his scalp.

"Yes. But they got it worse. And when the King and I faced off inside he claimed I'd 'killed his boys.'"

Rice frowned. "What did they have against you?"

"You remember the report I sent you about finding Heather Green in the trunk of that Monte Carlo? Course, I didn't know her name then. Anyway, the good old boys who came after me this morning were driving the green Jeep I described in that report. They were trying to get Heather then. I broke it up."

"Why?"

"I think King was trying his revolutionary game here but adding a new wrinkle."

"Kidnapping?"

"They wanted Heather for something. I'm just not sure what. And that was her inside just now. Shot. Bihn saw her."

Bihn winced.

"Damn," Rice said. "I didn't realize it was the same woman. She going to make it?"

Concho shook his head. "Modine killed her before I killed him. This," he hefted the baby he held, "is her daughter, Winona."

Rice glanced at Winona. Her sharp featured face softened for a moment, then hardened again as she looked back at Concho. "So somehow they picked up Green after she escaped from whoever tried to kill her yesterday. If they wanted her dead, why didn't they kill her immediately?"

Ten-Wolves shrugged. "Something we still don't know yet. But there's more we do know."

"What?"

"I didn't notice inside but did King Modine have any tattoos?"

"Not in our original reports on him."

She glanced at Bihn and he nodded. "I'll find out," he said, leaving them.

"You're thinking about that symbol we found written in blood on the wall at the Salas home," Rice continued to the Ranger.

"Yep," Concho said. "It was also etched on a shell casing Roland Turner found at the scene where someone *first* tried to shoot Heather. The two Modine sons I killed had the same image tattooed on their hands. I also saw it on a third man at a local bus station. I think he might be the third son. The symbolism didn't quite register until now."

"What is it? Some kind of token of their movement?"

"Exactly." He handed Winona to Isaak Parkland and took out his cell phone. Swiping through it to the pictures he'd saved from the morning wreck, he called up one image of the tattoo and enlarged it. "A straight razor. But you see the flair at the tip and the base of the handle? They curve in opposite directions."

"I see it," Rice said. "So?"

"I've been thinking about it. The familiarity of it. The razor is open at ninety degrees. And if you put two of these tats back-to-back, it looks like a variant of a swastika."

"What?" Rice demanded. She leaned closer to the image on the phone.

Roland Turner gave a grunt as if it had suddenly become clear to him as well.

A small gasp escaped Rice's mouth. "I see it now. I'd never have noticed."

"I should have," Turner said. You can't unsee it once you catch it."

"Better get Bihn to check the other dead men inside, too," Ten-Wolves said. "And did we take any of them alive?"

"Two," Rice answered. "They're in the back of our other SUV."

"Let's have a look."

The Ranger glanced at Parkland, who looked a little bit uncomfortable holding the tiny form of Winona Green. He took her back. Bihn returned and held up his own phone to show them a picture. A half open straight razor.

"It was on the back of King Modine's neck," he said. "Down low enough to be covered by a shirt."

"Thanks, Bihn," Della said. "Could you check the other dead perps, too? See if they have anything similar?"

"Will do."

Concho was already headed for the FBI's second SUV. The others fell in with him. An agent in a blue windbreaker opened the vehicle's back door as they approached.

"Bring them out!" Rice ordered.

The agent nodded. He reached in and pulled a man out by his arm—a thin fellow with sandy hair and fear written on his face. His hands were cuffed behind him. The razor tattoo showed on his lower right arm.

"What's your name?" Rice demanded.

The fellow opened his mouth but a hard voice from inside the SUV snapped, "Tell 'em nothin'!"

The sandy haired fellow clicked his mouth shut. The FBI

agent leaned back into the SUV and grabbed hold of a second man. This one struggled and Roland Turner had to help, but they got him out and shoved him against the vehicle. He was a big man, nearly as tall as Concho. Thick reddish chest hair curled out of the top of his shirt. Ten-Wolves recognized him immediately.

"Cleaned up some since I saw you at the bus stop," he said.

"What were you doing there?"

The man spat at Concho, who dodged it.

Turner drew his nightstick and pushed it up under the outlaw's chin. "Behave!" he ordered.

"Ain't answering any questions. I want my lawyer."

"You know this dude?" Rice asked Ten-Wolves.

"I saw him a couple of nights ago. At a local bus station. He pretended to be homeless, but I figure he was scoping the place out. Maybe to kidnap someone who wouldn't be noticed as missing. Pretty sure this is another of King Modine's sons. They were all hairy like that. Except the youngest. This one's got the razor tat on the back of his hand."

Rice nodded at the agent standing next to the perp, who twisted the big man around so they could see his cuffed hands. The tattoo was there.

"Separate the two of them," Rice ordered. "We'll talk to them one at a time." She glanced back at Concho. "We've still got questions but it looks like we're mostly done. You should go home, get some rest and...do whatever you need to do to see about the kid."

Concho shook his head. "It's a long way from over," he said as soon as the perps were out of earshot.

"What do you mean?"

"Two things. One, we still have an assassin out there. The one who shot up Sheriff Parkland's vehicle and killed Kerry Keegan."

"You don't figure he's one of this bunch at the farm?"

"No. From everything I've heard of him, he's a pro. He

wouldn't have been here and he wouldn't have been taken so easily."

Rice frowned. Parkland backed Concho up. "He's right. I got a glimpse of the fellow. He's a pro's pro. Cool as an icehouse."

"All right," Rice said. "But if he was hired by the Modines he's not gonna get paid and probably won't hang around."

"He might have been helping the Modines out with Heather Green but he's no homegrown terrorist. Somebody else trained him and set him on this track."

"And that's your point two?" Rice asked.

"Yeah, there's someone else out there we don't know about. And they're pulling the strings."

"Any leads as to who?"

"Just one. I believe Judge Janet Peregrino may have some idea. Somebody called in a favor from her regarding getting Martino Salas out of jail. And then Martino was killed. Probably by our professional assassin. When I talked to her before, she was closed mouthed, but with Salas's death, maybe she'll loosen up."

"All right," Della said. "Let's go." She paused. "Uhm, what are you going to do with..." she gestured, "the baby?"

"We'll take her along. The Judge has kids. But let's stop and get some formula and diapers on the way. I think she's a little damp."

"You know how to change a diaper?" Parkland asked.

"I can field strip an M16 or a Colt .45. Isn't it about the same thing?"

"I'll do it," Roland Turner said.

Everybody looked at him questioningly. He shrugged.

"That's right," Parkland said. "He and his wife volunteer at the pediatric clinic in Eagle Pass. I reckon he's got some experience."

Turner looked embarrassed but didn't say anything.

"OK," Concho said. "We've got every specialist with us we could need. Let's roll."

They started toward the vehicles. Concho paused. It felt as if something touched his neck. His scalp prickled. His head came up and he stared off into the distance. He could see nothing. Could smell or hear nothing. But something was there.

He'd felt the same touch only a day earlier outside the Salas home. The cold-eyed watcher from the shadows had come back. He was being stalked.

CHAPTER FORTY-FOUR

CONCHO CLEANED THE WARPAINT OFF HIS FACE AND THE BLOOD out of his hair as best he could on the drive to 111 Rio Grande Drive and the house of Judge Janet Peregrino. Peregrino didn't seem happy to see the Ranger back so soon, and she wasn't impressed with either Sheriff Parkland or Della Rice and the FBI either. Roland Turner and Bihn Bui remained outside with the vehicles. Turner was taking care of little Winona Green. They'd changed her and fed her on the way.

"I've already told Ranger Ten-Wolves everything I could," Peregrino said. "I'm not at liberty to discuss the issue further."

"Even though Martino Salas was killed because *you* signed his bail form?" Concho asked, allowing the anger he felt show in his voice.

Peregrino returned the anger note for note. "I'm sorry that occurred but Salas was undercover by his own choice. He knew the risks."

"What?" Ten-Wolves and Rice blurted at the same instant.

Peregrino looked chagrined as she realized she'd given them some information she shouldn't have. Her mouth worked back and forth but she held her tongue.

"Who told you Salas was undercover?" Concho asked.

"I'm not giving you that name. We've already covered that."

"He wasn't undercover with the FBI," Rice snapped.

"Nor any of the local police forces," Parkland added.

"Not my business," Peregrino replied.

'So who does that leave?" Concho asked. He kept his gaze laser focused on the judge.

"Homeland Security," Parkland said.

"Or the CIA," Della Rice added.

Peregrino's cheek twitched at mention of the CIA. In the next few seconds, a slew of memories exploded through Concho's mind and he knew why he'd been having his most recent flashbacks to Afghanistan.

In the aftermath of his best friend's death by IED in 2009, Ten-Wolves had rampaged through a group of Afghani fighters, killing every one that tried to kill him. He'd chased a last enemy up the stairs in a ruined house only to find an unknown soldier in army fatigues standing over the wounded rebel. Captain Jack Travers of the Green Beret was there as well.

Concho demanded the name of the Afghan, who was obviously important to Travers and the other soldier.

"You don't need to know that, grunt," the second soldier had said.

Concho bristled but Travers soothed the waters and introduced the man as, Hieronymus Gall, a name not easy to forget. It hadn't been the last time he'd seen Gall during the war. Only a few weeks later, he'd talked to both Travers and Gall again.

A US Ranger firebase. Nighttime; the base lay quiet. The 75th Ranger regiment had been pulled back from the front lines only a few days before. They rested, doing all the things soldiers do during the boring moments when they're not fighting or training to fight.

Concho had been practicing his usual activities: eating, reading, sleeping. Then he was summoned. He didn't know why. A private who was not a ranger woke him and told him to report to the Humvee he'd find parked next to the mess tent. It promised a break in routine so he went.

The back of the vehicle opened as Concho approached. The hand of a shadow gestured him inside. He didn't like it but he'd come this far. He swung into the Humvee. The back closed. A small light came on.

Two men faced him. One was Captain Jack Travers, although he wore the insignia of a lieutenant colonel now. He'd been promoted. The other was Hieronymus Gall. Concho didn't like Gall. It wasn't the eyes as pale as mother-of-pearl, or the flushed and jowly face. It was an aura the man gave off, almost a scent. Although not one that had any name.

"What's he doing here, Sir?" Concho asked Travers.

"He's part of what I want to talk to you about."

Concho forced his gaze away from Gall to meet Travers' agate eyes. "And what is that?"

"First, whether you accept what I tell you or not, our conversation can't be shared with anyone. You OK with that?"

Concho considered. He wasn't fond of secrets but he'd kept enough in his day. "All right."

Travers nodded, then continued, "You may have noticed this war is a little different than most the US has fought. Not many large-scale battles or offensives. Small strikes and counterstrikes. A few men going in to do a job and getting back out. It's a war for specialists."

"So?"

"So, we don't have enough specialists."

"You mean like the Green Berets and the Seals?"

"Exactly!" Gall said.

Concho ignored him, keeping his focus on Travers.

"As he says," Travers continued. "So, we're building a few more. Right here on the ground in Afghanistan. And we want you on a team."

"Why?"

"An obvious question. With an obvious answer. We've seen you in action. And," he grinned, "we've been checking up on you. You've got high marks in every aspect of modern warfare. You're obviously a very good soldier. But there's more—"

"You're a killer!" Gall said.

Concho felt a flinch but didn't let himself respond verbally. He kept looking at Travers, who gave Gall a glare. When the lieutenant colonel turned back to Ten-Wolves, he spoke softly.

"It's not about killing," he said. "It's about surviving. And about helping others survive while still doing a tough job. We're going to carve a few special units out of the rangers. They'll be organized in twelve-man teams, what we call ODA's."

"Operational detachment alpha."

"You know it?"

"I've read about the Green Berets."

"Yes. You'll be serving with some of the best soldiers who've ever lived. It'll be dangerous. I won't lie. But you'll be making a difference. More than you ever could as a soldier on the line. What do you say?"

Concho glanced from Travers to Gall, and back. "He gonna be there?"

"Major Gall is with army intelligence. He's involved with the recruiting, not with the training or deployment. Certainly not on the battlefield."

"I'll do it."

Concho came back to Judge Peregrino's study as his quick reverie faded. He'd seen Travers many more times during the war. Had worked closely with him. He'd also learned quite a bit about Hieronymus Gall.

He'd seen the intelligent officer's handiwork after interrogations, men with razor sharp cuts to the most delicate parts of their bodies, places where a little salt or other chemical rubbed into a wound could produce agony. Yes, the men were enemies, but they still didn't deserve that treatment.

He'd had only one contact with Gall after arriving home from the war. Three years after coming back to the States, Gall called Concho out of the blue and invited him to join the CIA. He'd told the man where he could stick his invitation.

"Let's leave the Judge alone for now," Concho said suddenly.

Parkland and Rice both stared at him. Rice looked irritated, but Parkland nodded and turned to leave. Ten-Wolves followed the Sheriff. Rice came reluctantly after. Peregrino merely watched them go with a confused look on her face.

"What was that all about?" Rice demanded as soon as they stepped outside under the late afternoon sky.

"The Judge is not going to give us a name," Concho said. "But she doesn't have to. I know it. As soon as you mentioned CIA and Peregrino's face twitched, I knew who we were dealing with."

"And that is?" Rice snapped, unable to keep the skeptical snideness out of her voice.

"Hieronymus Gall. But before we deal with him, we need to take care of his assassin. I'm pretty sure he followed us here."

"I didn't see any tail," Parkland said.

"Oh, don't worry, Sheriff," Rice quipped. "It's sure knowledge. Our Indian friend here just plucked it out of the cosmic beyond with his mystical powers. Like everything else he just told us."

"If I'm wrong, then no harm," Ten-Wolves said calmly. "But I met Gall during the war. I paid attention to the way he did things. He favored a straight razor for interrogations. And he's in the CIA now. He once tried to recruit me. As for the assassin, we know he's a pro and the CIA has the best. Even if the man's not trailing us at the moment, he's gonna keep coming. I'm not sure what he wants. Maybe me. Maybe it has something to do with Heather's daughter. But he's out there. I'm not taking a chance on the child being hurt."

"I'm with you," Parkland said.

Rice shook her head. "You've got no hard evidence of any of this."

"If I'm wrong, we're spinning our wheels. We waste a little time. But if I'm right..."

Rice breathed out a sigh that lasted for a good two seconds. "All right," she finally said. "What do you want us to do?"

"We convoy back to the sheriff's office. Then, Della, I'd ask that you and Bihn find out as much as you can about Hieronymus Gall and his current location. I'll bet it's in Texas. Leave the assassin to me."

"What are you planning?"

Concho flashed a grin. "I don't know yet but I'll figure something out soon enough."

CHAPTER FORTY-FIVE

Snow tracked the two law vehicles from Rio Grande Drive to the Maverick County Sheriff's office. He found an inconspicuous parking space at a nearby industrial site and settled in to watch. The SUV marked with the letters "FBI" drove off. Concho Ten-Wolves went inside the building with the Sheriff and a black deputy. He had the baby with him.

Time passed. Afternoon turned to evening. Vehicles came and went. As darkness fell, Snow prepared his motorcycle for quick unloading from the trailer. He'd seen a lot of bikes around Eagle Pass. In the dark, his would be no more noticeable than any other. And if it came to a chase, his Magna could run down just about any car. While he waited, he got a call.

"Where are you at?" the hoarse voice asked over the phone.

"Watching a sheriff's office. Ten-Wolves is inside."

"I've got news. The woman you were hired to kill. Heather Green. She's dead. King Modine shot her during a raid on the Modine compound. You've only got one contract left to fulfill."

"Gotcha. I'll take Ten-Wolves as soon as I can isolate him."

The phone voice dripped with venom as it added, "Extreme prejudice!"

"Noted."

"Oh, and King Modine is dead, too. Ten-Wolves killed him. He also killed two of the man's sons after they tried to ambush him on the road this morning."

So that's who they were, Snow thought. He might have guessed.

With Modine dead, the potential side jobs the older man offered Snow were off the table. It didn't matter. He'd find work. The idea of freelancing appealed to him and he knew where to look for those who wanted his particular specialty. However, he also knew King Modine had been one of his handler's secret assets.

"Modine's death going to cause you issues?" he asked.

"Changes some things around but his kind are a dime a dozen. I'll find a replacement soon enough."

"Good."

"Just finish Ten-Wolves!"

The phone went dead.

Snow tucked the cell back in his pocket. A few words spilled into his awareness. He murmured them out loud. "He writes in white lines with a razor, in the language of carnivores. And the white becomes red."

Almost immediately, a Dodge Ram 1500 pickup pulled around from the back of the building and parked out front. A man got out and Ten-Wolves came out of the building to join him. Ten-Wolves held the bundled-up child in his arms. The two men exchanged greetings and Concho took the keys, then climbed into the Dodge. It was just after 8:00 PM.

A few minutes passed, in which—Snow imagined—the child was strapped into some kind of car seat. Even the cops were supposed to obey those laws. Then the Dodge wheeled out of the parking lot and drove off in the direction of the Kickapoo reservation.

This was Snow's chance. The Modines would have rightly gotten the blame for their attack on Ten-Wolves. They'd probably been blamed for *his* attack against Heather Green and the

Sheriff on the road. With the Modines dead and the child recovered, the Ranger should figure it was all over. He'd be relaxing at case's end.

Under cover of darkness and on the sparsely traveled roads leading to the reservation, Snow could ambush the man and finish his final contract. Wheeling his bike out of the trailer, he fired it up and took off in pursuit.

They headed down FM 1021 toward Tierra Soberana Boulevard. An occasional car passed. Snow hung back. They reached the Shell station near where Ten-Wolves had been involved in that firefight earlier in the day. The wreckage had long since been cleared.

The Ranger turned onto Tierra Soberana and slowed to twenty-five MPH, the speed limit. Snow turned, too, after flicking off the lights on his bike. He came up behind the lawman's Dodge. No traffic now. He could feel the butt of the shotgun against his left leg.

Excitement fizzed in his bloodstream. His head seemed to expand. The thought of coming violence bit him like a shot of whiskey. Normally, he felt icily calm before a hit, but there was something about this Texas Ranger. The man was half feral, dangerous. It was almost a disappointment that he'd made himself so vulnerable.

"Even the tiger sleeps," he murmured, as he cranked the throttle on his Magna.

The big 750cc bike responded instantly. They surged up beside the truck. Snow flicked on his halogen headlight to startle the driver. The pickup slowed in surprise. Snow whipped up the shotgun into his left hand.

Something was wrong. He couldn't see the man behind the wheel. Something blocked his view. It took him an instant to realize. Bullet-proof vests had been strapped across the glass from inside.

A trap!

He grabbed for the throttle. A big shadow exploded out of the back of the pickup and swooped down on him.

———

IN THE FEW hours that Concho had been at Parkland's office, he'd hatched a plan. He'd called his mechanic friend from the Rez, John Gray-Dove. John swung by, one of the many vehicles the assassin would have seen coming in and out of the area. The Sheriff's Office owned their own garage out back of the building for vehicle maintenance. John used their tools to make a few modifications on an older model Dodge Ram pickup, which Concho had borrowed once before from Parkland.

When the Dodge pulled out of the garage and around to the front of the building where the assassin would be able to see it, it had two men in it. One lay on the floor in the extended cab area of the Dodge. The other got out and gave Concho the keys. The one on the floor was Isaac Parkland himself. The Sheriff wanted payback on the assassin who'd killed his deputy.

Concho climbed in and tossed the blanket-wrapped sack of sugar he carried on the floor. Little Winona Green wasn't coming along on this expedition, although Ten-Wolves wanted the cold-eyed watcher to believe she was.

Concho and Parkland switched places. Parkland drove as they left the parking lot and headed for the Rez. In the darkness, with no lights showing inside the truck, the exchange wouldn't be noticed.

Ten-Wolves climbed through the newly opened back panel of the pickup into the false tool chest attached to the bed. It was nothing more than thin slats of wood painted silver to look like steel. The space felt cramped for the big man but no more than flying coach with a modern airline. He reapplied his warpaint and waited.

When he heard the motorcycle accelerate alongside the truck, Concho pressed a latch inside the fake chest. It collapsed and he exploded up through it. A speeding shadow darted alongside the Dodge. Its lone headlight punched a hole in the darkness.

Concho had his guns strapped in their holsters but wanted to take the assassin alive. To question him about Hieronymus Gall. He dove over the side of the truck, slammed hard into the motorcycle and its rider—Snow.

The rider had drawn a shotgun but had no time to use it. The gun went flying. The handlebars on the bike twisted. The front end locked up in a screech of rubber. Concho and Snow crashed into pavement with the lawman on top. The bike flipped over them, shedding parts as it pirouetted from one wheel to the other.

Concho had prepared for his leap. He wore thick jeans and two heavy work shirts with the sleeves buttoned down. A bullet-proof vest had gone on over that. He wore gloves and a policeman's riot helmet. The front grill of his helmet smashed into the acrylic face plate of Snow's full-face helm. The assassin grunted as his back slammed into the pavement with two hundred and fifty pounds of Concho's weight on top of him.

But Snow's strength and reflexes were honed to a fever pitch. Even as the pain of impact shocked through his entire body, he was twisting his form, his arms and knees coming up. He flipped the big Ranger onto his side. His fist flashed toward Ten-Wolves' face.

The punch smacked into Concho's open palm. The Ranger closed his hand, trying to crush the smaller man's fist. Snow snapped a knee at his groin but caught his thigh instead.

The assassin yanked free, surged to his feet. Concho rose just as quickly. The motorcycle lay wrecked a few feet away but its headlight faced them and still burned, turning a small stretch of highway into an arena.

Snow's hand darted under his jacket for the pistol in his shoulder holster. Ten-Wolves lunged. His hand caught the assassin's wrist as Snow pulled his gun. A savage twist of his grip and the weapon went flying.

Parkland had brought the Dodge pickup to a sliding stop and bailed out. He had his service pistol drawn but Concho and the assassin were too close together to risk a shot. Besides, he knew the plan was to take the man alive.

Snow punched Concho in the side. The blow did nothing against the Ranger's bullet-proof vest. The lawman snapped a kick in return. It didn't look like Snow wore a vest. The Ranger's boot connected directly to the man's sternum. It knocked him back a few steps but seemed to have no other effect, even though Ten-Wolves put a lot of power into it.

Snow bent and whipped a knife free from his boot. It flashed like a six-inch fang in the light. Parkland fired to protect Concho's life. The bullet hit Snow in the side and the assassin took two steps to the left before regaining his balance. Then he lunged toward the Ranger, ignoring the Sheriff and his gun as the blade swung across for a disemboweling blow.

Ten-Wolves caught the wrist as the hand darted toward him. He twisted it upward, his fingers crushing down. Snow grunted. His fingers spasmed; the knife started to drop. Snow's other hand swept in, plucked the blade from his own loosening grasp. He stabbed upward, aiming for the Ranger's face.

The blade slid along Concho's vest. Concho jerked his head back. The knife tip sliced across his chin, leaving only a shallow scratch. Ten-Wolves powered forward, grabbing Snow's other arm to keep the blade away as he slammed the smaller assassin up against the rear end of the Dodge.

The two men strained with the blade. Concho let go of Snow's right hand and struck an open-handed blow up under the face shield on the assassin's helmet. The hit ripped the shield up and off, slamming Snow's helmeted head back against the truck.

In that instant while Snow was stunned, the Ranger recognized the man he faced as the strange bystander who'd spoken to him only this morning just a short distance from this spot. It didn't stop him from twisting his opponent's knife hand around and plunging the blade down into the right side of the killer's chest. The blow was meant to wound, not to kill, but the tip of the blade did neither as it struck metal and grated off to one side.

Surprise startled Concho. Snow got his feet under him. He grabbed at a scabbard on his belt for a second knife. Concho head butted him. The grill of Ten-Wolves' riot helmet pulped Snow's mouth and nose. He forced the big knife upward again, bending Snow's left wrist back, pressing the tip against the assassin's neck. The killer's right hand now grabbed the lawman's wrist, straining to hold it back and keep the knife from his throat.

Blood ran down Concho's face from the reopened gash on his scalp. He ignored it. "Give it up!" he snapped. "You're beaten."

"I'll kill everything you love," Snow growled.

Rage surged in the lawman's heart. A kaleidoscope of faces flashed across his mind. Kerry Keegan—dead. Isaac Parkland—wounded. Terrill Hoight—hospitalized. Heather Green—dead. With a snarl, he shoved upward on the knife with all his strength. Snow's wrist snapped. The blade sheared in under the chin and buried itself to the hilt in the assassin's mouth.

Snow choked, spewing blood that spattered Concho. His good hand flailed at the Ranger and fell away. His blue eyes filmed over. Concho stepped back, still holding onto the hilt of the knife. The blade came free of the assassin's mouth with a click of steel against teeth. The man slid slowly to earth.

Concho stood gasping for breath for a long moment, then bent down toward the assassin's body. He unsnapped the man's helmet strap, pulled it off, and let it roll away on the pavement.

Snow's long, white blond hair hung down his back in a ponytail. Still in a rage, hardly thinking, Concho grasped the hair just in front of the leather thong that held it together and cut the ponytail away with a single swipe of the bloody blade.

Parkland approached. He did not remark on his friend's act, only said, "I hit him when I shot. I know I did."

"He's wearing some kind of vest," Concho replied tiredly. "It turned the tip of the knife, too."

He grasped the neck of Snow's T-shirt and slashed it open. A very fine metallic mesh clung close to the assassin's skin under the shirt—apparently impervious to bullet or blade.

"That's gotta be government issue," Ten-Wolves said.

"The CIA," Parkland agreed. "Like you figured."

"Hieronymus Gall," Concho replied. He dropped the knife into Snow's lap, then straightened and walked past Parkland toward the front of the truck. "Will you call Della Rice? I've gotta sit down."

He still carried the length of hair he'd taken from the killer. His first scalp. He wondered if it would be his last.

CHAPTER FORTY-SIX

WORD WENT OUT. PEOPLE ARRIVED. BUT ONLY A LIMITED NUMBER and only those approved either by Concho or by someone he implicitly trusted. Even the ambulance that showed up to get the assassin's body was FBI. Ten-Wolves didn't want any word getting anywhere until he was ready for it.

A paramedic stitched up Concho's scalp wound again. He used alcohol swabs to remove the blood from the Ranger's face, some of it Snow's, some of it not. He didn't mess with the warpaint. Concho took off the top shirt he wore and the gloves, which were clotted with the assassin's gore.

"Without that paint you'd look vaguely presentable," Della Rice said to him when she arrived.

"You think I'd pass muster at Parrilla De San Miguel?"

"They might let you in at the KFC down the street."

Concho sighed. "This is probably the only time you'll ever hear me say this, but I'm not particularly hungry."

"You better go to the hospital. Clearly your concussion has returned."

"Did you get the information I asked for on Hieronymus Gall?"

"You were wrong about one thing. He's not in Texas."

"Oh? Where then?"

The woman's face dimpled, making her look younger and less hardened. "Mexico," she said. "Piedras Negras. Right across the bridge."

Concho offered a wry grin in return. "Two miles south of Eagle Pass. Doesn't seem I was too far off."

"I must admit, a lot closer than I expected. You have a way of being right even when you arrive at your conclusions by wrong means."

"That must have been hard for you to say."

"If you tell anyone, I'll deny it."

"I know you will. Give me Gall's exact location."

Rice didn't say anything immediately. She squatted next to the assassin's body and studied it.

"You see the letters C I A tattooed on his eyelids?" Concho asked.

Rice looked startled. She leaned closer to the body, then huffed a quick breath as she glanced back up at the Ranger with a bit of an eye roll. "You're an ass, Ten-Wolves."

"But I'm very good at it."

Rice shook her head, then added. "I've got Gall's address. But what do you plan to do with it? You were expecting this," she gestured at Snow's body, "to provide you with a link to Gall. That's not happening. And we don't have any hard evidence to arrest him on. Besides, you couldn't arrest him in Mexico anyway."

"I'm gonna do what I do best."

"Which is?"

"Shake some trees. Gall knows me and I know him. I'm sure he's got plenty of skeletons in his attic. And I'm not speaking figuratively. Maybe if I shake him, some will fall out."

"The FBI can't be involved. I can't go along."

"I understand."

"Who you going to take with you?"

"No one. I'm going in with the element of surprise."

"So you think. But if this guy is as dangerous as you say he is, he might be waiting for you."

"Guess I'll find out."

Rice rose to her feet. She drew a business card out of the pocket of her suit jacket and handed it over. The card was blank except for a typed address on one side, with no name attached. "That's it. But you didn't get it from me."

"Thanks."

"Be careful."

"As best I can."

———

HIERONYMUS GALL, who liked for his friends to call him "Hero," except he had no close friends to do so, mixed himself a third Scotch and water. He wasn't supposed to drink alcohol. But what did it matter now? He wasn't going to hurt his liver any more than it had already been hurt.

Besides, it was almost 3:00 AM and he had yet to hear from his operative in Eagle Pass. Not like Snow. The man was punctual almost to a fault, which was something Gall appreciated. He'd been that way himself before he got sick.

Possibly, the job of isolating Ten-Wolves and assassinating him was just taking longer than normal. Gall knew the Ranger and he'd be a wily target. It was also possible Snow had failed and the Ranger still lived. If so, he might have expected to hear from other assets in the area, but those—too—had been silent.

He made his way slowly upstairs into the room he'd been using as a bedroom, then stepped out onto the balcony. The villa where he was staying belonged to a colleague in the Mexican intelligence community. It sat upon a small hill looking out over the town of Piedra Negras, which translated as "black stones." Coal.

Piedra Negras was often referred to as a "sister" city to Eagle Pass, Texas, just across the Rio Grande, but it was certainly a big sister, with a population in the metropolitan area of about a quarter million. Eagle Pass held only about thirty thousand. At 3:00 in the morning, even this city seemed mostly asleep. Lights winked here and there but traffic was almost nonexistent.

Gall finished his Scotch. It had gone fast. He chewed the ice, then stepped back inside. He looked longingly at his bed but there was no way he could sleep now. Maybe if he had another Scotch. He went downstairs, stopping first by the bathroom, which dominated his life of late.

His next step was the study, where a spirits vault held just about every liquor imaginable. A dim light illuminated it, striking amber and burgundy and silver gleams across the bottles. As he started toward it, he noticed the top of the mahogany desk to his left. It had been clear of clutter when last he'd passed here. Now, something lay upon it, something like a cloth or scarf. He couldn't quite make it out.

A razor line of fear traced its way down his back. He spun, looking everywhere for an intruder. He saw none. His right hand slid into the pocket of his silk housecoat, grasping the butt of the two-shot Derringer pistol inside. He drew it.

"Who's there?" he demanded.

No answer came but he did not feel alone. He stepped over to the desk, to get a closer look at the object lying on it. His fear strengthened. His heart pounded and he panted for breath.

The object was a ponytail of human hair. Snow's ponytail.

"So, Ten-Wolves," Gall said, striving to sound calmer than he felt. "Why don't you come out? We can talk."

"Put the gun on the desk and step away. I've got two .45s pointed at you."

Gall tried to localize the voice but couldn't. The room was large, full of shadows from bookshelves, cabinets, and curtains. He did as told, laying the Derringer on the desk and moving away.

"How did you get in?" he asked. "This place is supposed to have good security."

"I can walk through walls, didn't you know?"

The voice had moved. Gall still couldn't pinpoint it. He chuckled. "I know you're capable, Concho. That's why I tried to recruit you for my agency. But I don't believe the stories I've heard about you being magic."

A large shadow detached itself from a wall of shadows and stepped into the dim light. Gall saw the face of Concho Ten-Wolves. Jagged lines of red paint streaked the cheeks, sending an icy stiletto touch down his spine. He watched the wide shoulders shrug. Very slowly, he turned toward the liquor cabinet and took a couple of unsteady steps.

"I could use a drink," he said. "Care to join me?"

"I'm picky about who I drink with."

"As am I," Gall replied. Still moving slowly, with his hands in plain sight, he opened the cabinet and took out a gleaming bottle of Macallan Double Cask 18-year-old single malt Scotch. He poured two fingers of liquor into two tumblers, set one of them down on the cabinet's serving table and moved away with the other one.

Lifting the glass, he toasted, "To your health." He sipped.

CHAPTER FORTY-SEVEN

CONCHO WATCHED HIERONYMUS GALL TAKE A SIP OF HIS SCOTCH. He stepped farther out of the shadows and walked over to the spirits vault where the other glass of liquor sat. Holstering his Colts, he picked up the glass, sniffed it, then took a very small swallow. He made a face, for Gall's benefit.

"Awful stuff," he said.

Again, Gall chuckled. "I suppose it is an acquired taste."

Concho slugged the rest of the whiskey back, let it burn its way down his throat into his stomach. He sat the glass down again with a click, then moved purposefully toward Gall. Gall lifted his hands.

"I'm unarmed!"

"I doubt that. I'm sure there's a razor on you somewhere. I remember how you liked to cut." But he stopped walking about three feet away from the other man.

"That was war," Gall said.

"It's always war."

After a moment, Gall nodded. "I suppose it is." He took another swallow of Scotch.

Concho's nose wrinkled. "Your breath stinks," he said. "Musty. Like a boarded up old brothel."

"Foetor hepaticus," Gall said. "A symptom of severe liver disease. You can see my color is bad, too. My abdomen swollen. Maybe a gift from Afghanistan. You know, you were there. Or," he hefted his glass, "maybe just too much of this. See, you don't have to kill me. I'll be dead in a month anyway."

"Drink up then," Concho said.

"You're a hard SOB, Ten-Wolves."

This from a man who just ordered me killed. And who set in motion events that led to the deaths of at least two other people I knew. One of them a young woman who never hurt anyone in her life, who was just trying to find a way to take care of her four-month-old."

"I don't know what you're talking about."

"That how you want to play it? You realize I can't arrest you here anyway. No matter what evidence I might have of your guilt."

"You've got no evidence. But you might be trying to manufacture some."

"Or maybe I just came to kill you. You called me a 'killer' once. Remember? In Afghanistan?"

Gall's voice turned placating. "I was wrong."

Concho pulled his right-side Colt and pointed it at Gall's face. He clicked back the hammer."

Gall recoiled a step. He shook, spilling his Scotch. His voice trembled as he bargained. "I...I can give you something."

"What?"

"The Modines."

"They're dead."

"Not all of them. You captured one alive. The oldest son. Derrick."

"Amazing what you know. Considering you weren't officially anywhere near that investigation. I figured you were getting information from somewhere. Probably got an agent inside the FBI."

Gall shrugged.

"It doesn't matter now," Concho said. "Derrick Modine is going to jail for a long time for accessory to the murder of an FBI agent. I'm sure we'll find some other charges, too."

"But the icing on the cake. I can give you that. And you can save a life. More than one. I know you like that sort of thing."

"Talk!"

Gall hurried to speak. "The Modines. I've been...following them."

"Working with them, you mean."

Gall didn't deny. He merely rushed his next words even faster. "They've been...taking women. Exotic women. That's why they wanted the Green girl. An Indian."

"Taking them for what?"

"They wanted to...they... Well, they're Nazis. And Nazis always have their neuroses. Some of their people. They like... non-white women. Feel like they can do anything to those women without guilt. They film it. They've got a place outside Eagle Pass. Not their farm. They call it the 'Red House.' They've got two women there already. I can give you the location. You might get some of the perps, too."

"Do it. Now!"

"I didn't have anything to do with them grabbing those women. I swear. But I found out. Snow found out. He told me."

"I don't believe you," the lawman said. He stepped even closer to Gall and placed the barrel of his Colt flush against the other man's forehead. The hammer clicked as he drew it back."

Gall's shaking intensified. "You've got to promise not to kill me."

"I promise nothing."

Gall chewed at his lips. He tasted the threat of vomit. Tears appeared in his washed-out eyes and began to drip down his cheeks. He blubbered an address.

Concho took out his cell phone with his left hand. He placed a call to Della Rice, though he didn't use her name when she answered. He just gave her the address Gall had given him and told her what to expect.

"On it!" she said.

"Call me back as soon as you know."

"Will do."

Ten-Wolves swiped off the call. He slid the Colt into its holster and turned his back on Gall to return to the liquor cabinet. He was aware that Gall stood almost against the desk where his Derringer lay. He hoped the CIA operative would grab for it. That would give him some excuse to finish everything tonight. It didn't happen.

Concho returned to Gall with the opened bottle of Scotch. He splashed three fingers into the man's glass. "Drink up!" he ordered. "Let's finish your liver off while we wait to see if you lied to me."

Gall gulped the whisky in two big swallows. Ten-Wolves poured him more, with a shark smile playing all the while on his face. And they waited.

CHAPTER FORTY-EIGHT

DAWN. SUNDAY. CONCHO CROSSED THE INTERNATIONAL BRIDGE back into Texas. Rice had called. They'd found the address Hieronymus Gall supplied. A farmhouse painted red. They'd freed two women being held prisoner at the site—one African American, one Asian—and had found plenty of pornographic video. They'd arrested three men with straight razor tats and one of them had already begun to spill the names of others in their group. The FBI was going to have a busy week.

Concho wanted to feel elation but was too tired—physically *and* emotionally. He'd left Gall in his borrowed villa, drunk and crying but alive. It had been a near thing. But he couldn't kill an unarmed, blubbering sot in cold blood. No matter how much the man deserved it. And he couldn't arrest him and take him back to the states. No such arrest would stick and a lot of innocent people would suffer for it.

He did leave the man with a quiet promise. "Keep drinking. If you're not dead in a month, I'm coming back."

Instead of going directly to his trailer and bed, Ten-Wolves drove to the Maverick County Sheriff's Office. He took a shower there and picked up little Winona Green to bring home. He fed her, and changed her, and played with her for a while. When she fell asleep, he made a soft pallet for her on the floor by his bed and tumbled into his own dreamless night.

Two hours later, he awoke again when Winona cried out. He held her and rocked her, and when she fell back asleep, he carried her to his truck and tucked her into the baby seat Roland Turner had obtained.

He drove through Kickapoo Village while the baby slept on. Some people ignored him, some waved. He waved back, though everything felt hollow and distant. The only thing that seemed solid and real was the child next to him. She was a cute little thing and she'd been through a lot in her short life. She needed calm. For a long time.

When he'd first held her, after he'd plucked her from the grip of her dying mother, he'd felt a longing that hit him physically. Since he'd met Maria Morales he'd begun thinking about having children. Now he had one. If he went to Maria with the baby in his arms, she'd accept her, embrace her.

But would that truly be in the best interest of Winona? Heather had entrusted him with her little one, to find a place for her where she'd not only be loved but safe. And he could not promise a safe life for any child, or for any woman he might marry. Not right now.

And so, he drove through Kickapoo Village. He came to a small red brick home near the outskirts and turned into the driveway. The place was well kept, with flower beds in the front and a garden to one side. As he stepped out of the Dodge, the sound of a machine came to him from around the back where he'd find a small work shed.

He opened the passenger side door and took Winona out of her seat. She was awake and looked up at him. Her eyes were so big and dark that he almost put her back and drove away. He couldn't. Someday there'd be a child for him, but it couldn't be this child. Not now.

He took a deep breath and started around the side of the house. A man met him. Tobias Escarra, husband to Temple. He must have been coming to see who was visiting. Tobias seemed surprised to see Ten-Wolves but smiled a welcome and offered his hand. They shook.

Tobias's gaze drifted to Winona. He smiled again as the baby looked back at him, but a questioning glint filled his eyes. "To what do we owe this visit?" he asked.

"I wanted to speak to you and Temple."

Tobias's gaze flicked once more toward Winona, but his words were not of the child when he spoke. "I believe she has been wishing to speak to you, too. Come."

He turned and Concho followed. From a long metal shed in the back yard came the sound of whirring machinery. The front of the shed stood open. Tobias led the way and called out loudly.

Concho stepped into the shed behind him. A woman in a gray cotton work shirt leaned over a grinding machine, sharpening the blade of a knife. She wore a welder's mask to protect her eyes.

At Tobias's call, Temple Escarra stopped her work and straightened. She flicked a switch on the metal table next to her and the machine burred to a stop. She pushed the welder's mask up on her face as she turned to look toward her husband and saw Concho and the burden he carried. Her eyes were brown, flecked with gold. She pulled off the mask and sat it down. She pulled off work gloves as she came toward the Ranger but did not offer to shake hands.

"Ten-Wolves," she said. Her glance flicked toward her husband. He stood inscrutable. She looked back at the Ranger. "Not many lawmen come to visit with a child in their hands," she added.

"I brought the child for you and Tobias to see."

Temple nodded. She stepped a little closer and peered down into the baby's face. Winona smiled at her and she smiled back. "It is...an Indian child," she said.

"Her mother was Navajo."

"'Was' means no longer is."

"She was murdered yesterday by a man who did not like Indians. Or blacks. Or...well, most people. Her name is Winona."

"How came you to have her?"

"Her mother was...becoming a friend to me. She asked me to look after her daughter. Specifically, she asked me to find a home for her, a place where she'd be loved and cared for."

Temple's gaze lifted to his. "And you brought her here?"

"Before...your own daughter died, I saw you and Tobias with her. I knew there was much love there. The kind of love that doesn't die. The kind of love that needs to be given away."

Temple looked abruptly away, her eyes damp. She beckoned Tobias, who came over to stand beside her. His face was impassive but feeling lay buried in the flesh. Temple touched the babe on the chin. Winona cooed and clutched at one callused finger. Temple seemed surprised and started to pull her hand back, then left it instead. She looked again to Tobias, then at Concho, and back to Winona. The wetness had gone from her eyes now. There was something else instead.

"What of the laws?" Tobias asked.

"I spoke to a social worker," Concho replied. "There'll be some papers to sign. I'll bring them to you in a few days. If you—"

Temple reached her other hand out and scooped up the baby. It gave a little startled cry but the woman cooed at it and burbled with her lips. Winona blinked and made a raspberry in return. Temple took a long breath. She tucked the blanket more carefully around Winona's shoulders. Her entire body seemed to curl protectively around the child.

"I've got some diapers and formula in my truck," Concho said.

Temple did not respond. Tobias did. "I will walk you there."

Concho nodded. He glanced once more at Temple, and at the babe. A little lump formed in his throat but he swallowed it down. He started toward the door.

"Ranger!" Temple said.

The lawman paused. "Yes?"

"Someday we'll speak of other things."

"Whenever you want."

She nodded and walked away toward the house. The two men went back around the front. Concho pulled a big brown paper sack off the floorboards of his truck and handed it to Tobias.

"If you need anything else," he said. "For the baby. Call me."

"We will."

"Well..." he started, but there was nothing left to say. He offered Tobias his hand again and they shook. Concho climbed into his truck and started it. He glanced at Tobias, then toward the house. "She's a good baby."

Tobias nodded. "You will have to come visit. Perhaps you will be its...godparent. As they say in the Christian churches. I think Temple will approve."

"I'd like that."

"Also..."

"Yes?"

"Thank you."

Tobias turned and headed for the house. Concho sat for a long moment, still and quiet, and then backed out of the driveway and turned toward home and his duties.

CHAPTER FORTY-NINE

In Mexico, Hieronymus Gall climbed into an ambulance to take him to a local hospital where he was scheduled to have a liver transplant. He hadn't been able to get on the list for such a surgery in the USA, but south of the border such opportunities could be more easily purchased. With money, or information. He was rich with both.

The doctors told him his recovery would take a long while, but afterward he'd have time to consider the future. Given the suspicions that Concho Ten-Wolves would no doubt fan among Gall's colleagues in the States, going home for his recovery might not be the best idea. But it wasn't as if a man of his talents couldn't find a sympathetic sanctuary elsewhere.

He'd have plenty of opportunities to consider payback.

———

In the late afternoon, with the light turning the low yellow that always left Concho feeling melancholy, he pulled into the driveway in front of his trailer and parked. A cool breeze teased him as he exited his truck and he went over and slumped down into one of the plastic lawn chairs around his firepit.

He didn't feel like going inside yet and facing an empty house. Maria wasn't scheduled to be home until tomorrow and he missed her. He found, too, that he missed the small bundle of Winona Green, though he'd scarcely known her.

The bushes rustled behind him and he turned. Meskwaa came walking out and slid into a second lawn chair across the fire pit from him. The medicine man wore buckskins and moccasins today, all of them red. A blue neckerchief around his neck made the only splash of a different color.

"Old man," Concho said. "What brings you all the way out here to visit me?"

"Just checking on my investment," Meskwaa replied.

"I didn't realize I was an investment."

"Pshaw," Meskwaa said. "Not all is about you."

"Then what?"

The old man reached out and stroked the bark of the big mesquite that grew over them. "I planted this tree, you know."

"As big as this tree is, it's probably more than a hundred years old," Ten-Wolves said.

A nod. "Yes. Like me, it is just now reaching maturity."

Concho chuckled. "Look at that, you've already lifted my mood."

Meskwaa shrugged. "If we must talk about you, how are you doing?"

"I'll be all right."

"You are thinking of what might have been."

"I suppose I am."

"Temple Escarra took the child?"

"She did. It was the right decision. She and Tobias will give her everything she needs."

"Sometimes, 'right' decisions do not feel right for the one making them."

"You get that off an inspirational poster, old man?"

"I do not even know what that is."

Ten-Wolves snorted. "Not sure I do either."

Meskwaa pushed up from his chair.

"Going so soon?" Concho asked, as the hollow feeling of loneliness pooled around him again.

"You are about to have better company than I can provide."

"Oh? Who?"

Meskwaa shook his head. "I despair. I had hoped, one day, you would sense such things yourself. It seems I am forever to be disappointed." He turned toward the brush he'd come from, but then paused and looked back. "There is still much ahead of you, Ten-Wolves. Much of it will be very good, and will fill that hole in your spirit. Be patient."

Concho took a breath. He nodded. Meskwaa melted away into the brush as if he'd never been. The Lawman scratched at his cheeks where a stubble of whiskers itched. He'd been several days without a shave. That would be something to do, to busy his mind.

He pushed up from his chair and turned toward his house. The sound of a vehicle coming up his long driveway caught his attention. A blue 2017 Ford Focus pulled into his yard and parked beside his truck. A woman got out.

All the hollowness inside Concho disappeared. He smiled. "Maria!" he shouted. He started toward the car as the woman he loved smiled at him, too. Her long dark hair flamed with gold from the setting sun. She wore black slacks and a silver blouse. Both rumpled. He didn't care.

"I thought you weren't coming home till tomorrow?" Ten-Wolves exclaimed as he reached her.

"I got an early flight. Somebody I wanted to see."

"Who is he? I'll beat him up."

Maria laughed, but then a look of concern clouded her face as she saw the shaved spot on his head and the stitches. "Are you OK?"

"I'm good. Much, much better now that you're here."

A tentative smile returned to her face. "Well, it *looks* like my other boyfriend beat you up first. What happened?" She lifted a hand, palm out. "No, don't tell me. I'm sure it's a long story and I've got something else on my mind."

"What's that?" he asked curiously.

"It doesn't involve your head. How's the rest of you working?"

"I am functioning within adequate parameters," he teased in a robotic voice.

Maria smiled, and this smile wasn't one of concern or friendliness. It was very much something else. She stepped closer to him. Her hand...drifted.

"Then take your woman to bed, Ranger."

A LOOK AT BOOK EIGHT
BLACK WOLF RISING

SADDLE UP FOR A WILD RIDE IN THIS ACTION-PACKED WESTERN FROM THE UNSTOPPABLE A.W. HART.

Texas Ranger Concho Ten-Wolves is about to meet his match.

Before he went to prison, Fulgencio Labante, known and feared as The Black Wolf, built a growing and influential drug cartel headquartered on Kickapoo land south of the Rio Grande. He was ruthless, known for ripping out the throats of his enemies in mimicry of a wolf attack.

With nine years behind bars doing nothing to tame his savage spirit, word on the street is The Black Wolf is set to rise again—and the one throat he wants to rip out most belongs to Concho.

Following up on a tip from a woman on the Kickapoo Reservation, Concho is staking out an abandoned building when he spots a bedraggled teenage girl. Now on the trail of a human trafficking ring preying on Native American girls, Concho faces a deadly showdown where justice, vengeance, and survival converge in a high-stakes duel under the unforgiving Texan sun.

COMING JANUARY 2024

ABOUT THE AUTHOR

Charles Gramlich lives amid the piney woods of southern Louisiana and is the author of the Talera fantasy series, the science fiction novel, *Under the Ember Star*, and the thriller, *Cold in the Light*.

His work has appeared in magazines such as *Star*Line*, *Beat to a Pulp*, *Night to Dawn*, *Pedestal Magazine*, and many others. Several of his stories have been collected in anthologies, such as: *Bitter Steel* (fantasy), *Midnight in Rosary* (vampires/werewolves), and *In the Language of Scorpions* (horror).

Charles also writes westerns under the name Tyler Boone. Although he writes in many different genres, all of his fiction work is known for its intense action and strong visuals.

Made in United States
Troutdale, OR
07/20/2024

21398064R00153